"You know what

"I have *amazing* powers of negotiation. If it weren't for this stupid eye condition, you would be signing papers right now. But instead I'm crying, and you think I'm weak, and I'm screwed."

"I don't think you're weak," he said, his voice soft. "My saying no isn't about you at all."

"Right." She looked up to see his face full of sympathy, and she started to cry harder. "Please don't look at me that way."

"What way?"

"Like you pity me."

He touched her hand. "Hey, I just turned down two million dollars. You should be pitying me."

She wanted to scowl at him, but instead a small laugh came out, and then suddenly, they were standing closer, although Freya had no idea who'd made the move. He pulled her into his arms, and she rested her cheek on his shoulder. The relief was almost instant. He let his hand run lightly down her hair and tightened his hold on her. It felt like falling and being caught.

It felt like heaven.

"This author is one to watch."
—*Romantic Times BOOKreviews Magazine*

*Please turn the page for more praise for
Lani Diane Rich and her novels...*

"Filled with humor where you don't expect it, murder, mystery, and mayhem. A fun, quick read that will keep you on the edge of your seat."

—ChicklitRomanceWriters.com

"Excellent pacing, good characterization, smart reading, and fine romance…[Rich] writes with confidence, humor, and creativity."

—PaperbackReader.net

"Delightful characters and plot make this a fun read."

—FreshFiction.com

"A masterfully worded tale, will keep you turning pages long into the night…Rich created a story filled with humor, romance, and adventure."

—BookLoons.com

"A delightful story that I truly enjoyed reading. This book is a must-have so go out and get yourself a copy!"

—TheRomanceReadersConnection.com

THE COMEBACK KISS

"A winner…Rich expertly blends romance and mystery [in] this charming, coming-home-again tale."

—*Booklist*

"An evocative treasure of a story…rife with passion, blazing hearts, and an intriguing mystery that goes to the heart of what makes a small town so very small, but so familiar and warm."

—FallenAngelReviews.com

more…

"Outstanding! This book has sharp and funny dialogue that will hook you from the first paragraph. Combine that with a well-plotted story and interesting characters and you have a winner."

—*Rendezvous*

"Absolutely wonderful...a sweet story about the importance of family, be it untraditional, and past love and new love...I loved this book and recommend it to anyone looking for a fun and thrilling read."

—*MyShelf.com*

"A must-read...page-turning, fun romance with a touch of suspense."

—*FreshFiction.com*

"Fast-paced...Readers will enjoy this solid, secondhand chance at love [and the] romantic suspense."

—*Midwest Book Review*

"A fun story with a serious mystery and lots of interesting characters."

—*RomanceReviewsMag.com*

"A quick, satisfying read that will leave you smiling when you finish."

—*The State* (Columbia, SC)

MAYBE BABY

"The merriment keeps the pages turning."

—*Publishers Weekly*

"This book has a lot of twists and turns and ups and downs. There is never a dull moment until you are finished with the ride and think, What the heck, let's go again."

—*Rendezvous*

"A sweet...book about following your dreams (and your dream man)."

—*Publishers Weekly*

"Funny...sweet...full of quirky, likable characters and the charms of small-town life...Will appeal to fans of Rebecca Wells's Ya-Yas."

—*Booklist*

"What raises this novel above many other chick-lit titles is its depth...You'll read it quickly for its sweet sass, but you'll reread it to savor its bittersweet truths."

—*Ventura County Star* (CA)

"Sweetly engaging. B+."

—*Entertainment Weekly*

"A fast, fun read, especially for those who enjoy the quirky characters of authors like Jennifer Crusie and Eileen Rendahl. Strongly recommended."

—*Library Journal*

TIME OFF FOR GOOD BEHAVIOR

"I love Lani Diane Rich's thirtysomething heroine, Wanda. The world hands her lemons, and she snarls and throws them back at the world. Fast, funny, and always true to herself, Wanda is one of those heroines you want to have lunch with."

—Jennifer Crusie, bestselling author of
Bet Me and *Faking It*

"A sparkling debut, full of punch, pace, and wonderfully tender moments. I devoured it in one sitting. Lani Diane Rich's gutsy, wisecracking heroine, Wanda Lane, speaks to any woman who has ever doubted her right to be loved."

—Sue Margolis, author of *Apocalipstick*

Also by Lani Diane Rich

Crazy in Love

The Comeback Kiss

Ex and the Single Girl

Maybe Baby

Time Off for Good Behavior

Wish You Were Here

Lani Diane Rich

FOREVER

NEW YORK   BOSTON

The characters and events in this book are fictitious. Any similarity to real persons, living or dead, is coincidental and not intended by the author.

Copyright © 2008 by Lani Diane Rich

Book design by Stratford Publishing Services, a TexTech business

Forever
Hachette Book Group USA
237 Park Avenue
New York, NY 10017
Visit our Web site at www.HachetteBookGroupUSA.com

Forever is an imprint of Grand Central Publishing.
The Forever name and logo is a trademark of Hachette Book Group USA, Inc.

Printed in the United States of America

First Printing: November 2008

10 9 8 7 6 5 4 3 2 1

To Rebecca, Cate and Sam.
This one's for you, girls.

ACKNOWLEDGMENTS

Like every book, this one couldn't have been done without the tireless support and beta reads of good friends. Lucky for me, my good friends are also excellent writers. Samantha Graves, Catherine Wade, Rebecca Rohan, Eileen Cook, Robin La Fevers, Jennifer Crusie, and Anne Stuart—I can't believe I'm so lucky as to have these amazing women cheering in my corner. Without them I would have never discovered how much unholy fun writing can be. You are all goddesses.

Thank you to the real Nikkie Cooper, who won a contest and then gave her gracious consent when I told her exactly what kind of character I was naming after her. For the record, the real Nikkie Cooper and the fictional one have nothing in common aside from the name. Thanks, Nik!

I am sad to say, I haven't actually spent much time in northern Idaho, but what time I did have there made quite the impression, obviously. It's a beautiful place, and while Deer Creek and its surroundings are works of total fiction, my research indicates that you can find the spirit of Brody Lake in a lot of places out that way. It's gorgeous country and I can't recommend it highly enough.

Wish You Were Here

CHAPTER ONE

FREYA DALY SWATTED at a fly buzzing her head as her left stiletto tottered on the gravel under her feet. The ancient log cabin in front of her was maybe four hundred square feet, if that. It looked like it had probably last been weather-treated sometime in the Nixon administration, and the number 4 over the front door hung upside down from one nail, waiting for the right moment to make a run for it.

Dig that, she thought. *Hell has a campground.*

She squared her shoulders, picked up her leather Louis Vuitton suitcase—no way was she dragging *that* over Idaho dirt—and started toward her cabin. Time to get to work. She walked carefully up the short path to the cabin and tried to imagine what the hell her father was thinking, sending her out here. Daly Developers acquired swank apartment buildings and five-star hotels and hot restaurants in big cities; they didn't go out into the middle of nowhere and purchase worthless campgrounds.

Except, apparently, they did. And this was it, the last of the flaming hoops of hellfire she had to jump through to prove to her father she was ready to take over when he retired in the fall.

Time to get jumping, she thought, and then her throat tightened and her eyes started to water and—

Crap.

She set her suitcase down on the porch and closed her eyes tight against the tears waiting behind them.

Not now. Not again.

"Useless doctors," she muttered, then reached into her purse, pulled out a box of Tic-Tacs, and shook three into her mouth. Three opthalmologists, a Lasik specialist, and the acupuncturist her sister Flynn had talked her into, and the only thing that could combat her odd condition were stupid Tic-Tacs, which she'd discovered on her own, anyway.

Concentrate, she thought, closing her eyes as she rolled the mints around on her tongue. *Minty fresh. Neutral. Unemotional. Calm.*

"There we go," she said as the heat behind her eyes simmered down. She blinked twice, sucked on the Tic-Tacs, and then took in a deep, minty breath. "That's it. Totally under control."

She rested her hands against the railing, looking out over the property. She could see three other cabins, and up a path behind the cabins was a massive but aged log home; the owner probably lived there. Another path led through the trees—she presumed to the lake—and beyond that, according to the map she'd seen in her packet of documentation, there was an acre or so of RV lots. The landscape was pretty enough, if you were into that kind of thing, but the infrastructure was crap. Old, decrepit, falling down. Why her father chose this for her last flaming hoop was beyond her.

Not that it mattered. Her job was to secure the place, go

home, and take over the company. And that was exactly what she was going to—

"Be careful there." The voice came from behind her, startling her. She spun around, losing her balance and slamming backward into the railing. She heard a crack, felt the world whoosh around her, and then suddenly, she jerked to a stop in midair. She looked up to see a man with dirty blond hair, two-day stubble, and sharp blue eyes looming over her, one hand fisted around the fabric of her jacket, the other hand braced against the support post that held up the overhang.

"*Shit*," she said, and swallowed her Tic-Tacs.

There was a quick yank at her midsection and then she was up onto the safety of the porch, falling into the Adirondack chair across from the railing.

"Ow," she said as her ass hit the hardwood.

The man took a step toward her, holding out his hand to help her up. "You okay?"

"Super." Freya ignored his hand and smoothed her skirt. "Thanks."

He retracted his hand. "Sorry. I didn't know you were coming in early until a few minutes ago. I'm just fixing some plumbing in the bathroom, and I'll be out of your way in a second."

"Really?" She pushed up from the chair, internally calculating how much plumbing issues might take off the asking price during negotiations; this handyman might come in handy. "There are problems? Are they systemic, needing a full rehaul, or just your standard leaky faucet kind of thing?"

He went silent for a beat before answering. "Hot water spigot needs replacing."

"I see," she said. "That sort of thing can be indicative of a systemic problem, don't you think?"

"Um…" He cleared his throat, then said, "This is the best cabin we've got at the moment." He glanced down over the side of the porch at the broken pieces of railing and shook his head. "Once I fix that."

"Well, if it broke that easily, it doesn't say much for the state of the place, does it? About how many repairs do you find yourself making in the average week here?"

He leaned in a little closer. "Who are you again?"

She held out her hand. "Freya Daly. I'm with Daly Developers, Incorporated. We're looking at the place for possible purchase, and have been in talks with your boss—"

"Let me stop you there," he said, taking her hand. "I'm the boss, and I've already said no, so save your pitch."

She stopped shaking his hand, but didn't let go. "*You're* Nate Brody?"

"Yep."

Damnit. She should have known that. In the old days, she would have known, she would have studied his picture, she would have memorized the research before she left instead of cramming it all in on the plane. She released his hand and reached for her Tic-Tacs.

"Sorry," she said, popping three. "Jet lag."

"Well, Ms. Daly—"

"Call me Freya. Please." She smiled tightly and clenched her teeth down on a Tic-Tac, scorching a peppermint burn into the side of her tongue.

"Freya. Look, I don't know what you've been told, but if your people sent you here to change my mind, it's a waste of your time. I'm not selling."

Great. A reluctant seller. Time to switch tactics. She smiled. "Actually...this is a vacation. My father told me about how beautiful it was out here, and I needed a little time off so I thought, where better to spend that time than Deer Gulch?"

"Deer Creek," he corrected.

Crap. "Right." These were rookie mistakes, and she never made rookie mistakes. Not even when she was a rookie. She felt the familiar rumbling of stress and panic in her gut and popped two more Tic-Tacs. She had to get away from Nate Brody and get herself together before she hosed this deal forever. "You know what? I think maybe I'd like to just take a shower."

"Sure. You bet."

He stepped past her and opened the door. She made a motion to reach for her suitcase, but he got to it first. He held the door open, inviting her to go in first, and then followed her, depositing the suitcase by the hearth.

Freya surveyed the cabin. There was a stone fireplace, which was nice enough. The dark wood floors were a bit creaky, and the decor consisted of a woven rag rug, a coffee table made from a slice of a mutant-large tree, and a 1970s-looking orange sofa. She imagined the demolition ball hitting it all, grinding it to dust to make room for the luxury cabins they'd replace it with before selling the land at a huge profit to the highest bidder, then she turned to Nate Brody with a genuine smile. "Thanks. I can take it from here."

"Yeah, I know, it's just..." He pointed toward the bathroom. "The hot water."

She waved her hand. "Oh. You know, that's fine..."

"You need hot water. It'll just take a minute to fix, and I'll be out of your way."

"Oh. Um. Okay," she said, and he disappeared into the bathroom. She followed to find him leaning over an ancient claw-foot tub with a middle faucet jutting out over it from the log wall. She glanced around, turning in a full circle before realizing...

"There's no shower?"

"No," he said, working his wrench on the faucet. "There's a tub. And a..." He clinked the wrench twice on a handheld shower head. "It'll just be a minute, I promise." And he ducked his head down and went to work.

She stared down at the tub, the panic escalating, for no acceptable reason, just like all the other times. On the heels of the panic came the choking helplessness, and then, like clockwork, her eyes welled up. She made a quick escape back into the main room, grabbed her purse off the coffee table, and rooted through it, finding her Tic-Tacs. She poured five into her hand and popped them, closing her eyes.

Minty. Cool. Unemotional. Calm.

"Dad?"

Freya turned her head toward the open front door to see a slight brunette girl poke her head in the doorway. She was about ten or eleven years old, with ragged pigtails and skinned knees peeking out from her cutoff shorts, and she wore a pink T-shirt that read "Don't Call Me Cute," in glittery, swirly silver lettering that shot out stars from each end.

"Wow," the girl said, her eyes going wide as they went from Freya's head to her shoes and back up again, as if she'd never seen someone dressed in silk before. "*You're* staying here?"

"Can I help you?" Freya asked, sniffling.

The girl stepped into the cabin. "I'm Piper." She held out her hand, arm straight, head high. Freya took it and shook.

"I'm Freya." She released the girl's hand, but the kid just stared up at her, her head tilted and her eyes assessing, making Freya uncomfortable. Freya crossed her arms over her stomach and said, "Uh, is Nate your father? He's fixing something in the bathroom. He'll be out in just a second." She turned her head toward the bathroom and said, "Nate?" right as the water turned on. Freya looked back at the girl, who was still staring at her. "You're welcome to go in there and hang out with him if you'd like."

Piper didn't move. "Are you okay?"

"Me?" Freya swiped under her eyes and bit down on a Tic-Tac. "I'm great."

"It's okay if you're crying," Piper said. "I cry all the time. It's no big deal."

"I don't," Freya said. "I'm not the emotional type."

"Everyone's emotional."

"Well, I'm *not*." Freya crossed her arms over her stomach, feeling oddly exposed in the girl's crosshairs.

"Ruby says it's just a matter of whether you express your emotions or not, and it's unhealthy not to express your emotions, because then when they do come out, they're all explosive and everything. Like diarrhea. Your chin is trembling a bit. Are you sure you're okay?"

"Would you like a Tic-Tac?" Freya said quickly, holding out the tiny plastic box.

Piper smiled. "Sure."

Freya stuffed the box into the kid's hand. "Take the box. I've got a stash."

Piper popped a bunch in her mouth, but unfortunately,

it didn't keep her from talking. "So why are you crying? Is everything okay?"

"I'm not crying. I just..." Freya sighed. "I have a condition, okay? My eyes start tearing every now and again, for no reason." *Like driving to work. In staff meetings. During diabetes fundraisers with the Red Sox.* "But I'm not really crying. I'm not sad. I have nothing to be sad about. It's just... my eyes."

Piper gave her a dubious look. "There's a disease where you cry when you're not sad?"

"It's not a *disease*." Freya blinked hard. "It's a *condition*."

"What's it called? Because I've never heard of anything like that. Are you sure it's real?"

"It's *real*." Just because she hadn't found a doctor who could confirm it yet didn't mean it wasn't real. "Don't you have homework to do or something?"

"Sorry that took so long, but everything's—" Nate stopped talking as he stepped out into the main room and saw Piper, his face brightening at the sight of his little girl. Freya's throat closed up and her eyes filled again. Luckily, Nate and Piper were focused on each other.

"What are you doing here, Pipes?" he said.

Piper skipped over to him.

"Ruby wanted me to tell you that Number Four checked in early."

Nate shot a light smile at Freya, and then his smile faded a bit as he focused on her.

I'm not crying, goddamnit, Freya thought.

Nate looked back at Piper, and Freya took the opportunity to swipe away the moisture under her eyes.

"Thanks for the heads-up, kid," he said, ruffling her hair. "Your homework done?"

"Not yet," she said. "Hey, Dad, have you ever heard of an eye condition that makes people cry when they're not sad?"

Nate looked at Piper, then at Freya. Freya tried to smile through the thin veil of her disintegrating dignity but, based on Nate's expression, her success was limited.

"Uh…" he said, "you know what, Piper? We should go get that homework done, leave Ms. Daly alone."

"We can call her Freya," Piper said. "So, have you ever heard of it?"

Nate looked at Freya again and she averted her eyes, humiliation raging through her. *Just leave, just leave, just leave…*

"Yeah, sure, I've heard of that."

Freya raised her head to look at Nate, but he was still focused on Piper.

"There was a guy who played for the Redskins a few years back who had it," he said.

Piper hit her dad playfully on the arm. "Shut up!"

"No, really," he said. "Big guy. Linebacker. Six feet tall, 285 pounds, happiest guy in the world. Cried all the time." He met Freya's eye quickly, then looked back down at Piper. "Made a miraculous recovery when people left him alone about it." He chucked her under the chin. "Got it?"

"Got it." Piper turned to Freya. "Sorry I didn't believe you."

"No problem," Freya said, then met Nate's eyes and smiled. "Thanks."

Nate nodded and put one hand on Piper's shoulder, directing her toward the door. "Homework."

Piper turned her head over her shoulder and kept talking. "You can come up to the house later if you want. We can play Slap. It's this card game—"

"Freya's a guest," Nate said. "We don't harass guests, remember?"

Piper angled her head to look up at her father. "I wasn't harassing. I was inviting."

"Sorry," Nate said to Freya as he nudged Piper out the open door.

"It's okay." Freya walked with them to see them *out, out, out*. She had them all the way out the door when Piper stopped suddenly and peered over the edge of the porch.

"Oh, shit, what happened to the railing?"

"Don't say 'shit' in front of the guests," Nate said, then looked at Freya and said, "I'll be back later to fix that."

Piper turned back to her father. "You're coming back? Oooh, I can help!"

"No, you've got homework," he said, then turned to Freya. "Ruby's in the office until five, so if you need anything, just dial nine on the phone. There's also a grocery store in town if you need anything we don't have, on 2nd Avenue. Just follow Route 8 back into town and take a left, you can't miss it."

Piper grabbed her father's sleeve. "I can go with her, show her around."

Nate took her hand. "*Homework.*"

"But she's *sad*," Piper said in a stage whisper she probably thought Freya couldn't hear.

"She's *fine*," Nate said.

Piper sighed and reached around her dad to wave. "Bye, Freya! It was nice to meet you!"

"Bye, Piper," she said.

Nate pulled the girl away, and Freya heard her say, "She needs friends. We should be her friends," as Nate shushed her and walked her down the front steps. Freya shut the door, then closed her eyes and took a deep breath to relieve the tension in her shoulders as she leaned against it, hoping it was in better shape than the porch railing. *When I open my eyes, it won't seem so bad.*

When she opened her eyes, her focus went straight to the ugly orange couch, and she was hit with the sudden realization that there was no bedroom. *That* was her bed, and it was the color of fiery brimstone. She was in Hell's campground, and she'd be sleeping on Hell's pull-out couch.

She felt the panic start to swell within her, then stamped her foot on the floor.

"This is *not tougher* than me." She went to her suitcase, pulled out a pair of pajamas and her toiletries, and headed for the bathroom. "I'm Freya Goddamn Daly, and *I am not emotional.*"

Then she trudged into the bathroom and eased herself into the hot water. A box of Tic-Tacs later, the tears finally abated, and she considered it a win.

Nathan Brody stared down at the sizzling salmon steaks in front of him and tried to clear his mind. The day had been long and—as usual—unproductive, and even cooking wasn't making him feel any better about the lack of progress he'd been making.

That wasn't a good sign.

"Oh, shit, he's doing gourmet again," Ruby said, ruffling Piper's hair as she entered the kitchen. She tossed the day's office mail on the breakfast bar and looked at Nate. "What happened? You didn't find the"—she glanced at Piper, who sat hunched over her math homework—"*toolbox,* did you?"

Nate shot Ruby a warning look, nodding toward Piper. He'd asked Ruby a thousand times not to talk about it in front of Piper, but it didn't much matter what you asked Ruby. Ruby was salt-of-the-earth Idaho, and Ruby did what she damn well pleased.

"Whatcha workin' on there, kid?" she asked Piper.

Piper scratched some numbers down and lifted her head. "Percentages. I'm supposed to be counting M&Ms."

Nate looked up from the salmon. "Then why aren't you counting M&Ms?"

Piper sighed heavily, and Nate felt a whiff of cold terror for the teenage years to come.

"Because based on the estimated number of M&Ms per bag, I can just roughly guess and save some time." She chewed briefly on the edge of the pencil, then casually jotted a figure into her notebook and said, "And then I can go with you to fix the railing on Number Four."

"Nice try. No."

He inhaled, but instead of smelling the salmon, he remembered the warm, clean scent of woman he'd caught when he pulled Freya off that railing. Excitement sparked within him, and he knew it had been way too long since he'd done anything but fix broken cabins and take care of his kid. One beautiful woman shows up in his path, and his synapses start misfiring.

He shook his head, inhaled again, and it was all salmon this time. He cleared his throat and looked at Ruby.

"Speaking of Number Four, Ruby, I thought we decided that we were going to keep the cabins empty this summer."

Ruby sat back, rearranging the fabric of her T-shirt over her wide frame. "It's just one weekend. We could use the money. And there's plenty of time to find the—"

"*Salmon's ready*," Nate said loudly over her.

"—toolbox," Ruby continued, nonplussed. They stared at each other in a silent stalemate for a moment until Piper shut her notebook and said, "I'm not stupid, you know."

Nate let his eyes travel from his sort-of-stepmother to his daughter.

"I know you're not stupid." Nate pulled the roasted rosemary potatoes out of the oven, plated them with the salmon, and drizzled the reduced wine sauce over it, wiping down the edges of the plate with a towel before delivering it to the table. "Eat."

Piper sighed and picked up her fork. "Some parents make hot dogs."

"Good for them. Eat." Nate kissed her on the top of the head and returned to the counter for the other portions.

Piper took a bite, chewed for a moment, then said, "I know you're not looking for a toolbox."

Nate froze at the table, holding Ruby's plate in the air. The older woman reached for it and he pulled it back out of her reach, his eyes hitting her with accusation.

"Don't look at me," she said. "I told you to tell her everything in the first place."

"Right." He put the plate down and walked back to the counter to get his own, then placed it at the seat next to Piper before speaking.

"So, what else do you think you know?"

Piper played it cool for a second, but then a light sparked in her eyes and she leaned forward in excitement. "I know you've been looking for this"—she made air quotes with her hands—"'toolbox' since we got here. And I know you've already searched most of the land and haven't found it."

"You know a lot," Nate said, glancing at Ruby, who shrugged and dug her fork into her salmon.

"So…" Piper said, leaning forward eagerly, "what is it?"

Nate shook his head. "Piper…"

"Look, if I know what you're looking for, maybe I can help. I'm small. I can crawl under things. Plus, I'll see things you don't see. Like, you know that story about the truck that gets wedged under a bridge and no one can figure out how to get it out until a kid says to let the air out of the tires? Like that. I can help."

He glanced at her, half amazed at her intelligence and enthusiasm, half wishing he could magically make her three years old again. "You figured all that out on your own?"

Piper speared a potato. "Yep."

"Smart kid."

Piper's face lit up. "So. You're going to tell me what's going on?"

"No," Nate said. "I don't want you to worry about that, okay?"

"But I can help." She set down her fork and sat back. "It's bad enough that you've lied to me this whole time, the least you can do now is let me help."

"Hey," Nate said, pointing his index finger at her. "I never lied. Maybe I didn't tell you everything, but you don't need to know everything."

He met Piper's eye, and knew he'd won that part of the argument. Pretty much from the beginning, it had been just the two of them, and while he might stonewall her on occasion about some things, he'd never lied to her, and she knew it.

Ruby stood up and put her hand on his shoulder. "Lemme get the wine."

"Get the Pinot, it's what I used in the sauce," Nate said, then looked at his daughter. Ruby was right; Piper was going to figure it out on her own eventually, anyway. At this point, the best he could do was cap his losses. "You really want to know?"

Piper's eyes went wide. "You're gonna tell me?"

"Is there any chance you're gonna drop it?"

Piper shook her head. Nate dropped his napkin on the table, ran his hand over his face, and looked at his kid. "Then go ahead. Ask me whatever you want to know."

Piper watched as Ruby placed wine glasses in front of each of them, filling Piper's with milk and hers and Nate's with the wine. Once Ruby was seated, Piper spoke.

"Why didn't you and Mick get married?" Piper said, her eyes on Ruby.

Nate sat forward. "Hey, I said you could ask *me*—"

"It's okay," Ruby said. She nodded at Piper, her eyes filled with respect. "Your grandfather never asked me, and I never asked him."

"Did you love him?"

Nate looked at Ruby. "You don't have to answer that."

She raised one eyebrow at him and said, "Thank you, counselor," then looked at Piper. "Your grandfather could be a very charming man." She met Nate's eyes and he could see in her expression the word she deliberately left out.

Sometimes.

Nate had a thousand questions of his own that he'd wanted to ask Ruby since the day she'd called him to his father's deathbed. Had his father hit her, the way he had hit Nate's mother? Had he changed at all in the last fifteen years of his life? Or was he the same son of a bitch he'd always been, and if so, why the hell had Ruby stayed with him?

"Dad?"

He glanced back at Piper, who was watching him expectantly.

"What?"

"I just asked you — what's the toolbox?"

Oh. Yeah. That. He shook his head. "I don't know."

Piper's face fell in disgust and disappointment and she threw herself back in her seat. "Come on, Dad."

"I'm serious, Pipes. I don't know what the toolbox is. That's what makes it so hard to find. We just called it a toolbox to keep you from getting interested." He raised his glass to Ruby before taking a sip. "Here's to that raging success."

Ruby ignored him and looked at Piper. "We think it might be treasure."

"Or a dead body," Nate muttered. Ruby stiffened and he felt a touch of guilt. "Sorry."

"A dead body?" Piper's eyes went wider than Nate thought possible.

"No, that was a dumb joke," Nate said. "This thing is just some object, about..." He held out his hands approximately twelve inches away from each other the way his father had in those moments before he died. "...this big. It's purple. My father made me give my word that I would get it before I sold the place, and then he died before he could tell me where it was."

Piper looked at Ruby. "And you don't know anything? He never told you?"

Ruby reached for her glass of wine. "Your grandfather wasn't a big talker."

Nate saw a flash of something go across Ruby's face, but it was only for a second, and then her standard wry and world-weary expression returned. She was one tough old girl, Ruby, and she was the only reason Nate had any hope that maybe his father had changed toward the end. Ruby did not seem the type to take the kind of crap his father doled out to women.

"Well." Piper nibbled her lip, but then stopped before Nate could admonish her. "If you don't know what it is or what it looks like, how can you possibly find it?"

"That's a good question." Nate raised his glass toward Heaven but then, on second thought, glanced downward. "Care to field that one, Pop?"

"So, what happens if you don't find it?" Piper asked.

Nate didn't want to think about that. "I'll find it."

Piper took a bite of her salmon, chewed carefully and swallowed. "Or... you know, maybe we could just... stay."

Nate's salmon stuck in his throat and he grabbed for his wine to wash it down. "Sorry, what?"

"Well, we could just... stay." She raised her eyes tentatively to Nate's, and he could see the pleading in them. "Forever?"

"I have the restaurant in Cincinnati," Nate said. "And I have to get back to it. I know you've made friends here, Piper, and you're gonna be able to finish out the school year with them—"

Piper huffed. "That's only two more weeks!"

"—but I'm gonna find this thing, and then we're going back home. You have friends there, too."

"I know, but..." She put her fork down and crossed her arms over her stomach. "I like it here."

"You liked it in Cincinnati just fine."

"I like it *here*, where you're around."

The room went silent and Nate closed his eyes. "Honey, you know my work—"

She shifted forward, anger radiating from her tense limbs. "We go fishing here. We hang out. We have dinner together. If we go back to Cincinnati, it's going to be the restaurant again all the time and the next time I see you will be my high school graduation."

He eyed her, letting her know she was approaching the line fast. "That's not fair and you know it."

"You know what's not fair? Most of my life, I've barely had one parent. Here, I've got almost two." She motioned toward Ruby, and Ruby's face went as soft as it ever got. "For the first time in my life, I almost have a real family, and you want to take that away."

Nate stared at his kid, unable to believe she was playing this dirty. Apparently there was a bit of Mick Brody in her after all, which was yet another reason to get them out of that place as fast as possible. "I'm a chef, Piper. Not a campground manager."

Piper leaned forward, her eyes pleading. "You can open a restaurant here. People need to eat everywhere."

"It's not the same. Between Deer Creek, Alabaster, and Noley, there are maybe ten thousand people. This area can't support the kind of cooking I do, you know that."

"Then cook something else," she huffed, throwing her

fork down and pushing back from the table. "I'm sick of stupid salmon, anyway."

She ran to the front door and slammed it behind her. Nate leaned forward where he could get a view of her through the living room window; she was heading down the path to the office. It was safe enough to let her sit out her fit there. He could go get her in a little while after she'd had time to cool off. He sat back in his chair and ran his hands through his hair. Ruby got up, topped off his wine, and set the bottle on the table next to him.

"You could just sell it," she said carefully. "Rip off the Band-Aid. The longer you stay here, the harder it's going to be."

Nate shook his head, staring out in the direction Piper had gone. "I gave my word."

Ruby let out a snort. "Your dad would have sold it in a minute and never looked back."

Exactly.

"When Number Four checks out," he said after a while, "we're closing down the cabins and tearing them up. I've looked everywhere else. It has to be there some-where. Shouldn't take more than a week, and then you'll be free, too."

After a protracted silence, Ruby nodded. "Sounds like a plan."

"Then it's a plan." Nate pushed back from the table. "Meantime, I've got a railing to fix."

CHAPTER TWO

*F*REYA SAT cross-legged on the sofa in her red satin pajamas, clean and comfortable and staring down at her laptop screen. She hit the play button on her media player and closed her eyes.

Eastern music played, and she set her hands on her knees, sitting the way the woman on the CD artwork was sitting.

"Visualize," the soft female voice said. *"Visualize what you want, and you shall have it."*

Freya took a deep breath, tried to visualize herself with Nathan Brody, shaking hands on this deal. Instead, all she got was his face smiling at her as he led his little girl out of the cabin.

"If you can see it, you can achieve it."

Freya pulled her shoulders up and released them, then rolled her head around to relax her neck. *Visualize.* She saw herself in her father's offices, head held high, everyone amazed and intimidated by her, the way it used to be. No one whispering that she'd lost her edge. No secretaries handing her tissues and asking her if she wanted to talk about her feelings.

"Agh!" She opened her eyes, flexed her hands as if flicking the bad away, and rolled her shoulders.

The audio file on her computer continued, *"Inside you is a light so bright, it is almost blinding. This light will help you achieve what you need to achieve. Visualize."*

Oh, crap. The light thing again. This part always made her feel stupid. ET had a light inside. People had intestines. Why had Flynn sent her this nonsense, anyway?

"Visualize. The light within—"

"Oh, screw it," she said, leaning forward and closing out the media player. The whole idea was stupid, anyway; the fact that she would even try using visualization techniques to get back to her old self was just more proof of how far she'd slipped. The fact was, the only thing that would make her feel like herself would be getting Nathan Brody's handshake on this deal, and going home with orders for Contracts to draw up the papers. Anything less, and she'd be going home a failure.

And that was unacceptable.

There was a light knock at her door and she called out, "I've got everything I need. Thanks anyway. Go away."

A small voice came from the other side of the door, but Freya couldn't understand what was said. She sighed, pushed up from the couch, and walked over to the door, pulling it open to find little Piper Brody staring up at her.

"Hey," Freya said.

"Hey," Piper parroted.

The kid stood in silence, staring up at Freya. Freya crossed her arms and leaned against the doorjamb. Piper scuffed her sneakers on the porch, then looked back up at Freya.

"You did knock, right?" Freya asked finally.

"You wanna ride bikes?"

Freya almost laughed, but there was a look of need in the girl's eyes that threw her off her guard. No one ever looked at Freya like that, mostly because Freya made a point of avoiding needy people. It was more hassle than it was worth, in her experience, and since she herself needed no one, it usually ended badly.

However, it was a damn sight better than having the kid pity her.

"I'm in my pajamas," she said finally.

Piper looked at her. "Those are pajamas? They look like a suit."

Freya glanced down at herself. Granted, the set was finely tailored, but who wore red satin to the office? She looked back at Piper. "Trust me."

Piper shot big brown eyes up at Freya through her lashes, her lip set in the slightest of pouts.

"Don't do that," Freya said.

"Do what?"

"Give me the pretty eyes. I've already got pretty eyes, kid, I don't need yours."

"Okay," Piper said, her shoulders slumping. "Well... bye."

"Oh, now that's just sad," Freya said.

Piper blinked. "What?"

"The big eyes, the pout, the slumping off. That usually works for you?"

Piper paused for a moment, then said, "Yeah."

"It's below you, kid," Freya said. "The second you use your girlness to give you the edge in negotiations, you remind everyone that you're a girl, and no one will take you seriously. Use your brain. Argue to win. Try again." Freya straightened up. "I'm in my pajamas."

Piper took a tentative step forward. "They look like clothes."

Freya raised an eyebrow, waiting for more. It took a moment, but she could see the lightbulb go on over the girl's head as she stepped even closer.

"And no one else is even around to see you," she said, sounding more like she was asking a question than making a statement, but still. It was progress.

Freya looked down at her feet. "I don't have any shoes on."

Piper pointed to the pair of slip-on Keds Freya used for slippers, which she'd left sitting by the couch. "There's a pair of sneakers right there."

Kid's got a good eye. "I'm tired."

"Exercise gives you energy."

"I don't have time."

"We'll just ride down to the lake and right back."

"Good." Freya leaned over, putting herself eye to eye with Piper. "As long as you've got a brain in that head, I don't want you to rely on pretty eyes again. If you want something, you argue for it, and don't take no for an answer, you get me?"

"Yeah." Piper hesitated. "So . . . you wanna ride bikes?"

Freya straightened up and eyed the kid for a moment, then said, "Can't say no now, can I?"

Piper's eyes lit with happy surprise. Freya slipped into her sneakers and followed the kid down the path toward the office where they retrieved a small pink bike for Piper and a larger, blue ten-speed for Freya. She and Freya hopped on and Piper led the way down the pine-needle-covered path into the woods, the tree branches overhead thick enough to mute the mellow glow from the predusk sky. It had been some time since Freya had been on a bike that went anywhere and she'd forgotten how much fun it could be to actually ride. Between the green, earthy smell of the forest and the warm early summer air on her face and the endorphins from the simple exercise, she was almost in a good mood by the time they broke through the woods to find the small lake peacefully reflecting the warm colors of the sky above it.

"Wow," Freya said, overtaken for a moment by how very pretty it all was. She didn't have long to appreciate it, though; Piper sped up, and Freya found herself having to work to keep up with the kid. The lake was surrounded by grass, but there was a well-worn dirt path circling it that made for relatively easy riding. Piper lifted up from her bike seat and pumped her legs hard, gaining speed, and Freya did the same, feeling the exhilaration of escape as they raced in silence around the lake. Piper finally slowed down when they reached a small shack near the dock. The little girl leaned her bike against it and walked out toward the dock, and Freya followed along.

At the end of the dock, Piper took off her shoes and socks and sat, her feet dangling into the water. Freya stood stiffly next to her.

"Aren't there fish and bugs in that lake?"

Piper nodded. "Yep. Wanna put your feet in? It's fun."

"No. Thanks." Freya stared down at the rippling pinks and oranges and pale yellows in the surface of the water. "Is it cold?"

"My father's so stupid," Piper said suddenly. "He never talks, and then when he does, he doesn't listen."

"Hey," Freya said, laughing lightly. "Who knew we had the same dad?"

Piper looked up at her. "Your dad is like that, too?"

"My dad is…" She sighed. "…not like yours. But yeah, listening is not his strong point. But maybe it's just harder for fathers to listen."

"Do mothers listen?" The child's voice was so light that Freya wasn't sure she'd heard her right, but when she looked down, she could tell by Piper's expression that she'd heard exactly right.

"Where's your mother?" Freya asked.

Piper shrugged, playing tough, and focused on swirling her right foot in a figure eight in the water. "She left when I was a baby."

"I'm sorry," Freya said.

"I don't remember her." The girl looked out at the water. "She's coming back, though."

"Really? So she's been in touch?"

Piper shook her head. "I just know she will. Someday."

"I see." Freya stepped a little closer to Piper. "My mother was a pretty good listener. I was only twelve when she died, though, so who knows?"

"I'm going to be twelve," Piper said. "In August. And I'll probably be back in stupid Cincinnati by then."

Freya perked up at this. Nathan Brody was moving, which meant that he must not be terribly attached to his craphole. As a matter of fact, money from the sale of the craphole might be welcome. Freya felt a surge of hope.

"Cincinnati," she said. "Nice town. I was there for a business trip a few years ago."

"I like it *here*."

Piper said it with such brutal finality that Freya took a moment before responding.

"Well, here's… nice, too."

"It is, right?" Piper said.

Freya took a deep breath and stared out at the lightly rippling surface. "I like the way it smells."

Piper pulled her feet out of the water and swiveled on the dock to face Freya. "You're very pretty, even without makeup," Piper said.

Freya wasn't sure how to take that, but said, "Thanks."

"What's it like being pretty?"

"Um. Nice. I guess."

"Have you ever been in love?"

Freya had to laugh. "Wow. That's a topic leap."

"How do you know when you're in love?"

"Whoa." Freya held up her hands to halt the barrage. "Hang on, there, Piper. One serve at a time."

Piper went quiet and stared up at Freya with those bright eyes, expecting...God only knew what. Freya knew she was way out of her depth dealing with kids, but she knew women pretty well, so she squatted down until her eyes were almost level with Piper's and said, "What's his name?"

Piper nibbled her lip for a moment, then seemed to come to a decision as her shoulders relaxed. "Matthew."

"Matthew what?"

A small smile appeared at the edge of the girl's lips. "Hartley."

"Right." Freya sat up straighter. "I think I get it now. You've got a thing for this Matthew Hartley, and your dad's getting set to pull you out of school here and take you to Cincinnati, and you don't want to go."

Piper rubbed at her big toe and shrugged. "It's not the only reason."

Freya nodded. "And your dad doesn't know about Matthew Hartley, does he?"

Piper's back went stick-straight and her eyes widened. "No! Oh, God, no. I can't talk to him about *boys*. He'd lock me in my room forever. He'd *home school* me."

"Right." Freya adjusted herself on her toes; squatting wasn't comfortable, but there was no way her satin ass was touching that dirty wooden dock. "So, this Matthew Hartley. He's cute?"

Piper nodded. "Really cute."

"And he likes you, too?"

Even in the waning sunlight, Freya could see Piper's cheeks flush. "I don't know."

"Well, let me tell you something about boys, Piper, which you'll figure out sooner or later but I say the sooner the better." She paused for dramatic effect. "Boys are stupid."

Piper's eyes widened. "Oh, not Matthew. He's really smart. He's on the honor roll and everything."

"No, I don't mean school-stupid," Freya said. "They're girl-stupid, and I'm sorry to tell you, it never gets any better. And the thing is, the ones who are girl-smart are only that way because they want to get in your pants, so they're no good, either. Basically, we're all screwed."

Piper's face suddenly froze up hard, and Freya realized what she'd said.

"Maybe I didn't say that right. What I mean is—"

"Yeah, explain," a voice cut in from behind her. "I didn't quite catch all of that."

Freya swiveled around to see the dark form of Nate Brody standing on the dock, his arms crossed over his chest and his face taut. She felt like a kid getting caught after curfew, and she didn't like the feeling. She stood up and held her hand out to pull Piper up to standing. Nate glanced past Freya at Piper.

"Since when do you ride down to the lake without telling me?"

"I was with an adult."

"She's not an adult," Nate said.

"Pardon me?" Freya said.

Nate gave her a dull look, then shifted his glance back to his daughter. "She's a guest. Guests are not babysitters."

"I'm not a baby!" Piper shouted, but instantly shifted a little behind Freya as she caught her father's dark look.

"C'mon, Nate—" Freya started but, on catching an intense look of warning from Nate, thought better of it and shut up.

"Piper," Nate said, his voice hard and even, "you get on that bike and go back to the house. *Now.*"

Piper slid out from behind Freya and stamped down the dock toward her bike. Nate watched her go, obviously waiting to unload on Freya until Piper was out of earshot.

Panic built in Freya's gut as they waited; how the hell was she going to fix this to the point where negotiations could start? The worst part—she was better than this. She'd been better than *this* when she'd first started working for her father as a freakin' intern.

What the hell had happened to her?

Piper rode out of sight, and Nate turned on Freya, his eyes dark. "What the hell do you think you're doing?"

"Look, just let me explain—"

"You don't have kids, do you?"

Anger rose, pushing the panic aside, and her jaw clenched tight against it. "No, but—"

He advanced on her, his voice rising. "Maybe you don't understand how these things work, but you don't just run off with someone else's kid without telling them."

"*Hey*," Freya said, advancing on him in turn. "First of all, I didn't come looking for your kid. She asked me to ride bikes, and for all I knew, she got your permission first. And maybe I don't know much about kids, but I'll tell you one thing—if it was my kid, I'd listen to her so that she didn't have to grab some random stranger just to have someone to talk to."

Never get personal. Always be friendly. Freya swallowed as she remembered the two most basic rules of negotiation. Less than twelve hours, and she'd managed to violate both of them with Nate Brody. If someone under her had ever screwed a deal up that badly that fast, she'd fire her on the spot. The anger seeped away from her and she turned her suddenly exhausted mind to her only tool left—walking away before she could screw anything else up.

"I have to go," she said, her voice cracking. Nate's face softened and he opened his mouth to say something, but she pushed past him and ran down the dock. She hopped on the bike and rode it back fast, her limbs shaking as she pumped harder, speeding through the woods back up to the cabins, a host of emotions running through her so fast she couldn't even recognize them all. Had she gone crazy? Riding bikes with some kid when she should be preparing for a negotiation... that wasn't like her.

But then, *she* wasn't like her, and hadn't been for a while.

Feeling a bit calmed from the exercise, she put the bike back at the office and walked to her cabin, where she saw that the stupid railing pieces had been roughly nailed back into place. She stared at it for a moment, focusing all her anger and frustration on the the hasty workmanship.

Great job, she thought. *You got a hell of a craphole here, Brody.*

Then she walked inside and found a vase of fresh-picked wildflowers on the coffee table next to a box of Kleenex. A yellow sticky note was fixed at the base of the flowers: *Will be back to really fix the railing tomorrow. Be careful.* —*N.*

"I was right," Freya said, ripping open the box as the first tear slid down her cheek. "Boys are stupid."

She grabbed her purse, withdrew her cell phone and dialed her father's office. Of course, despite the late hour, he answered on the second ring.

"Richard Daly."

"You really want this place?" she asked, then sniffled.

"Freya?" There was a pause. "You're not crying again, are you?"

"No." She crumpled up the tissue and tossed it into the garbage can in the corner. "I asked you a question. Do you want this place?"

Say no, change your mind, because I've already fucked this up beyond recognition and this guy is never going to sell to me.

"Yes, you know I want it, Freya."

She closed her eyes and took a deep breath, trying to work up the will to finish this thing. She'd had a killer instinct; it was just a matter of finding it again.

"Freya?" her father said in the silence. "Are you still there?"

Barely. "How much can I offer?"

"Have you talked the owner into selling?" he asked, surprise in his voice.

"No. And thanks for the heads-up that he already said no, by the way."

Her father sighed. "That information was in the documentation I gave you."

Great. Add that to her list of screwups. "Whatever. Look, he's planning on moving, so if he doesn't already have an offer, he's looking. He's probably just playing hard to get, waiting for the best deal. I can do some research tomorrow morning, but if I need to hop on an opportunity, I just want to know how long a rope I have to hang us with."

"Two million dollars."

Freya sat up straight, her heart pounding. "What— seriously? This place isn't worth half that."

"Then it should be easy to close the deal."

Right. Easy. Except it didn't make even the tiniest bit of sense. She ran her hand through her hair and took a deep breath. "Dad, what am I doing here? We shouldn't even be buying this place at all, but that kind of money—"

"I didn't send you out there to advise me," he said. "I sent you out there to make the deal. So make it."

There was a click on the line. She held the phone out and stared at it. "What? No pony?"

She flipped the phone shut, tossed it onto the coffee table, and lay back on the sofa, staring at the ceiling. Two million dollars. For this place. Good thing the man was retiring; he was obviously insane.

On the bright side, it was almost over. There was no way Nate Brody could possibly turn down an offer like that for land like this. She'd be on her way back home tomorrow afternoon at the latest.

She grabbed the afghan off the back of the sofa and wrapped it around herself, then spoke to the phone on the coffee table.

"Every girl should have a pony, you know."

Then she closed her eyes and fell asleep.

Ruby Vane heard the front door slam, followed by thumping footsteps, but by the time she ducked her head out of her bedroom door, all she saw was Piper's bedroom door slamming shut. There was no sign of Nate yet. She gently shut her door and locked it, then lifted up the rug on her bedroom floor, counted the wide oak floorboards until she hit the right one, and pushed her foot down on one end until the other end popped up. She grabbed it with her hands, set it aside, and then sat down cross-legged next to the hole in the floor. She reached down into the floor and withdrew the foot-long plastic, purple ladies' tackle box. She set it on her lap and ran her fingers over it, then slowly undid the latch and opened it. In the deepest part of the box was a dinner plate wrapped in plastic. Taped to it was a yellowed piece of paper with *Deliver to the Boise Police* scratched on it in Mick's jagged hand.

She reached in and picked it up. Through the aged plastic she could see it was kinda ugly. Ornate gold trimmed the scalloped edges. The rim was a deep pinkish purple, and in the center was an eagle with its wings spread out as it stood on a shield sporting the stars and stripes.

"Ugh." She turned it over and read the gold imprint on

the back again. "Haviland and Company. Lime-o-gees." She set it back down in the tackle box. "Huh."

She had no idea what it meant, what it was, or why it had been so important to Mick that Nate find it and bring it to the authorities. All she knew was that as long as the box stayed hidden, Nate and Piper would remain in Deer Creek, and Ruby wouldn't have to leave her home. And, yeah, Mick's dying wish went unfulfilled, but she could live with that.

"Sorry, babe," Ruby said quietly as she shut the box. "Payback's a bitch."

She tucked it back into the floor, replaced the board, and moved the rug back into place.

CHAPTER THREE

$\mathcal{N}$ATE SPENT most of his morning run trying to figure out exactly how he was going to apologize to Freya. The look on her face after he'd unloaded on her made him feel like shit. He had no right taking his panic out on her; Piper was his responsibility, and if he couldn't keep tabs on her, it certainly wasn't Freya's fault. The truth was, he hadn't even been *that* panicked; when Piper got upset, she always went either to the office or to the lake, and he'd been pretty sure he'd find her there. What had really thrown him for a loop was finding his baby girl getting advice on boys from Freya Daly.

That had kept him up all night.

Even so, when Nate emerged from the path in the woods to see Freya—wearing a well-tailored gray pinstripe power suit and heels that could perform an appendectomy—beelining toward his office, his first instinct was to avoid her. He slowed to a jog and thought briefly about ducking back into the woods, but her eyes locked on him and he was stuck. He bent over to stretch a bit as she changed course; he had a feeling it couldn't hurt to limber up before this interaction.

"Good morning, Nate." Her posture was ramrod-straight, her hair pulled back tight. In her right hand, she clutched a briefcase. Her smile seemed calculated, almost stiff, and his guard went up.

"Morning, Freya."

They stared at each other for a moment, then she said, "I'd like to start by apologizing about last night. It didn't occur to me that Piper hadn't asked you first. I wasn't thinking."

"I appreciate that," he said, feeling oddly formal, "but it wasn't your fault. I was out of line, talking to you like that. I'm sorry."

She gave a small nod. "That's very kind, but really, I should have—"

"No, it's fine," he said. They stared at each other, silence fueling the awkwardness, and Nate wondered what the hell was going on. This woman in front of him was all sharp angles and cold agendas, nothing like the warm, vulnerable woman he'd yelled at yesterday, and suddenly he wanted to be cleaned up and in a suit before trying to get an apology past her.

"Well," he said, shifting toward the house. "I should probably go take a shower."

"Wait," she said, stepping a bit closer. "I think we got this whole thing off on the wrong foot yesterday, and I was hoping I might be able to take you out to breakfast this morning."

"Um," Nate said, not sure if he was more amused or surprised by this turn of events. "No. That's not necessary. Just...enjoy your stay. When are you planning on checking out, by the way?"

He realized that had come off a little rude, but Freya only smiled wider.

"Actually, that kind of depends on you," she said.

"Right," he said. "Look, I told you. I'm not selling. It's a waste of your time."

"Why don't you let me be the judge of what wastes my time?" She pulled the briefcase in front of her, using both hands to hold the handle, looking a bit like a little girl with a treasured lunch box on the first day of school. It was cute as hell.

"All right," he said. "We can talk, I guess. But there aren't many places around here that are..." He searched for a word that wouldn't make him sound like a food snob, but gave it up. "The food in this town is total crap."

"Wow," she said. "Way to support the locals."

"There was a decent diner in the next town for a while, but a McDonald's moved in next door and they closed down. And the other places here I've been to weren't great, to be honest."

"Well, let me take you out to coffee, then," she said, taking another step closer. "It's hard to screw up coffee, isn't it? And I don't think this will take long at all."

He was suddenly overcome with a desire to make this take as long as possible. "Why don't you come on up to the house and let me make you breakfast?"

"Oh," she said, looking a little surprised by the offer. "I kind of wanted to talk to you alone. Since this is a business discussion."

"Well," he said, suddenly determined to win at least this part of the negotiation, "Ruby's in the office and Piper's not speaking to me, so she went along with her. We'll be alone."

"Oh." Her posture softened as she glanced toward the house, then back to him. "I just wanted to keep things...you know. Professional."

Her eyes met his, and she was back, the vulnerable woman he'd met yesterday. He smiled, hoping to keep this Freya in play. "I can charge you if you want."

She raised an eyebrow at him, but her eyes were bright with amusement. "Are you making fun of me?"

"A little."

"All right. Fine." She nibbled her lip a little, and it took Nate a moment to meet her eye again.

"Great." He motioned toward the path that led to the house. "It's just through here, beyond the trees."

They started down the path in silence, Nate following behind her and wondering a little what he'd just gotten himself into, but not caring much.

Freya picked a grape off the bunch that Nate had set out on the breakfast bar for her and closed her eyes as the cool juices shot into her mouth. The sounds of the shower had stopped a few minutes before, and she could hear his feet pounding through the hallway. She grabbed one more grape and popped it into her mouth.

"These are amazing," she said when he appeared in the kitchen. "I don't think we have grapes like these in Boston."

"If you've got a farmers' market, you've got them," he said, grabbing a plain white bistro apron off the wall and tying it around his waist. "You just have to get out of the supermarkets, start buying fresh."

Freya nodded, as though she had the slightest idea where a farmers' market might be. Her entire pantry at her apartment consisted of two cans of tuna, a few packets of Crystal Light lemonade, and menus for all the takeout places within a one-mile radius. But for now, she needed to make nice with Nate Brody, present the offer, get the deal done, and get gone.

"So," Nate said, his head deep in the open refrigerator. "How do you feel about goat cheese in your omelet?"

"Very good," she said. "I feel like I should offer to help, but I'm a disaster in the kitchen."

"Everyone says that," he said, his head still in the fridge, "but they're never as bad as they think they are." He popped up, arms full with a hunk of cheese in Saran Wrap, a clear plastic package containing six brown eggs, and something green and leafy. He shut the fridge door with a quick kick.

"No, no, I'm as bad as I think I am," Freya said. "I once set a pot of boiling water on fire." He stopped and looked at her, and she held up her hand in an oath. "Scout's honor, I'm useless in the kitchen."

"Oh, well. Now you just sealed your own fate." Nate unloaded his ingredients onto the counter, then reached behind him and grabbed another apron off the wall. He tossed it at her and she barely managed to catch it before it hit her in the face.

"And what am I supposed to do with this?" she asked.

"Put it on. You're cooking breakfast."

She laughed out loud and threw the apron back at him. "Funny."

He tossed it back, eyebrows raising in challenge. "Not kidding."

She watched him for a bit, decided he was serious, and stood up to show off her suit. "This is Ann Taylor."

"Hence the apron."

He walked over to her, expertly slid the jacket off her shoulders and laid it on the stool next to her. Then he grabbed the apron and slid his arms around her waist.

"I'm not sure…" she said, feeling oddly out of breath with him so close. He smelled like the hot shower he'd just stepped out of, and it was making her a little dizzy. "I…um…oh!" she said as he cinched the apron tightly around her waist and tied it, his hands floating over her body expertly, making her flush a bit at the sudden odd intimacy. "I…don't…"

"Yeah?" he said, then he took her left arm, undid the button at her wrist and began rolling up her blouse sleeve. "You got a full sentence in there somewhere?"

She didn't. His movements were strong, confident, professional, and her skin was starting to feel hot as his hands worked over her. He finished with her right sleeve, then stood back and took her in.

"Perfect," he said, his eyes raising to meet hers. He swallowed quickly then stepped back, motioning toward the stove in invitation.

Freya hesitated. "You're serious?"

"Yep."

"Look, I'm not being modest. I really can't cook."

"People think they can't cook because they burned one meal and quit." He jerked his head toward the stove. "I'll watch over you the whole time, tell you exactly what to do." He met her eye again. "There's nothing to be afraid of."

"I'm not afraid," Freya said.

He smiled. "Prove it."

She stared at him for a moment, then decided to concede. It'd soften him up for negotiations later, presuming she didn't burn the house down, which was a minimal risk if he was right there watching over her.

"All right." She popped one last grape into her mouth and scooted around the breakfast bar into the kitchen.

She stopped in front of the stove and he angled himself behind her, close enough that she could feel his breath on the back of her neck. He pointed to a knob on the stove. "Turn that to medium."

Freya reached tentatively toward the knob and turned it. It clicked a few times, a sharp tang hit her nose, and then the gas hissed on, all flickery and blue. "Oooh, pretty."

"Tell me you've seen a gas stove before."

"Up close? No."

"*Hell*," he said under his breath. He stepped aside, grabbed a large pan off the wall, and handed it to her. "Okay, let's get this frying pan on, let it heat up a bit."

She took it and put it down over the fire. So far, so good.

He shifted to her right and started dealing with the green leafy stuff, then reached with one hand, grabbed a white plastic squeeze bottle and handed it to her. "Here. Put a couple turns of olive oil in the pan."

He ran the green leafy stuff under the water, and Freya looked at the bottle, hoping for something on it that would explain what a "couple turns" was. Unfortunately, the bottle was blank. Nate was already dicing the cheese before he noticed she was standing there, frozen.

"Everything okay?"

She turned to him. "A couple turns? What does that mean?"

He wiped his hands on the apron and put his hand over hers. "Turn it over, squeeze it, and run your hand in a circle twice, like you're tracing the numbers on a clock." She did as told, trying not to jump back as the oil hit the pan and sizzled. From behind her, Nate guided her hand around in two efficient circles, then let her go.

"Couple turns," he said, then went back to where he'd been working. He held up a handful of the green stuff. "Spinach." He tossed it in the pan, so much that it was almost overflowing. She barely had time to ask what was next before he put a wooden spoon in her hand. "Stir it around. It'll cook down, and then we'll add the eggs and the cheese."

She stirred, and next to her, he whizzed around the kitchen like an expert. He diced the cheese with a speed that made her a little nervous, then cracked a bunch of eggs into a bowl, whipped them up, and seasoned them with salt and pepper. Then he wiped his hands on his apron and walked over behind her, his expression relaxed and happy as he observed her work.

"Good job." He lowered the flame a bit, then poured the egg mixture in over her spinach. He handed Freya the cheese cubes. "Sprinkle these on top."

Freya did as told, trying to get them evenly into the eggs. She wiped her hands on her apron and said, "Now what?"

"Now, we wait for a minute."

"Okay." She looked down at the eggs. It felt weird to just stand there. She raised her wooden spoon. "Should I—?"

"No." He put his hand on hers and lowered it. "Sometimes the hard part is doing nothing."

She turned a bit to look at him. Their eyes met and held, and then he said, "Now."

"Hmmm?"

"Shut the flame off."

She glanced at the eggs. "But they're not cooked in the middle."

"Exactly. Shut the flame off."

She did as instructed.

"Good," he said. "Now grab the pan and put it in the oven."

"Okay." She reached for the pan handle. "But the oven's not on, is it?"

"It is. I turned it on when I first started."

"Wow." Freya pulled the oven open and inserted the frying pan. "Guess I missed that part." She closed the oven door and turned to face him. "So. You're really good in the kitchen."

"Should be," he said. "I'm a chef."

"A chef?"

"Yeah," he said. "I have a restaurant in Cincinnati."

He missed it, she could tell by the look on his face. This was almost going to be too easy. "Well, if you have a restaurant in Cincinnati, what are you doing here?"

"Good question," he said, but didn't seem at all inclined to answer it. Still, the opening was right there. All she had to do was walk through it.

Child's play.

"So, hypothetically, if someone offered you a lot of money for this place, would you sell it?"

He raised an eyebrow. "Depends. Is this hypothetical person insane?"

"Does it matter if the check clears?"

He smiled at her, and Freya's breath caught. "I don't know. How much are they hypothetically offering?"

Freya hesitated for a moment, gave Nate a moment to let his imagination fly. She'd been looking forward to this part all morning, and the excitement built as she laid it out for him.

"A million dollars."

Nate laughed. "For this place? You've got to be kidding."

He was reacting just like she'd expected, and now she was seconds away from a yes, and a million bucks under budget to boot. She could practically taste the champagne on her first-class flight back home.

"Not kidding," she said, unable to keep the seductive tone out of her voice. "Would you take that offer?"

He shrugged. "Well. Hypothetically, yeah. I'd be crazy not to."

God, she almost wished her father could be there to see her. "Great! I'll head back to Boston tonight and have the papers drawn up. I'll need the name and contact information for your real estate agent and your attorney—"

He held his hand up. "Wait. Whoa. What happened to hypothetical?"

Her heart skipped as she looked at him, his forehead creased, his smile gone.

This was not what she'd planned.

"Oh, come on," she said. "You knew I was making an offer."

"We were talking hypotheticals," he said.

"Well, now we're not. One million nonhypothetical dollars are right here on the table, for the taking. We can shake on it right now. There will be some details for the lawyers to work out, obviously, but I don't see why you can't have a check in your account before the month is out."

Nate stared at her in silence, then said simply, "I'm sorry. I didn't mean to lead you on."

Freya's body went slack. "What...*lead me on*? You just said—"

He ran his hands over his hair and said, "I know. I was…flirting. I wasn't…I mean, you shifted gears kinda fast there and I lost the thread." He cleared his throat, looking almost as unhappy as she was feeling. "I'm sorry, but the answer is no. I'm not selling right now."

"Okay. Fine. You want to play hardball? One-point-two-five." It was an embarrassing offer to have to make, but hell. She was still under budget.

Nate shook his head. "I don't think you understand. I'm not playing hardball—"

Damnit. "One and a half. But I'm telling you, that's my final offer. I cannot go higher."

"Freya," he said, shaking his head. "You're not listening to me. I'm not selling the campground. The answer is no."

She bit her lip. She couldn't. She *couldn't* pay two million dollars for this property and go home with her head held high. She just…she couldn't.

But if she went back without a deal at all, scorched in the ass by her last flaming hoop, passed over for the promotion that was hers after all this work…

Well. That wasn't an option.

"Fine," she said through clenched teeth. "Two million, but seriously, I really can't go any high—"

"*Stop,*" he said, putting his hands on her arms. "Please, stop before I have to kill myself."

Her heart beat hard and fast in her chest, and her throat tightened as she realized with a cold panic that she'd left her purse, with her Tic-Tacs in it, in her cabin.

Fine, if you can't fight it, use it.

Hating herself, she looked up at him through her lashes. "Nate, you don't understand. My father is retiring.

If I don't close this deal, he's gonna pick Charlie Taggert over me to run the company, and *I'm family*." Her throat tightened, and she swallowed hard. "I won't be able to still work there if that happens, it'll be too humiliating." She blinked hard and took a breath, then did her best to smile up at him, show him the pretty as her stomach turned. "Nate, I can't go home without this deal."

He looked away, then shook his head. "I'm sorry. The answer is no."

She stared at him in total disbelief. A few seconds ago she was on a plane back to Boston, victorious and confident. And now...

Now she was a failure. A failure who'd stooped to *pretty*.

"This isn't happening," she muttered.

"Oh, shit," Nate said suddenly, then darted past her and opened the oven. He wrapped his apron over his hand and pulled the pan out, then set it down quickly on the stove top, where it smoked heartily. The entire top was blackened, and the acrid smell of burning goat cheese filled the room, matching Freya's mood in both foulness and intensity.

"There you go," she said, swiping under one eye and hoping Nate wouldn't notice. "I told you I couldn't cook."

"No, that was my fault." He looked up at her and his face grew concerned. "You okay?"

She sniffled. "It's my stupid eyes."

"Ah." He nodded. "Right. The condition."

She kept her eyes on the black, smoking top of their crap omelet. "Yep."

"I have more ingredients," he said flatly. "If you want to try again."

Freya reached down and tried to untie the strings on her apron. "No. That's fine." Her voice was squeaking, and the tears were coming fast and she couldn't get the strings undone. "What the hell kind of sailor's knot did you put this in, anyway?"

"Let me." He reached forward, gave a quick tug and pulled the apron off her, then set it on the kitchen counter.

"You know what's really infuriating?" she said, snatching a paper towel off the roll on the counter and wiping at her face. "I have *amazing* powers of negotiation. I have brought CEOs to their knees. If it weren't for this stupid eye condition, you would be signing papers right now. But instead I'm crying, and you think I'm weak, and I'm screwed."

"I don't think you're weak," he said, his voice soft. "My saying no isn't about you at all."

"Right." She looked up to see him watching her, his face full of sympathy, and she started to cry harder. "Please don't look at me that way."

"What way?"

"Like you pity me."

He touched her hand. "Hey, I just turned down two million dollars. You should be pitying me."

She wanted to scowl at him, but instead a small laugh came out, and then suddenly, they were standing closer, although Freya had no idea who'd made the move. The next thing she knew, he pulled her into his arms, and she rested her cheek on his shoulder. The relief was almost instant, like air being let out of a tire that was too full.

"I'm not crying," she said and sniffled. "It's just a stupid condition."

"I know." He let his hand run lightly down her hair and tightened his hold on her. She closed her eyes and let herself fully lean into him. It felt like falling and being caught. It felt like not having to be responsible for everything.

It felt like heaven.

Just one more second of this, she thought. *One more second, and then I'll go.*

The problem was, for the first time since her plane touched ground, she suddenly didn't want to go anywhere.

"Better?" he said, his voice barely above a whisper.

She pulled back, dry-eyed. "Yeah."

Then she stepped back, keeping her eyes on his. Slowly, wordlessly, she picked up her briefcase and suit jacket and escaped out the front door, grateful that Nate didn't say a word to stop her.

CHAPTER FOUR

$\mathcal{R}$UBY FLIPPED the card from the top of her stock pile into the center waste pile and Piper slapped the pile hard, the sound bouncing off the wood paneled walls of the small back office.

"Put some shoulder into it, why don't you?" Ruby said, glancing down at Piper's hand with suspicion. "You sure that's a legal slap?"

"Plus one." Piper shifted the five of hearts that Ruby had just played to reveal the four of clubs beneath it. "Legal slap."

"Oh, fine." Ruby sat back and watched Piper slide the pile of cards toward her off Ruby's beaten-up old desk and neaten them up before putting them on the bottom of her stock pile. Kid was gonna beat her at this game again.

Which was okay. Ruby didn't ever like losing, but losing to Piper was different. That, she didn't mind so much.

Piper flipped the top card into the middle. Six of clubs.

Ruby flipped her card. Eight of diamonds. "So, you haven't talked to your dad since last night?"

Piper laid down her card. King of spades. "Nope."

Ruby took her turn. Two of diamonds. "You know he just wants what's best for you, right?"

Piper shrugged and put down a four of hearts. "He just wants his restaurant. He doesn't care about me or what I want."

Ruby put her palm down on the center pile, and Piper raised her eyes. "That's not a legal slap."

"I'm not slapping. I'm pausing." She leaned forward, leveling her eyes with the girl's. "Your dad is a good man and he loves you, and if you don't know that, then you're not near as smart as you think you are."

Piper rolled her eyes, and Ruby fixed a hard stare on the kid. "Do I roll my eyes at you, little miss?"

Piper sat up straighter, her lip set in a small pout, and shook her head.

"Right. And why don't I roll my eyes at you?"

Piper sighed. "It's disrespectful."

"Right. I show you respect, and you show me respect. That's our deal." Ruby sat back. "Let me tell you something. I grew up with one man who didn't give a crap, then I ran out at seventeen and married me another one just like him. Since then, it's been hit and miss, mostly miss, so I know men that don't care, and I'll tell you this, your dad is not one of them. He's got his life back in Cincinnati, and he's got the right to miss that. It doesn't mean he doesn't love you."

Piper slumped back in the folding chair. "If he loves me so much, why doesn't he care about what I want? I like it here. I don't want to go back to stupid Cincinnati. I want to be a real family, here."

Ruby eyed the girl for a short while, then said, "I might be able to help you with that."

Piper raised hopeful eyes to Ruby. "Really? Are you going to talk to him?"

"No," Ruby said. "Your dad's got his mind made up, and it's not my place to try and change it. But..."

Ruby pulled open the desk drawer, grabbed the key ring, and pushed back from the desk, her bones creaking as she stood up. Goddamn, it was a bitch getting old. She walked over to the filing cabinet, unlocked the top drawer, and reached into the back until she felt the soft fabric under her fingers. She shut the cabinet and sat back down at the desk.

"The only man in my family who was ever worth anything was my grandfather," she said, loosening the purse string on the old pouch. "He was from Ireland, and I only saw him a few times before he died. But one of those times, he gave me this." She pulled the silver coin out of the pouch and flipped it back and forth between her fingers, studying the Irish harp on one side and the horse on the other.

"He gave you a quarter?" Piper asked, and Ruby could tell she was trying not to sound disappointed. She was such a good kid, this one.

"It's an Irish half crown, minted the year I was born." She passed it on to Piper, who took it gingerly and turned the coin over in her hands, then furrowed her brow and nibbled her lip.

"Don't hurt yourself with the math. I'm sixty-two. The point is, the coin is magic."

Piper raised doubtful eyes to Ruby's. "Magic isn't real."

"Now who told you that?" Ruby said. "Magic is real enough, but you have to really believe in it, which pretty much means you have to find it when you're a kid. When my grandpa gave me this, I was still young enough to believe in it, and you know what?"

Piper's eyes went wide as she shook her head. "No."

"It works."

The child went still. She looked down at the coin in her palm, then back up at Ruby. "What does it do?" she asked, her voice high and quiet.

"It grants wishes."

Piper picked it up, holding the coin by the edge and examining it. "How?"

"Well, first, there has to be something you really want, so much that it makes your heart hurt to think of it. You don't use it to wish for a Barbie doll or a new bike or something stupid like money, you know what I'm saying?" Ruby paused for a moment until Piper met her eyes again. "Do you have something you want that bad?"

Piper hesitated, but then nodded.

"Okay, then." Ruby pushed up from her chair and walked over to stand next to Piper. "You need to face east."

Piper stood up as well. "Which way is east?"

"You know which way is east."

"No, I don't."

Ruby sighed. What the hell were they teaching kids in school these days? "Where does the sun rise from?"

Piper closed her eyes for a second, then opened them. "Over there," she said, pointing toward the big window at the front of the office."

"Okay." Ruby felt a wave of love rush through her. Kid was smart. "Now you know where east is. Face it."

Piper turned to face the window.

"Close your eyes. Good. Now cup it in your hands, place your hands over your heart, and make your wish, but don't say it out loud. Just think it in your head, three times."

Piper cupped the coin in her hands and pulled them in to her chest, her brow furrowed in concentration. After a long moment, her face smoothed out.

"Now what?" she asked, her eyes still closed.

"That's it. You can open your eyes now."

The girl opened her eyes. "How long does it take?"

"It takes as long as it takes," Ruby said. "But it will happen, if you believe it. Do you believe it?"

Piper let out a deep breath, but then a soft smile broke on her face and she nodded. "Yes."

"Good."

Piper held the coin out to Ruby. "Thanks."

Ruby shook her head and walked back to the desk. "It's yours now. If anyone else touches it, it'll break the wish. Keep it in the pouch, and carry it in your pocket during the day and put it under your pillow at night. Then, when the wish comes true, you put the pouch somewhere safe and hide it until you need it again."

She watched as Piper gingerly took the pouch, tucked the coin inside, and put them into her front pocket.

Ruby sat back in her chair and tried to remember the words the way her grandfather had said them all those years ago. "Now, I don't know what you wished for, but whenever you feel like you don't have any control over your life, you just remember that wish, and try not to get upset. You've got old Irish magic working for you now, and that's the most powerful thing on earth." Something like that, anyway.

Piper sat down in the chair opposite Ruby. "Whose turn was it?"

"Mine, I think." Ruby flipped her card over. The four of spades. She slapped, getting her hand in just under Piper's.

"Damnit." Piper pulled her hand back, but she was smiling, and her face was a hell of a lot brighter than it had been all day.

"That's what happens when you get cocky," Ruby said as she gathered her winnings from the center of the desk. "I may be old, but I've still got a trick or two left in me, and don't you forget it."

Two million dollars.

It had been all Nate had been able to think about all day. At the lumber yard, at the farmers' market, driving back home, those three words repeated over and over in his head. *Two million dollars. Two million dollars.* He couldn't believe he'd gotten the offer, and what he couldn't believe even more was that he'd turned it down.

Two million dollars.

He pounded another nail into the support post on Number Four as hard as he could. Freya's car was gone, so there was no one to be bothered by it, but even pounding nails wasn't making the pit in his stomach any less hollow.

Two. Million. Dollars.

That money could get Piper through college. Twice. He could set Ruby up with enough to be comfortable for the rest of her life and still have some left over to get state-of-the-art everything for the kitchen in the restaurant.

But instead, he was here, in Crap Creek, Idaho, fixing the stupid railing on a stupid cabin in a stupid campground he didn't even want, all because he'd given his word to a man who had no familiarity with the concept of honor.

He pulled another nail out of his tool belt, lined it up, and raised his hammer.

Two.

Million.

Doll—

"Ow!" He threw the hammer down and jammed his smashed thumb into his mouth, cursing. With the palm of his uninjured hand, he hit at the new railing. It held, so he hit it again. Didn't budge. He pulled his smashed thumb out of his mouth, wrapped both hands around the new railing, and shook it, yelling out his frustrations as he did. Yelling at his dead father, his damn bad luck, the woman who left him to raise a kid by himself, the world.

"Having a bad day?"

Nate turned around to see Freya standing next to the open door of her rental car. She was wearing her skirt and blouse from that morning, but she'd lost the blazer, and her hair was loose around her shoulders. Over her blouse, she wore a T-shirt that read "Kiss me, I'm from Idaho" with a big smooch mark over her left breast.

He cleared his throat. "I like your outfit."

"It's called retail therapy," Freya said, then turned around and dived back into her car. When she popped back out, she was laden with various shopping bags boasting logos he recognized from the tourist shop strip off Route 8. She used her hip to shut the car door and made her way over to him. "I was all depressed, you know, after you shot me down this morning, and then I thought—hey, I'm in Idaho. Time to shop." She glanced at the railing, then back at Nate. "Nice job."

Nate bent down and picked his hammer up off the ground, slipping it back into the loop on his tool belt. "You seem pretty cheerful for someone who's depressed."

She smiled, lifting her laden arms high, and despite the desperation at the back of her eyes, she had a radiance about her that brightened his own mood.

"Let me tell you something about me, Nate," she said. "When things get bad, I get badder. I fight it out, I scrap, I dig in my heels until I'm the last one left standing. But now, you know, between us . . . I just don't have the energy, so I figured I'd change tactics. This time, I'm gonna steep myself in denial, pretend that everything I've worked for my entire adult life isn't imploding before my eyes, and get drunk."

He eyed her. "Is this an attempt to guilt me into taking your offer?"

She went still, her eyes focusing sharply on him. "I don't know. Is it working?"

He looked at the railing, feeling bleak. "Sorry."

"Well, then, back to Plan A." She raised one arm, bags dangling. "Somewhere in here, I have a bottle of Blue Ice Idaho Potato Vodka. I'm gonna go inside and get sauced."

He watched with amusement as she walked up the steps and went into the cabin, leaving the door wide open behind her. He stood there, listening as she dumped her bags on the floor, mumbling to herself. He knew he should leave, but being around her cheered him, so he made slow work of clearing out the nails and tools he'd left spread around his work area. When he looked up again, Freya was standing in the doorway, blue bottle in one hand and two glasses in the other.

"What, were you raised by wolves?" she said. "You don't know an invitation when you see one?"

She turned and disappeared back into the cabin. Nate stood where he was for a minute, thinking. Ruby and Piper were back at the house making dinner; they wouldn't miss him. And hell, if ever he needed a drink, now was the time. What could it really hurt to have one drink with a pretty woman? He was a single father, not a goddamn monk.

Freya reappeared in the doorway. "Hey. Brody. Are you coming in or not? You're letting the bugs in."

Nate unbuckled his tool belt and dumped it on the porch floor. Two minutes later, they were facing each other on opposite ends of the couch, each nursing a glass of vodka. Freya had set a shopping bag on her lap, and she pulled out a small souvenir spoon in a tiny plastic case.

"I never understood those," Nate said. "What's the point?"

Freya snorted. "I have no idea." She flipped it around so he could see it. "But it says Idaho, so I bought it." She held up a small plastic bag full of small, round, white candies. "Idaho Snowman Poop. I mean, who thinks up these things?"

"People who get paid too much," Nate said, taking a sip of his drink and watching her closely, amused by every movement she made. She might be having a mental breakdown, but she was doing it beautifully.

She pulled out a ceramic potato on a red ribbon, running her hand under it in the air like a television spokesmodel. "A potato Christmas tree ornament." She glanced around, surveying the room, then pointed to the corner behind her. "I think my tree will look nice right there, don't you?"

"You plan on being here at Christmas?" Nate said, surprised.

"Why not?" she said, shifting around again to face him. "Isn't that what people do when they fail miserably? Start over in a new place?" She glanced around. "And this place is new. To me."

He looked at her. "I find it hard to believe you can't bounce back from this. It's just one deal."

"It's not," she said softly. "It's the last flaming hoop. And it doesn't matter that I got through all the other flaming hoops. It'll just matter that I fucked up the last one." She lifted her glass and sipped, and her forced smile faded a bit.

"I'm sorry," Nate said.

"So," she said louder, her cheerfulness returning, "are you gonna tell me why you can't sell me this place, even though you're a chef with a restaurant back home that you can't wait to get back to?"

"This is my father's place. He was dying. I hadn't spoken to him in years, never wanted to talk to him again, but he was dying." Nate shook his head. "He made me give my word that I'd do something for him before selling the land. I still haven't done it, so I can't sell."

Freya stared at him blankly. "You turned down two million dollars to keep your word?"

Nate took a drink. "Don't remind me."

"You know there's honorable and then there's just stupid, right?"

He raised his eyes to see her smiling at him, and then shook his head. "I know which one I am. I don't need you reminding me."

She sighed. "Okay, we'll take it from another angle.

You just have to do something, right? What is it? Maybe
I can help."

"I have to find something."

"I'm good at finding things," she said, shifting closer
on the couch. "What is it?"

"I don't know."

"You don't know?"

"He started to describe it, and then he died. All I know
is that it's purple, and about"—he held his hands twelve
inches apart—"this big." Nate laughed at how ridiculous
it sounded when he said it out loud.

Freya was silent for a long moment, then said, "Forgive
me for being indelicate, but was he on . . . maybe . . . painkillers when he elicited this promise?"

"My dad was on a lot of things in his life, but no. This
time, he was lucid. Whatever this thing is, it's here and
until I find it, so am I."

"So, I take it you're a man of your word, then? You
won't go back on it? Even for the kind of money that
could keep you and yours comfortable for the rest of your
lives?"

Nate took a large gulp of the vodka. "My word matters
to me. I'm sorry if that makes things harder for you."

Freya put her drink on the coffee table, then leaned
back, resting her head on the back of the couch and looking at him.

"You're not stupid," she said.

He angled his head to look at her. "Gee. Thanks."

"I mean, from before. I said you were either stupid or
honorable. You're not stupid."

"Well, that's a matter of opinion." Nate rested his head
on the back of the couch as well, looking at her, and the

air between them seemed to heat up. Her eyes were soft from the vodka and seemed to glisten in the low light. She was so beautiful, so close that he'd just have to move the tiniest bit and he'd be kissing her, and she smelled like heaven. All he had to do was put that damn glass down and give in, let himself have what he wanted, just this once...

"Don't feel bad about screwing up my deal, okay?" she said softly. "You did the right thing, and I'm gonna be okay."

"I know."

She raised her head, looking surprised. "What?"

"I know you'll be fine," he said. "You're a strong woman, Freya, anyone who sees you knows that. You seem like the type of person who can bounce back from anything."

She sat up. "I do? Even after...all the tears and burning the omelet and my total failure to swing what should have been the biggest cake deal of my career?" Her chin trembled slightly and she pushed up from the couch, walked over to the door, and grabbed her purse. Nate set his glass on the coffee table and followed her.

"Did I say something wrong?" he asked.

She shook a few Tic-Tacs into her hand and popped them in her mouth, her back to him. "No. I just need a moment." She took a few deep breaths, then turned to face him, her eyes dry as they locked on his. "Thank you."

He reached up and touched her face. She stepped closer and angled her face up toward his and she was so close, all he had to do was—

"I should go," he said softly.

She blinked. "What?"

He swallowed, unable to think. "It's…it's getting late."

"It's six o'clock," she said, but then threw her hands up in the air. "Okay. You know what? I'm not going to get shot down by the same guy twice in one day. Even my ego doesn't have that kind of fortitude." She scooted around him, putting her hand on the doorknob. "Forget it. Bye."

"Freya—" he began, but she cut him off.

"Don't worry," she said. "It's nothing a little Idaho potato vodka and some snowman poop won't cure. What the hell is in that stuff, anyway?"

"Freya—"

"Run along." She pulled the door open.

He shut it.

"Stop playing games," he said. "It's unattractive."

She raised an eyebrow. "Oh, *I'm* playing games? Nice. I'm not the one giving the sexy eye and then running out the door."

"I have a kid," he said. "And…sexy eye?"

"I know you have a kid," she said, then made a face. "And you know what I mean."

"All right," he said. "Forget the sexy eye. My point is, I have a kid. It complicates things. Her mother abandoned her when she was really small. I've let her meet exactly three women in the past ten years and she got attached to each one, only to have her heart broken when it didn't work out."

"I understand that. It's just…" She let out a heavy sigh. "It's been a crap day, for both of us. We're both…itchy." She raised her eyes to his, and one side of her mouth twitched up in the sexiest smile he'd ever seen. "It might be nice to…scratch. That's all."

One arm went toward her, almost out of his control. The idea of scratching with this woman seemed like...damn. A really good idea.

Except it wasn't. He pulled his arm back.

"Look. Piper...she already likes you. If I stay here long enough to...scratch...Piper'll know. The kid always knows everything. And she'll start building castles in her head and—" He sighed, focused his thoughts on his daughter, and achieved a certain level of peace with what he was giving up for her. "Look, you and me, we can do this and walk away unharmed, but I've got a kid. What I do affects her, and I won't hurt her if I can help it."

Freya watched him, her eyes softening. "Okay. I won't take it personally." She held up her hand. "But, for the record, and my dignity, if it wasn't for Piper, you'd stay, right?"

"Oh, hell yeah," he breathed. Raw want rose in his gut as he looked into those smoky eyes, and he exhaled roughly. "I have to go. Now."

"All right." She pulled the door open and he stepped into the doorway. "You're a good man, Nate. That's a good thing."

She leaned back against the doorjamb and looked up at him, her lips slightly parted and her blue eyes soft from vodka and being itchy, and he couldn't believe his fucking luck. It had been a long time since a woman like that had looked at him like that, and he knew the odds were good it would be a long time before it happened again. And here he was, turning down money for his dad, turning down Freya for Piper and who would it kill if he touched her, just for a second?

He reached up one hand, just wanting to know the

feel of her skin. She nuzzled her face into his palm, just a slight movement, and everything else melted away but her. He stepped closer and she took in a deep breath as the warmth from their bodies built a raw heat between them. He moved slowly, knowing these few seconds would have to last him a long time. He slid his hand slowly from her face to her neck, letting his fingers twine in the softness of the hair at the back of her neck. He lowered his head, grazing his lips so lightly over hers that they barely touched. Freya moaned and his body hardened in response. He pulled her to him and kissed her as if it was the last thing he'd ever do, and if his heart didn't stop pounding like that, it just might be.

Her hands ran over his shoulders, her fingers pressing into his skin, sending waves of heat shooting through him, intensifying his need. She pulled him tighter against her, pressing her abdomen against him, making him so hard so fast that he thought his entire body would explode right there. Oh, God, if the itching was this good, how good would the scratching be?

"Oh, man," he said, pulling himself away with the last bit of strength he had left. "That was . . ."

"Yeah." She let out a breath, looking a little stunned herself.

He stared at her for a moment, willing some blood to return to his brain. She stared back, breathing heavily, and put her hand to her neck.

"Maybe you should go," she said.

"Yeah. Right." He pushed himself away from the doorjamb. "Good night."

"Night." She smiled, then stepped inside and shut the door. Nate knelt, gathered his toolbelt and box of nails from the porch, and started back for his house, the heady mix of Freya and vodka still on his lips. He walked slowly, concentrating on the taste of her, the smell of her, the memory of how she'd felt in his arms.

By the time he got to the house, he was sure.

That kiss had been worth the two million.

CHAPTER FIVE

FREYA SWIPED the bottle off the coffee table. She took one giant swig, coughed for a few minutes until her face was red, and still, even after a near-death experience by vodka, she was so turned on she hardly knew what to do with herself.

Well, she did have *one* idea, but... she glanced around at her immediate environment. A lumpy orange couch. She supposed she could pull out the bed inside, but by the time she...

The shower head.

"Oooh, smart girl, Freya." She walked into the bathroom and leaned against the doorway, staring at the tub. She couldn't believe it was just yesterday that she'd stood in that same place, watching Nate fix the leaky faucet there. If she'd had any idea how that man kissed, she would have thrown him down on the floor and had her way with him right then and there. Remembering the heat of him on her skin set her body back into overdrive, and she hurried out to her suitcase to get something comfortable to change into after her bath. If Nate wouldn't scratch her itch for her, she'd just have to scratch it herself.

It would be a far second to the real thing, but desperate times—

Her cell phone went off. Her shoulders tensed, and she hesitated, then said, "Better things to do," and went into the bathroom. She whipped off the "Kiss Me" T-shirt and her blouse, baring down to the silk camisole she had on underneath. She unzipped the side of her skirt and stepped out of it. The cool air of the bathroom on her skin felt good, and she eyed the shower head with some anticipation as the cell phone gave one last chirp, then cut off.

"Thank God for voicemail," she whispered. She closed her eyes and leaned against the sink, trying to bring her mind and body back to what Nate had made her feel. She imagined his lips on hers again, the feel of his hand on the small of her back as he pressed himself against her, her breasts pressed up against his strong chest, the cool taste of vodka on his tongue as he explored her—

The cell phone rang again. She opened her eyes, looked at herself in the mirror.

"Hold that thought," she said, then stormed out to the living room where she tossed the bags aside, trying to find her purse. It chirped off, going to voicemail just as she pulled it out of its case. She flipped it open, checked the missed calls log.

Dad. Talk about a mood killer. She hit dial, and waited. He answered on the second ring.

"Richard Da—"

"What? What is it you want, what is it you must have *at this exact moment* that can't wait??"

"Freya." He was using his stern voice.

Freya really didn't give a crap. "What is it? You got me, what do you want?"

"I was expecting to hear from you on the Idaho deal. Are you on your way home?"

She put her hand to her forehead, anticipating the headache that was sure to come. "No, not yet."

There was a slight pause. "Did you make the offer?"

"Yes. No deal. He won't sell."

Her father let out a half laugh. "Well...that's ridiculous. The property isn't worth near that much."

"No, Dad. It's not. I seem to recall pointing that out once or twice."

"Then what's the delay?" Her father's voice shifted from surprise to anger. "Freya, you should have had this deal sewn up in five minutes. I sent you because I thought you could close this one without a problem. I would expect this kind of thing from your sister, but you've always been one of my most dependable people."

Her shoulders slumped and she sighed. "I can close this deal. It's just...complicated." She plunked down on the couch where Nate had been sitting. "The guy has some family issues he needs to deal with. I just need a little more time—"

"Freya, this is a simple deal. There's no reason for it to drag on like this, not with that kind of money on the table. I'm beginning to think I should have sent someone else."

Someone *else*? Was he under the impression she was *vacationing* out here? Jesus. She blinked hard, then reached for her Tic-Tacs. "You don't need to send anyone else. I can handle this."

From the other end of the line, she heard her father's heavy sigh. "Come home. I'll send Charlie Taggert."

She crunched down on the mints, flipping the box over in her fingers. "And what happens when I come home?"

"What do you mean?"

"You know what I mean. If I don't come home with this deal signed, are you still going to recommend me to the board as your replacement?"

There was a long silence. Too long.

"Freya. I already made my recommendation."

"What?" The air went still around her, and then, like puzzle pieces clicking together, she finally got it. "You recommended Charlie."

Her father didn't answer.

"Bastard," Freya breathed.

"Freya, I'd like to pass this company on to you, but you and I both know that's just not a reasonable expectation."

"Really? We both know that?"

"Your performance has been uneven. You've been emotionally unstable." There was a long pause, and then he said, "You've lost your edge, Freya. Surely you've noticed that."

"Everyone struggles sometimes, Dad," she said, but he went on as if he hadn't heard her.

"Charlie's record, on the other hand, is above reproach, and he's got seniority—"

"*Seniority*? It's Daly Developers. I'm a Daly. You're gonna have me work under *Charlie Taggert*? The man thinks it's acceptable to goose his assistant. No one's ever going to respect me again if my own father picks him over me."

"Charlie has a strong record. The board feels comfortable with him. In a few years, when he's ready to retire, if you work hard—"

"If I *work hard*? What the hell do you think I've been doing?" Freya cleared her throat. "All right. Forget it. You know what? I'm gonna close this deal. If I don't, you can send Charlie. Or, you know, maybe come and close it your damn self, since you seem to think it's so easy."

There was a stony silence, then he said, "Don't forget who you're talking to, Freya. I'm not just your father. I'm also your boss."

Not for long, she thought. "I'll be home in a few days. We'll talk more then."

She flipped the phone shut, her hand shaking. That was it. She had to make this deal now. She needed to come home victorious and drop the damn paperwork on her father's desk, right under her resignation.

She reached for her glass and downed the last bit, reeling with determination as it scorched its way through her. She'd find what Nate was looking for, if she had to tear up every inch of the place to do it. Then she'd sign that deal. She might lose her father, her job, her apartment, but goddamnit, she was going to keep her dignity if it killed her.

As the vodka snaked through her, the energy she'd worked up drained away. She kicked her shopping bags off the couch, lay down, and pulled the afghan over her, snuggling into its softness. Once this deal was done, her life as she knew it would be over. She could travel. Visit her sister. Decide what she wanted to do with the rest of her life. She closed her eyes, trying to imagine what her life might be like, but all she could see was Nate shaking his head, turning her down.

Again.

She reached for her Tic-Tacs, emptied the last of the box into her mouth, and started crunching desperately to stop the tears.

It didn't work.

* * *

Malcolm Brody downed the last of the diner sludge people in these parts called coffee, keeping his eyes on the front door of the diner. He checked his watch.

She was late. He should have expected as much.

"Would you like a refill on your coffee?"

He glanced up at the waitress. She was young and blonde, but tragically overweight and with an unfortunate mole on her chin that didn't help matters much. He let loose with a wide smile; the nice thing about homely girls was they were easy as hell to charm.

"I sure would, lass. You're a pretty young thing, now, aren't you?" The Irish brogue was fake, sure, but at his age, Malcolm Brody had learned the inestimable value of tiny deceptions.

The waitress giggled self-consciously and filled his cup. "You know," she said, "we've got a fabulous peach pie here. You really should give it a try."

And you should maybe try it a little less, Malcolm thought, glancing at her sizable rump, but instead he said, "I will certainly take that under advisement."

"Okay." She smiled and walked away. Malcolm watched her go, sad to see that the view of her wasn't much improved from the back. Poor girl.

The bell on the door jingled and a woman with short dark hair dragged a heavy, wheeled suitcase in behind her. She wore a well-tailored tweed business suit and a pair of sunglasses, which Malcolm found amusing. Although Nikkie hadn't grown up in L.A., that was where he'd tracked her down, and she appeared to have picked up the Angeleno quirk of expecting the sun to follow her wherever she went. She pushed the sunglasses to the top of her head, glanced around the diner, and finally locked eyes with Malcolm. He smiled, stood up, and gave a small wave. She rolled her eyes, jerked at her suitcase, and headed his way, not bothering to apologize when she knocked her massive haul into the various patrons unlucky enough to be in her path.

When she reached him, Malcolm smiled wide, hoping he looked like he was pleased to see her again.

"Nikkie, darlin'," he said, putting his hands on her shoulders and placing a kiss on each cold cheek. "You're lovely as ever."

"Cut the crap, Malcolm. I flew coach for this." She tossed herself into the booth, leaving her suitcase out so that the poor fat waitress had to step around it.

"Good evening," the waitress said, flashing a wink at Malcolm, then turning to Nikkie. "What can I getcha?"

Nikkie raised one eyebrow at Malcolm. "You're paying, right?"

Malcolm nodded, and Nikkie looked up at the waitress. "Bring me two of whatever alcohol has the highest proof."

The waitress lowered her pen and pad in apologetic supplication. "Oh, I'm sorry. We don't have a liquor license."

Nikkie's eyes closed slowly and she pressed her thumb and forefinger to the bridge of her nose. "Just bring me some tomato juice with a celery stalk and a splash of Worcestershire sauce, okay?" She pulled her hand away from her face and looked up at the waitress. "I'll use my imagination."

"Oh. Um. Okay." The waitress stepped awkwardly around Nikkie's suitcase and hurried to the back.

"Well, Nikkie girl, I must say you're quite the vision. As bonny a lass as ever."

"Knock it off, Malcolm. The closest you've ever gotten to Ireland is Hennessey's of Boston, and you and I both know it."

He sighed. The woman was beautiful, but she had no appreciation for the theater of life. He leaned forward. "I trust your flight was pleasant?"

"No. It sucked. They fucked up my reservation and I ended up in coach, and I'm really pissed off about it. So tell me what you dragged me out here for, and it better be good or I'm gonna ask mole girl for a nice big fork so I can stab you with it."

Malcolm widened his smile. "Charming as ever, Nikkie."

"Fuck you, Malcolm."

"Well, I see pleasantries are going to get us nowhere." Malcolm reached into his satchel and pulled out a manila envelope. "There's a thousand dollars in there."

Nikkie huffed and sat back. "Oh, fuck, Malcolm. A thousand dollars? Are you serious? I live in L.A. now. My manicures cost a thousand dollars." Despite this, she snatched the envelope off the table with remarkable speed and slammed it down into the seat beside her. "Talk."

"That, m'dear," he said, nodding toward the envelope, "is merely a down payment. There's more where that came from, you can trust that."

She eyed him for a long moment and said, "Well, keep going. What the hell do you want?"

The waitress scooted in and placed Nikkie's drink in front of her. Nikkie took a sip and cringed.

"I'm sorry. Is it not good?" the waitress asked, genuinely concerned.

"Not yet." Nikkie pulled a tiny, clear bottle out of her

pocket, dumped the contents into the drink, and mixed it with her straw. She took a long drink and still cringed, but it was less noticeable this time.

Malcolm looked at the waitress, who was staring at Nikkie.

"Um," the waitress said, "I'm not sure it's legal for you to—"

"Oh, lass, don't you worry yourself," Malcolm said. "It's quite the lost cause."

The waitress smiled a bit, but her eyes were still worried as she backed away.

Nikkie sat back from the drink and seemed to relax a bit. "I'll tell you right now, Malcolm, I don't care how much you offer me, I'm not sleeping with you. Or Mick."

"As flattered as I am by the fact that such a thing would even cross your mind, that's not what I'm after," Malcolm said. "And Mick's dead, so I feel confident you won't have to worry about any unwanted advances from him."

Nikkie straightened. "Mick's dead? Then what the hell are we doing in Idaho?"

Malcolm sighed. He had hoped this could be handled with a little more delicacy, but it seemed that Nikkie had hardened significantly since he'd last seen her, and she'd hardly been a marshmallow back then. "There's an item that Mick had, and I need it."

"And why can't you get it yourself?"

Malcolm gave a slight nod. "My nephew has inherited the land, and we've had trouble seeing eye to eye since that time he threatened to cause me bodily harm if I ever darkened his door again."

Nikkie's face went white. "Nate...um..." She cleared her throat. "Nate's here?"

"Yes. So is Piper. They're living at Mick's campground and that's where this item is, I believe. So you see my predicament."

She stared at him for a while, her eyes narrowed, then sat back and crossed her arms over her stomach. "You are one shitty piece of work, you know that?"

"It's been brought to my attention on occasion, yes."

"You want me to use Nate and Piper to get you some stupid 'item' because you're too much of a coward to get it yourself?" She downed the last of her drink, slammed it on the table, and stood up. "Fuck off, old man."

"Let's not be rash."

"I'm not being rash." She pulled up the telescoping suitcase handle. "I'm coming to my senses. Why I ever thought this might be a good idea is —"

"There was no mistake with your reservation, Nikkie, was there?"

Her grip on the handle of her suitcase tightened, but she didn't move away. Malcolm stood up and moved closer, careful to keep the smile on his face and the gentle tone in his voice.

"You and I both know that, even if you could afford first class, you wouldn't fly out here from Los Angeles to see me unless you were beyond desperate. I know about the debts, dear, and I know that, despite all your posturing, you will do this for me, because I will pay you, and you've never been choosy about where your money comes from, so long as it comes. Am I right?"

Nikkie muttered something foul at him, but she didn't leave. Malcolm put a fatherly hand on her shoulder.

"All I'm asking is that you go for a short visit, under the aegis of checking up on your ex-husband and daughter after their devastating loss. While you're there, you will find this object for me. Once you do, you'll have enough money to get rid of those pesky debts, and maybe have a little left over to do something about that nose." He touched the slightly upturned tip of her nose with his finger. "I know you've always wanted Sharon Stone's nose. Here's your chance."

She turned her face away from him for a moment, but he could still smell her desperation. Even before she turned her eyes back to meet his, he knew he'd won, and was already smiling.

"That's my girl," he said, motioning toward the booth seat. "I knew you'd see reason."

She let out a hefty sigh and threw herself back down into the booth. "I'm still not sleeping with you."

"Believe it or not," Malcolm said, "the idea is almost as repugnant to me as it is to yourself."

He raised his hand, and the waitress appeared almost instantly.

"My companion will be requiring a refill," he said.

"Don't bother," Nikkie said, pulling two more stolen airline vodkas out of her pocket and placing them before her on the table. She whipped the top off one, threw it back, and then looked up at the waitress, who was staring at her. "What?"

"Um," the waitress began, but then Malcolm touched her gently on the arm.

"You know," Malcolm said, putting his hand on the waitress's arm to draw her attention away from Nikkie, "I think I'll break down and have some of that peach pie after all."

The waitress smiled uneasily, then jotted the order

down and hurried off. By the time Malcolm turned back to his companion, she'd already downed the second vodka. Then she shook her head like a dog coming out of the rain and leaned forward.

"Here's the deal. You give me another three grand, cash, for a down payment, and I'll give you two days. If I find this 'item,' you give me fifty grand. If I don't find it, I'm outta here and keeping the down payment for my trouble. Understood?"

Malcolm smiled. "It's going to be a pleasure working with you, Nikkie. I can feel it in me bones."

CHAPTER SIX

*N*ATE WHIPPED the eggs in the bowl and yawned. Sleeping last night had been almost impossible. Even after taking a long shower and relieving what tension he could on his own, he hadn't been able to stop thinking about Freya. He'd never met a woman who could be so tough and so vulnerable at the same time. He ran the night over and over in his head, remembering how funny she'd been when going through her tourist loot, how irresistible she'd been when she'd pressed against him in that doorway...

"Okay," he said, and tried to concentrate on the eggs, to limited success. Giving up a social life for Piper was having a stark side effect, in that his desire for this one woman was so powerful, he could hardly think of anything else.

But he needed to think of other things. Like Piper, and her future. At three in the morning, he'd shot up in bed, fully realizing what a jackass he'd been to turn down Freya's offer. It came down to stubbornness and pride, and he had so much of both, he couldn't see what he was doing, which made him more like his father than he cared to admit. Still, there was a little time for it all to work out. If he could keep Freya there for just a little while longer, he might be able to find the damn toolbox—or whatever the hell it was—before she and her offer skipped town. Then he could go back to his restaurant in Cincinnati and set up the world's most kickass trust fund for Piper, Freya'd go back to Boston and get her promotion, and Ruby'd have enough to start over wherever she wanted and never need to put up with a man like his dad ever again.

He'd try to do it and keep his word, but if he had to betray his promise to his father in order to make it happen, then he'd betray his promise.

In a heartbeat.

"Morning, Dad."

He turned around to see Piper practically dancing into the kitchen, looking sweet in her pink pig pajamas and matching slippers. She walked over to him, put her arms around his waist, and squeezed.

Apparently, he was forgiven. Good to know. He put the bowl down, wrapped his arms around her, and lifted her high enough that he could kiss the top of her head, inhaling the sweet scent of the strawberry shampoo she used. He knew it was just a matter of seconds before she wasn't a little girl anymore, and his heart flushed with gratitude that they weren't wasting any more of that precious time being mad at each other.

She released him, humming a happy tune as she pulled the orange juice out of the refrigerator. Nate poured his eggs into the hot pan and grabbed his whisk.

"So, you're in a good mood this morning," he said.

"Yep," she said. "I'm not mad anymore."

Wow. Things were so much simpler with little girls

than with grown ones. "Good to know, Pipes. I hope you're in the mood for scrambled."

She sat at the table and took a sip of her juice. "No goat cheese."

He laughed. "Deal." He turned back to the stove, checked the heat on the second frying pan, and put the bacon on, feeling for the first time in a long time as if anything was possible. He was in the middle of a fantasy that involved searching for the toolbox with Freya on one of the pull-out couches when Ruby's voice brought him back to the moment.

"Good morning," she said as she stepped into the kitchen. "Anything I can help with?"

Definitely no. "Thanks, but I'm almost done. Go ahead and sit down and—"

Just then, the doorbell rang, and Ruby looked at Nate. "Expecting someone?"

Nate smiled. "No." But he had an idea who it might be, and he did owe Freya a breakfast. He wiped his hands on his apron and turned to Ruby.

"Do me a favor," he said. "Plate this up; I'll get the door."

He ruffled Piper's hair as he passed her into the living room, and had just enough time to whip the apron off and run his hands through his hair before pulling the door open. After that, his mind went blank for a second until it could connect reality with what he saw standing before him.

She was still beautiful, he had to give her that. She'd cut her hair short, that was different, but aside from that, she looked almost as if no time had gone by. For a moment, he thought maybe he had some kind of brain tumor and was hallucinating, because who wore severe business suits on a Sunday morning? Even Nikkie hadn't been that driven.

"Hi, Nate," she said. Her voice had gotten a little rougher, a little deeper. She smiled at him, and he could tell she was nervous, which meant she was real. In all the scenarios he'd played in his head where she'd suddenly come back, she'd never been nervous.

And that woke him up.

He glanced behind him; Piper was still in the kitchen, with her back to them. Thank God. He stepped outside, pushing Nikkie back, and shut the door firmly behind them.

"What are you doing here?" he asked, his voice low.

"I heard about Mick." She put one hand on his arm. "I'm so sorry."

He glanced down at her hand, and she pulled it back.

"Piper's had ten birthdays you couldn't bother to send a card for," he said, "and you want me to believe you give a crap about Mick?"

Nikkie glanced at the house behind him. "Is she in there?"

"Yes, she is, and you'd better get the hell out of here before she sees you, or—"

"Or what?" Nikkie raised her eyes to his. "Or you're gonna toss me out on my ass? Without ever telling Piper I was here? Come on, Nate. We both know that's not the kind of man you are."

The kind of man he was seemed to be causing more problems than it solved. "How'd you even find out about Mick, anyway?"

She sighed. "I have a Google alert set up for all your names. I've been keeping track of you. I know about the restaurant. Congratulations. That was always your dream."

Her smile was tight and her eyes cold. No way was this a social visit; she was after something. "Mick didn't have any money, Nikkie. And even if he did, I paid you off a long time ago. You don't have any claim on anything I have. And that includes Piper."

"I'm her mother, Nate."

"Yeah, and as I recall, all it took to get you to give her up was a cashier's check. Legally, you have no rights here, and you know it."

"I'm hoping it won't come to lawyers," she said. "I just want to see my daughter."

He closed his eyes. His world was spinning, and he couldn't think fast enough what to do, how best to protect Piper. Nikkie was right; there was no way he was going to kick her out and not tell Piper. That would be a lie, and he didn't lie, not to his kid. But to let Piper see her again, especially when he had no idea what Nikkie wanted, was just reckless.

"She's going to be wondering who's at the door."

Nate opened his eyes. Looking up at him were the same brown eyes he'd been staring at for the last eleven years. He saw them as more Piper's than Nikkie's, but he couldn't deny they were the same. He knew the day would come when he couldn't protect Piper anymore, but he'd hoped it wouldn't come so damn fast.

He sighed, reached for the doorknob, and opened it. Nikkie allowed a small, victorious smile to quirk at the edge of her lips. She still loved winning, more than anything else.

She hadn't changed.

He followed her into the living room, where Ruby and

Piper stood, waiting. They had obviously figured out something was up, and Ruby stood with her hands on Piper's shoulders, both of them still as they watched Nikkie walk in the room.

Nikkie eyed Ruby, then looked back at Nate, her eyes glittering with cold amusement.

"Just when I thought you couldn't surprise me, Nate," she said under her breath.

He shot her a warning look and whispered, "That's Mick's widow." Close enough to it, anyway. If Mick had been enough of a man to marry her, she would have been. Nate cleared his throat and spoke louder. "Um, Ruby, Piper. This is—"

"Nikkie?" Piper's voice cracked on the word, and Nate took a step toward his girl, only he didn't know what to say. The look on her face almost killed him, and it was going to get a hell of a lot worse before it got better.

Nikkie stepped out from behind him. "Yes, Piper. It's me."

Piper looked at Nate, who nodded. The few pictures he'd had of Nikkie had been in an album Piper had kept in her bedroom since she was a toddler. Nate watched, his stomach roiling, as his daughter's face registered everything she was thinking. First, there was a kind of shock, then a hint of a smile, then shock again. The hurt would come later. Not now, not when the one thing she'd always wanted was finally right in front of her, but later, when Nikkie revealed herself for the person she really was, the person she'd always been. He'd been too blind to see it coming the first time, but it was all too clear for him now. Only now, it was his baby's heart that was going to get broken, and there was nothing he could do to stop it.

Ruby, he noticed, kept her hands firmly clamped on Piper's shoulders, and when Piper started to step forward, she hesitated before letting her go. Slowly, Piper made her way across the room to stand in front of Nikkie. Nate watched, his stomach in knots, as Nikkie leaned over to look at Piper.

"You're pretty," she said, then straightened up. "The last time I saw you, you were bald."

Piper's lip trembled and she threw her arms around Nikkie's waist.

"I knew you'd come," she sniffled into her mother's stomach. "I knew it."

Nikkie put her arms awkwardly around Piper, patting her back.

Nate walked over to stand next to Ruby, biting the inside of his cheek as he watched his daughter bawl in her mother's arms. Ruby put her hand on his arm, showing solidarity; she didn't know much about Nikkie, but she wasn't stupid, either. He could tell by the look on her face that Ruby knew Nikkie was no good. It was a comfort, knowing Ruby had his back, knowing that someone would be there to help him pick up the pieces after Nikkie got whatever it was she wanted and broke his daughter's heart.

"It's okay," Nikkie said, still patting Piper. She looked up at Nate, a mildly helpless look in her eyes. Nate made a motion with his arms. *Hug her.*

"Oh. Right." Nikkie knelt to Piper's level and put her arms around her. Piper rested her head on Nikkie's shoulder and Nikkie said, "It's okay. I'm here."

Nikkie met and held Nate's eye, and she looked scared to death, which was good, because if she hurt his kid again, he'd kill her.

*　　*　　*

Freya sat in the Adirondack chair on her cabin deck and sipped her coffee, which was getting cold. She'd been out there for almost an hour, trying to decide what she was going to do, how she was going to convince Nate to let her help him find the whatever his father wanted him to find. She figured she could keep the offer on the table for about five more days before her father got too antsy. In that time they could find the whatever, soothe Nate's conscience, and still put the deal through.

She might even get Nate to talk her up to two-point-two-five. There seemed a ceratin poetic justice about making her father pay five times what the place was worth.

She heard distant footsteps and looked up to see Nate coming down the path. Her heart leapt at the sight of him—which made sense, she always got excited before finishing up a big deal—but then she grinned and waved like an idiot, gestures inspired by emotions that were decidedly not professional. She lowered her hand, relieved that he didn't seem to have seen her; he just walked with his head down, flipping through a set of keys in his hand, and then took a sharp left and turned into Number Two.

"Oh," she said, lowering her hand as she realized he wasn't coming to see her.

Which was fine. He didn't need to want to see her for her to make this work. She got up, hesitated a minute over her wardrobe—she'd never closed a deal in silk capri pajama bottoms paired with a T-shirt that read "Idaho Snow Bunny," but hell. There was a first time for everything, and she didn't want to waste any time making this happen. She slipped her Keds on, headed over to Number

Two, knocked on the door, and poked her head in. Nate stood at the back corner of the main room, keys clanging in his hand.

"Good morning," she said.

He barely glanced at her. "Yeah."

She walked over to stand by him. He opened the padlock and swung the door open on the fuse box, his face hard as he pulled out one fuse and replaced it with another.

"I was wondering," she said, "if maybe later we could talk about—"

"Do me a favor," he said, motioning toward the front door. "Switch on the main light."

"Um. Okay." She hesitated for a moment, watching him, then crossed the room and did as he asked. The light came on for a second, then there was a pop from the fuse box, and it went off again.

"Goddamnit." He slammed the fuse box shut, locked it, and muttered, "Fuck it. She can use candles." Then he leaned against the wall, crossed his arms over his chest and hung his head. Freya walked back to him and touched him lightly on the shoulder.

"Nate? Are you okay?"

He looked up at her and took a deep breath, as though he had just realized she was there. Then he let out a soft, sad laugh and said, "No."

"Don't worry about me," a voice called from the front door as it swung open to reveal a pretty brunette in a business suit dragging a tremendous suitcase behind her. "I'll get my own luggage."

Nate pushed himself off the wall and walked toward her. "Ruby's getting you clean linens for the pull-out, but the electricity is fucked and I can't get it fixed today. The front door doesn't lock, and the water's gonna be cold because the water heater's electric."

The woman looked around the cabin with an expression of such disdain that Freya had to smother an urge to smack her. Finally, her dark eyes landed on Freya—eyes Freya recognized as colder, older versions of Piper's—and Freya's skin broke out in goose pimples as she realized she was looking at Piper's mother.

Nate's ex.

The woman gave Freya a quick once-over, then raised her eyebrows at Nate. Nate raised his eyebrows back. Finally, the brunette stepped forward and held out her hand. "Hi, I'm Nikkie Brody—"

"Nikkie *Cooper*," Nate said quickly.

"—and you are...?" Nikkie said smoothly over him, keeping her hard eyes locked on Freya.

"She's a guest," Nate said, stepping between them.

Nikkie's eyebrows shot up. "Oh, really? Is that what they call it in Idaho?"

"Excuse me?" Freya said, stepping out from behind Nate, ready to take the woman's head off, she didn't care who she was. But then Nate put his hand on the small of Freya's back, pressing slightly. Freya looked up to see the request on his face and bit her tongue.

"Get settled, Nik," Nate said. "I'll be back in a little while. Stay here until I come get you."

He led Freya out, slamming the door behind them. As soon as they reached her cabin, she turned to face him.

"What the hell was that about?"

For the first time that morning, some of the angry tension drained from his face, leaving just the naked stress.

He ran his hand over his face and leaned against the exterior wall of Freya's cabin.

"I don't know," he said. "Ten years, we've heard nothing from her. Then she just shows up out of nowhere. She wants something, but hell if I know what it is. And now Piper..." He went silent, and Freya could feel the tension coming off him in waves.

"Hey," she said, "it's gonna be okay. Piper has you. She'll be fine."

"It's just...you don't know Nikkie," he said. "We met when she was a waitress and I was a prep cook, and I knew exactly what kind of girl she was, but I was twenty-three and she was hot, so what the hell did I care? But then she got pregnant."

Freya nodded. "So you married her."

"Seemed the thing to do. Doomed from the start, but goddamned honorable. Anyway, Nikkie got every last penny in the divorce, but I got Piper, so I won." He released a deep breath, and the muscles in his face tightened. "I can't keep her from Piper, that's not fair to Piper. But it's not going to end well, and Piper's gonna take it on the chin."

Freya watched him, knowing what she had to do. Now was her moment. He was weak, he was confused, and two million dollars would go a long way toward getting rid of his ex. All Freya had to do right now was be his friend, make arguments that would lead him to the money. No mater how honorable Nate Brody was, his daughter's happiness was more important to him than his word, and Freya knew it would be so easy...so easy...

If only the very idea didn't make her want to throw up.

Dad's right, she thought as she reached out and took Nate's hand. *I've lost my edge.*

Well. Fuck it. She squeezed his hand and said, "You know what? Piper's gonna be fine."

He didn't look convinced. "You didn't see her face this morning."

"No," she said. "But I've seen her face when she looks at you. It's the face of a kid who knows that, no matter what happens, someone will be there to catch her."

"I don't want to catch her," he said, staring down at his feet. "I want to keep her from falling in the first place."

"Can't do that," Freya said. "But trust me. Having a father who's there, no matter what... it matters. A lot."

Nate looked up at her, his eyes searching hers as his fingers tightened around hers. Freya's breath caught as he watched her, and she stepped back and dropped his hand.

"Hey," she said, "I need you to do something for me."

He nodded and pushed himself off the wall. "Something wrong with the cabin?"

"No," she said. "Well... yes, but that fix would require a bottle of bourbon and a wrecking ball. No..." She glanced at the cabin across the way from her own, then looked back at him. "I need you to keep the idea open in your mind that maybe Nikkie's really here to connect with Piper."

Nate shook his head. "Freya, you don't know—"

"I know what it's like to be betrayed, trust me. It's just..." She took a deep breath. "My mother died when I was a little girl. I spent so many nights wishing so hard that she could come back to me, even if it was just for a minute. I would have given anything, *anything*, for the chance Piper has right now."

"I'm sorry," he said, and she could tell by the look on his face that he meant it. "But your mother and Nikkie, they're two different people. Your mother didn't choose to leave you."

"Doesn't matter," Freya said. "Not to a little girl. And if there's even a slight chance that Nikkie is really here for her, you have to let it play out, okay? And if Nikkie's up to no good, then you'll just have to be there for Piper when it's over."

Nate stared at her for a while, and Freya held his eye until she could see that first hint of surrender she'd seen so often around the negotiating table. He was on the ledge; all she had to do now was push him over.

"Go get Nikkie and bring her back to Piper. It's the right thing to do."

He stared at Number Two for a long time, his expression intense and angry, and then he sighed and nodded. "Okay."

He turned back to Freya like he was going to say something, but then just reached out and touched her face, a small smile on his lips. Their eyes held for a moment, and then he kissed her forehead.

"Thank you," he said.

"Get out of here," Freya said. She watched as he walked over to Number Two, got Nikkie, and walked back with her to the house. Once they were out of sight, Freya started toward cabin Number Two.

She didn't care what she had told Nate. That woman was up to something. Nate needed to give Nikkie a chance for Piper's sake, but Freya didn't. She glanced behind her to be sure Nikkie wasn't coming back for anything, then slipped inside. She took a moment to memorize things exactly the way Nikkie had left them, then went for the suitcase.

She might have lost her edge where Nate and Piper were concerned, but when it came to playing dirty with the likes of Nikkie Cooper, she still had a few tricks up her sleeve.

CHAPTER SEVEN

$\mathcal{N}$ATE AND RUBY sat at the kitchen table, watching Nikkie and Piper perched stiffly next to each other on the living room couch. It was all Nate could do to stay where he was and let it unfold, but Freya was right. He had no choice.

Whatever her mother really was, Piper had to find out for herself.

"So ... you're doing well in school?" Nikkie asked for the fifth time.

Piper nodded. "Yeah."

And they fell into silence. Again. Nate looked at Ruby, who looked back, her face as stony as ever. She was still in mother bear mode, believing she could prevent whatever hurt might be coming Piper's way. Nate kind of missed that illusion.

"Where did you go?" Piper asked finally.

"What?" Nikkie said.

"When you left. When I was a baby. Where did you go?"

Nate stiffened; small talk was over. He felt Ruby's hand on his arm, and he touched her fingers lightly before she withdrew.

"Well...um. First, I went to Des Moines. It's where I grew up. I spent some time with..." She glanced at Nate. "...an old friend for a while."

Greg had been the name, Nate thought, although he couldn't be sure. There hadn't been a lot of time for proper introductions when he'd gone after Nikkie to get some final documents signed and found her living with the guy.

"And then?" Piper asked. "Where'd you go after that?"

"Well, I...floated for a while. Spent some time in Arizona. Then, a few years ago, I ended up in Los Angeles." She brightened. "Oh, do you know Rodeo Drive?"

Piper shook her head. Nikkie's shoulders slumped a bit.

"It's a place with a lot of shopping. Really expensive stuff. High fashion, stuff like that. I used to work there. And I met a man there who I was seeing for a while. Did you ever watch *Sex and the City*?"

"No. Dad says it's inappropriate."

"Oh, please. They cleaned up the reruns—"

Nate cleared his throat and Nikkie looked up, rolled her eyes lightly, and looked back down at Piper.

"Anyway, his brother was a producer for that show."

"Oh. Neat."

Another painful silence. Nate curled his hand into a fist and pressed it into the table, locking himself into his seat.

"I thought you were in the Congo," Piper said. Nate shot a confused glance at Ruby, who shrugged. When he looked back, Piper was sitting with her hands tucked under her knees, lower legs kicking out from the couch, her eyes on the floor.

"The Congo?" Nikkie laughed. "Why in the world would I go there?"

Piper stopped kicking. "I saw a movie once where a guy went to the Congo to find some plant to cure cancer. And his daughter came down to find him. She was mad because he'd left their family, but he'd gone because he wanted to save people. And they didn't have phones or mailboxes or anything." She straightened up and looked up at Nikkie. "But you were in California?"

Nikkie nodded, her face tense. "And Arizona."

Nate felt as if someone had just dropped a heavy stone on his gut. All these years, Piper had never mentioned the Congo to him. They'd talked about Nikkie very little, except for Nate's rote explanation that her mother loved her, but wasn't able to be around. Here Piper had been building this whole scenario in her head, a reason why her mother had left her that made sense, and he'd never even known. He wanted to run over there, throw Nikkie out the door, and pull his little girl into his arms, but he knew he couldn't. He had no choice but to sit there and watch as the last of his daughter's precious illusions were shattered.

Piper stood up from the couch and walked over to him. He smiled as brightly as he could, but her face was flat.

"Hey, Pipes," he said. "How ya doin'?"

"I'm going to ride my bike down to the lake, okay?"

He nodded. "Okay. Be back for lunch."

He watched as she gave a short, halfhearted wave at Nikkie, then walked out the front door, closing it quietly behind her. Nate sat where he was for a while, watching Nikkie as she sat on the couch, not moving. She looked beaten up. Nikkie had never been one for showing emotions, so for her to look beaten up meant that something was really going on inside. She wasn't all cold; he knew that. In there somewhere was a beating heart, it was just buried under so many layers of shit that by the time you got to it, it was hardly worth the digging.

And the fact that it was his little girl trying to wade through all the shit made him a lot less sympathetic than he would have been otherwise.

He shot a look at Ruby and pushed up from the table, walked over to Nikkie, and stood a few feet away from her in silence. The truth was, he was so far out of his depth that he wasn't sure what to say or do. Finally, Nikkie raised her head.

"Should I go after her?" she asked.

Nate shook his head. "No."

"Do you think she'll ever forgive me?"

Her voice was so quiet that Nate wasn't sure if he'd imagined it, but when she looked up at him, he could tell by the look in her eyes that she was torn up. As torn up as Nikkie ever got, anyway.

Good.

"I don't know," he said honestly. "I guess it all depends on what you're willing to do to earn it."

Nikkie nodded again. "Right." She pushed up off the couch. "Well, I guess I should get back to my cabin. Take a shower. Get some rest." She looked at Nate. "When can I see her again?"

Nate took in a deep breath. "Come back for dinner. Six-thirty."

One edge of her mouth quirked up. "You cooking?"

Nate shrugged. "Me or Ruby."

Ruby's eyes lit a bit with gleeful malice. "I make excellent mac and cheese. Straight from the box."

Nikkie held a cold look with Ruby, then turned and left. Nate walked over and sat down next to Ruby, suddenly exhausted beyond the telling of it.

"You're doing the right thing," Ruby said. "A girl needs to know her mother, for better or worse."

Nate nodded. So he'd been told.

"It's a California driver's license," Freya said, holding up one of Nikkie's receipts on which she'd scribbled the paltry information she'd gleaned from going through Nikkie's purse. Through her cell connection, she could hear her sister's boyfriend, Jake Tucker, typing the information into his computer. "The name she's going by is Nikkie Cooper, but she might also use Brody."

"All right," Jake said. "I can run a basic check on her; it'll give you what jobs she's had, any criminal record, aliases, that kind of thing. We'll see what comes up."

"I also need you to track down a number," she said. "I got it off her cell phone and it just said 'private number,' but she'd gotten three calls from it in the past two days." She read the number off; it was a 208 area code, which narrowed its issue down to anywhere in Idaho.

"Got it." Jake paused for a moment, then said, "So, what's going on out there, Freya? You're not in any trouble, are you?"

Freya stiffened. "What makes you ask that?"

"You're calling me to track down odd information for you, for one thing. Plus, you share genes with Flynn."

"It's no big deal. It's just a tiny thing I have to work out on the property I'm going to buy. Send the bill to my apartment, though, okay?"

"Right," Jake said flatly. "I'll get right on that."

"I'm serious, Jake. We hire private detectives to check on things for us all the time. It's standard operating procedure. Bill me."

"No," he said. "You want me to get Flynn for you?"

There was a light knock at the door, and Freya put her hand over the phone and called out, "Who is it?"

"It's me," Piper's little voice called through the door.

"Just a minute," Freya said, then spoke into the phone. "Gotta go. Give Flynn my love. Keep her out of trouble."

"Easier said than done," he said, and Freya said goodbye and powered off her phone. As soon as Flynn found out that Freya had hired her boyfriend to look into something, she'd call, and Freya didn't feel like explaining anything. Not now, anyway. She opened the door to find Piper standing there, staring up at her, her eyes red-rimmed but dry.

"I asked my dad if I can ride down to the lake, and he said yes," she said.

"Ah. She can be taught." Freya crossed her arms over her stomach and leaned against the doorjamb. "How are you doing, kid?"

Piper shrugged then looked up at Freya. "You wanna come?"

"Sure." Freya shut the door behind her and followed Piper to the office, where they got the bikes. Without speaking, they rode fast down to the lake, zipping through the paths so fast that Freya thought she was going to get thrown from the bike just trying to keep up with Piper. Finally, they reached the lake and set their bikes against the shack. Freya followed Piper's lead, walking quietly behind her until she sat at the end of the dock and looked up at Freya, who pulled the back of her oversized T-shirt down over the butt of her silk capri pants to protect them and sat next to Piper. She pulled her knees up to keep the silk from touching the dock and waited for Piper to speak first, which she finally did a few minutes later.

"Do you have kids?" she asked.

Freya stared out at the water and shook her head. "Nope."

Piper turned to face her. "Did you ever want kids?"

"Nope," Freya answered honestly. "I don't think I'm the mommy type, you know? Some people are good at that kind of thing, and some people aren't, but it ends up being the kid who takes it on the chin when they screw up."

Piper nodded and then her face crumpled and tears streamed down her face. Freya put an arm around her and Piper curled into her, her body shaking on the shocks of a fresh grief. Freya simply held her, remembering the exact same grief she'd had at that exact same age. In a different way, but just as real, Piper was grieving for the death of a mother as well, and Freya knew there was nothing to do but just be there. She held the girl in silence as she cried, running her hand over her hair until Piper straightened up and swiped at her face with the back of her hand.

They sat in silence for a long time, and then Freya said, "For what it's worth, if I could get a guarantee my kid would turn out like you, I'd go for it."

"Right," Piper sniffled, and her eyes filled again. "You're just saying that to be nice."

Freya tapped Piper's wrist until the kid looked up at her. "You don't know me well, so I'll let you get away with it this time, but I don't say things to be nice."

Piper shrugged and swiped at her face, not meeting Freya's eyes.

"Hey," Freya said. Piper didn't look at her, so she said it again. "*Hey.*"

Piper finally looked up. Freya crossed her legs in front of her as she shifted around to face her.

"You're a great kid, Piper, but if you start feeling sorry for yourself, you're gonna end up being just another whiny little brat who's pissed off that life didn't go how she wanted, and that'd be a hell of a waste."

Piper sniffled. "Is this supposed to be a pep talk?"

"Close as I get to one, yeah," Freya said. "My point is, if she didn't want you, that means something's wrong with her, not you. You understand me?"

Piper straightened a bit. "Yeah."

"I mean it," Freya said. "You're stronger than that and better than that. You need to know, without a doubt, that none of this is because of you."

Piper met her eyes, and slowly the doubt in them seemed to recede. "Okay."

"Okay." Freya stood up and held her hand out to pull Piper to her feet. "You've just gone through a hell of an emotional growth spurt, one your future therapist will be hearing about for years to come, and I think we need to celebrate, which means near-lethal doses of fat and sugar." She eyed Piper. "You like chocolate, right?"

"Yeah," Piper said.

"Good woman. Unfortunately, all I've got is snowman poop." She crinkled her nose. "What's in that stuff, anyway?"

Piper shook her head. "I don't know. It looks kinda gross to me."

"Right." Freya sighed. "What can I say? It was an impulse buy. You got some kind of chocolate back at the house?"

Piper nodded. "We have Rocky Road. And hot fudge."

Freya put her arm around the kid's shoulder and led her off the dock.

"All right, then," she said. "Last one back does the scooping."

CHAPTER EIGHT

*N*ATE LAY BACK on his bed, staring at the ceiling. He'd
been trying to gather his thoughts for an hour, but
they were impossibly jumbled. He'd been so close, *so
close*, to having it all figured out. That morning, it had
seemed so clear—screw his word, take the money, leave
his goddamn father and his father's goddamn dying wish
behind and go back to Cincinnati. It had seemed the obvious best thing for all of them. But Nikkie's sudden appear-
ance had thrown a new light on everything. Piper didn't
need money, she needed *him*, she needed his time and
attention, and uprooting her from a place where she was
happy, where she *wanted* to stay, to go back to his fifteen-
hour-a-day job in a city she hated...it was wrong. Selfish.

Impossible.

Almost as impossible as staying there, spending the
rest of his life managing a run-down campground in a
two-bit town where the only cooking he'd do would be
for his tiny family of three. His miserable martyrdom
wouldn't do Piper any good, either.

Fuck. He rubbed his eyes and, for the millionth time in
his thirty-four years, quietly cursed his father.

The phone rang, and Nate grabbed it off the nightstand.

"Yeah," he said.

"Hey, shithead."

It was Clint, one of his partners from the restaurant. Nate pressed his fingers on the bridge of his nose.

"Hey, Clint. Look, I'm kind of in the middle of something right now. Can I call you back tomorrow?"

"Can't, man, sorry. I've got Eddie here. Gonna put you on speakerphone."

There was a click, then the naked hiss of speakerphone, and Nate heard his other partner's voice coming over the line. "What's up, asshole?"

"Eddie. What's going on?"

There was a pause on the line, and then Eddie said, "We got a problem, Nate. Lulu's getting restless. She wants head chef permanently, or she's walking."

Fuck. Nate closed his eyes. "Right."

"When are you coming back?" Clint said. "Any idea yet?"

"I'm working on it." Nate sat up and put his feet over the edge of the bed. "I can't really say for sure, though."

"Look, man," Eddie said. "I don't know what's going on there, but we can't lose Lulu. She's been great for us, stepped right up when you left, and it's been six months. She got an offer from Bridge's. Either you come back, or we gotta give her head chef."

"Right," Nate said. He'd known this day was coming, and soon. He just wished the hammer could have come down on a day when his ex-wife hadn't shown up out of nowhere.

"You'd still be part owner," Clint said, "unless you

want to take our offer to buy you out. That's still on the table, too."

"Thanks. I appreciate that." When they'd first made that offer, Nate couldn't say no fast enough. Losing his restaurant felt like losing a limb, but if he wasn't going to be cooking there, what was the point?

Except, he could be cooking there. He could take Freya up on her offer and be out of there in a week. He could cook again and give his daughter everything money could buy.

Except time with her father.

Eddie's voice came over the line. "Look, you know we wouldn't screw you, man, but I don't know what the fuck else we're gonna do. We need a head chef or we're fucked, and no one else is gonna do the job Lulu's gonna do, not if you're not here. It's this or we lose the restaurant."

"I know," Nate said. "You're right. How long do I have?"

Eddie sighed. "I don't know, man. We can hold her off, maybe one more week. Can you be here a week from Monday?"

Nate looked at the calendar. It was Sunday. That gave him eight days to make a choice.

Christ.

"I gotta think. Can I call you back?"

Another hesitation, then Clint said, "Yeah, man, but we need an answer. Soon."

"I know."

Nate hung up the phone and stared at it, his mind winding in circles again. He had to choose between his daughter's happiness now and her security later, choose between keeping his word and being a stubborn ass like his dad, or breaking it and being a dishonorable shit. Like his dad.

Not to mention that taking the two million dollars would only keep Nikkie around longer, looking for a way to suck the teat dry, and not taking it would screw Freya out of her promotion.

Tick tock, Nate. Pick a door.

The sound of laughter drifted up from downstairs, jarring Nate out of his thoughts. He glanced behind him at his bedroom door, and there it was again—the raucous giggling of women.

"What the...?" He got up from his bed and headed down the stairs, the sound of the laughter broken intermittently by banging noises. He rounded the corner into the kitchen to find Piper, Freya, and Ruby all playing Slap. Messy piles of cards littered the tabletop, along with the empty ice cream bowls they'd shoved to the side to make room for the game.

"Hey, Dad!" Piper said, giggling as she pounded her hand down on the center pile. Smiling, Nate leaned against the wall and watched her happy, carefree face.

"Hey!" Freya said. "That's an illegal slap!" She turned to Ruby. "You should have warned me she was a cheater, Ruby."

Ruby held her hands up. "I take no responsibility for her."

"I'm not cheating!" Piper wailed, then practically threw the top half of her body over the table as she picked up the cards in the center of the pile. "See? Seven of hearts, six of—"

"Five!" Freya picked up the card underneath. "*Five* of clubs! You think you're gonna pull something over on me because I'm older than you, is that it? I may be in my thirties, kid, but my eyes still work."

"Is that how you've been winning all these games?" Ruby said, laughing. "Taking advantage of my bad eyes?"

"I am *not* a cheater!" Piper laughed and shot the seven across the table at Freya, who caught it handily. "I made a mistake. I'm a kid. I can't make a mistake?"

Freya raised an eyebrow at Ruby. "Oooh, playing the innocent-child card. She's good."

"She is," Nate said.

Freya turned and their eyes met and held for a moment before Ruby put down another card in the center and set them all to giggling and slapping cards. Nate picked up the dirty bowls and brought them to the sink to wash them, listening as the women giggled and slapped cards and accused each other of cheating. He ran the water and let the happy sounds of family roll over him, one voice in particular calling to him, making his heart jump every time she spoke. He wanted to kiss her more at that moment than he'd ever wanted to do anything in his life, but instead he stood with his back to the festivities, letting her entertain and cheer his daughter.

He put the last dish away just as a peal of screeches came from the table. He turned to see Freya standing up and dancing to her own song, looking ridiculous and beautiful in her short green pants and silly tourist T-shirt.

"I won, I won, I shot the BB gun," she sang as she gathered up the last of the cards while Ruby and Piper threw out random accusations of cheating and taking advantage.

"Oh, shut up," Freya said. "Nobody likes sore losers. Do they, Nate?"

She turned to look at him and their eyes met again and

her smile faltered a bit. It turned him on even more knowing that it was obvious, at least to her, what he was thinking.

"No," Nate said, keeping his eyes on hers. "Nobody does."

She took a quick breath, then turned back to Piper and Ruby and said, "See? Told you."

"Best two of three," Piper said, gathering up the cards.

Nate cleared his throat. "Sorry to break things up, but Freya and I actually have some business to discuss."

"We do?" Freya turned to him. He widened his eyes a bit, hoping she knew an invitation when she saw one.

She flushed slightly and said, "Yes. I think we do. Overdue business."

"Well," Ruby said, keeping her eyes on the cards, but Nate caught the slight upturn at the edge of her mouth. "That's the most pressing kind."

She had no idea. "Why don't I walk you to your cabin and we can...discuss it?" he said, taking off his apron and throwing the wet dish towel he'd had slung over his shoulder onto the counter.

"Okay," Freya said. She turned to Piper and Ruby. "See you guys at dinner? We'll have a rematch and I'll kick your asses again." She looked at Nate quickly and her eyes widened a bit. "Butts. I mean butts." Then she mouthed "sorry" at him and he held his gaze on her mouth, her lips soft and full and pink.

"It's okay," Piper said. "You can say ass. Dad says it all the time."

Freya grinned and turned to him. "Really? Captain Cleft Chin allows bad language? Just when you think you know a guy..."

"Captain *what*?" Piper said, giggling.

"All right," Nate said. "I'm gonna walk Freya to her cabin so we can talk. We'll see you guys later."

"Step carefully," Ruby said, her eyes on the cards she was straightening in her hands.

He put his hand on the small of Freya's back and led her out toward the living room, through the front door, and to the path to the cabins.

"Everything okay?" she said quietly once they'd gotten out of sight of the house. "You look a little . . . urgent."

"Everything's fine, but we need to hurry."

"Why? What's going on?"

"This." He stopped short, turned to her, and cupped his hand at the back of her head, pulling her to him. He kissed her hard, putting everything he was feeling at the moment into it, loving the way his head cleared when he did. For the moment, he needed to hold back nothing, think of nothing but what he wanted. She responded, putting her hands on either side of his face as they made out on the path like hungry teenagers, until they stumbled into a tree and had to part before they fell over. They caught their breath for a second, staring at each other, smiles growing on their flushed faces.

"Let's go." She grabbed his hand and yanked him toward the cabin, making him laugh and stumble and feel like a carefree kid. Not that he could remember ever feeling quite like this as a kid, but if he never had, it was long overdue.

They reached the cabin, and Freya made quick work of unlocking the door and they were all over each other again before they'd even kicked it shut. She grabbed a fistful of his shirt and pulled her to him, her mouth exploring his as his blood roared in his ears. And elsewhere. He teased her tongue with his as he wrapped his arms around her waist, pulling her tighter against him with every bit of strength he had. It had been so long, too long, since he'd wanted anyone this badly and...

Piper. Nikkie. Dad. Ruby.

He relaxed his hold on her for a second and she pulled back, her eyes smokey and heavy-lidded.

"Stop it," she said.

Right.

"Yeah. Okay. I'm sorry. I don't know what came over me." He released her, expecting her to help him, slap him, push him away, tell him why it was wrong for him to ravage her like that, but instead, she grabbed his hand and put it on her ass.

"Stop it," she said.

He shook his head, trying to get a grip on the moment, but was only able to say, "Mixed signals."

There wasn't a lot of blood in his brain.

She put her hands on either side of his face and said, "Stop thinking." Then she gently bit his lower lip and pulled it ever so slightly and...

"Oh, God," he breathed and dived into her again. The smell of her, the feel of her, overwhelmed him. She was everything in the world, there was nothing else—

"Ow!" he said as pain shot up his leg. He looked down—okay, so there was a big fucking coffee table. He kicked it out of the way and they fell onto the couch, him underneath her as she straddled him, kissing and touching, and she ran her hand up under his shirt and did something to his nipple, he didn't even know what the hell she did but it felt so—

The restaurant. The new chef. The toolbox.

She pulled back, grabbing a fistful of his shirt. "*Stop it.*"

"Right," he said. "I just—"

"Stop *thinking*," she said. "You're a good man. I get it. You have a kid. I live in Boston. We hardly know each other." She made a chattering mouth with her right hand. "Blah blah blah, who gives a crap?"

He took a deep breath. "I'm sorry. I think I just need a minute to think."

"No," she said. "The last thing in the world you need is a minute to think. If you do, you'll remember that you're the kind of guy who waits until he's sure no one's gonna get hurt and he can marry the women he sleeps with. Well, fuck that. You see how well that worked for you."

She whipped off her shirt, revealing a light green silk camisole. Under it, her nipples were peaked and hard and—

"Touch me," she said.

He raised his hand, cupping it under her breast. So soft, so full, so warm. He ran his thumb lightly over the nipple, watched it tighten under the light fabric. She groaned and arched against him.

"Not thinking is good," he said. She laughed, then leaned down and kissed him, her body hovering over his, moving against all the right places.

"We've both had shit weeks," she said, her breath hot on his lips. "And we both need this. I'm not gonna get hurt and we're not gonna get married and so help me God, if you think about anything but being inside of me for the next fifteen minutes, I'll kill you where you stand."

She got up, grabbed her purse, pulled a condom out,

and tossed it at him. "Get prepared, Boy Scout. This is not a drill." She tucked her fingers in the elastic waist of her pajama bottoms and shot him a look. "What are you thinking about?"

He sat up, facing her. "You."

She stepped closer, her knees straddling his as she stood before him, and slowly lowered the bottoms, revealing the sharp edge of her naked hip bone. "And now?"

He reached for her, hooking one finger under the elastic and tugging it down farther, then laying a light kiss below her belly button.

"Oh," she said breathlessly. "Good man."

He pulled her underwear and pants to the ground and she daintily stepped out. He grabbed her hips and lifted her until her knees were on the couch next to him, then he kissed her belly, working lower until she made a little squeaking noise that let him know he was on the right track.

Like riding a bike, he thought, and tasted her some more until she patted him on the shoulder and said, "Put the damn condom on."

He slid out of his jeans and boxers and put the condom on, and she straddled him again, pressing herself up against him and grinding her hips in a small circle.

"What are you thinking about?" She shifted her weight forward.

"Oh, God," he said, stars breaking behind his eyes at her every slight movement.

She cupped her hand around his chin and shook his head no.

"You," he said.

"Good man." She leaned into him and kissed him, her

pelvis shifting away from him, making him groan with pure want. There was nothing else in his head, nothing but her, the desire to fill her, to be inside her. He put his hands on her hips, shifting her closer, and she let out a moan as their bodies grazed each other, pressing against each other in all the right places. He slid one hand under her camisole and slowly crawled up to her breast, taking it full in his hand. She arched against him as he squeezed and rolled the nipple between his thumb and forefinger.

"Oh, God," she said.

"No," he said.

She smiled and looked at him. "Nate."

"Good woman." He put his other hand on the back of her neck and pulled her to him, tasting her as deeply as he could, drinking her in.

She pulled back and he groaned and reached for her, but she pressed her palm against his chest and pushed him back against the couch, keeping her eyes locked on his as she slid herself over him. For a moment she stayed completely still, taunting him with the anticipation. When he was on the verge of exploding inside her, she started to move, slowly at first, then faster and faster, working him into a frenzy of heat and want. He watched her, his mind wonderfully, blissfully blank as his body screamed for her, into her, until she tightened around him in wild spasms, sending him into hot blackness as he released into her, letting it all go, letting his world reduce down to nothing but how she smelled, how she felt, how rough and spent her voice sounded as she screamed his name.

They held on to each other for a while and then she shifted off him and curled into his arms, a relaxed smile on her lips as she closed her eyes and rested her head on his chest. Her body shuddered in a mild aftershock and he tightened his hold on her.

She let out a light, happy hum and laid a soft kiss on his neck.

"I'm not going to marry you, so don't even think about asking," she murmured.

He laughed and ran his hand over her hair.

"I wasn't thinking anything," he said. It was the truth.

"Good man," she said, and a moment later, he fell asleep with her in his arms, his mind as blank and happy as it had never been.

Malcolm Brody sat on the bed in his rented RV, leaned his back against the thin, faux-wood wall, and took a drag of his cigar. He tasted the smoke in his mouth for a bit and released it, then held the cigar out to take a look.

It wasn't Cuban, but those would come. All in good time.

He reached for the glass on the foldout bedside table, filled with the finest Irish whiskey he could afford, which wasn't all that fine. But that was all right, for now. He couldn't drink it anyway; it was against the rules.

There were no rules about sniffing it, though, and he stuck his nose in the glass, inhaling the sharp fumes deeply. He'd been sober for eight months, and that sobriety had served its purpose. He'd thought clearly, devised a plan, and was going to live like a king for the rest of his life. Once he was there, he could drink all he wanted. Being a drunk wasn't a problem if you were rich enough to keep the whiskey flowing. In a few days, he would be that rich.

And, now, it was time to get that plan rolling.

He put the glass down, picked up his cell phone, and dialed. It rang twice, and then the man answered.

"Richard Daly."

"Hello, Richard," Malcolm said, not bothering with the Irish accent. He wanted to make sure Richard recognized the voice on the line. "How have you been?"

There was a long, tense silence. Malcolm waited; he knew Richard would put it all together. Richard Daly was a lot of things, but stupid was not one of them. As a matter of fact, if Malcolm were a betting man, he'd put cash money down that Richard Daly had been expecting this very call.

"Malcolm," he said finally. "What do you want?"

Malcolm chuckled. "The same thing you do, I expect. The only difference is, I have it and you don't."

Richard cleared his throat. "I don't know what you're talking about."

"Richard, let's not play games. Your daughter isn't in the middle of Idaho for no reason. You know exactly what I'm talking about."

There was a short silence, then Richard said, "My daughter has nothing to do with this. I'm busy. You have five seconds to tell me what you want, Malcolm, and then I'm hanging up."

"The same thing my brother wanted," Malcolm said. "Only lots more of it." Malcolm picked up the bank records he'd stolen from his brother's desk drawer two days before his death. "I'm afraid Mick lacked vision. That, or he didn't know what you're worth. It's good for me I don't have either of those problems, isn't it, Richard?"

"How do I even know you have it?"

Malcolm reached for the cheap ceramic plate he'd picked up at the dollar store specifically for this call and held the phone out as he hurled it to the floor, where it shattered. He put the phone back to his ear.

"That wasn't it," he said. "Good thing, too. Well, good for me."

Richard was dead silent. Malcolm had known that silence well back in the day, and if he and Richard were in the same room at that moment, he might be concerned that he'd pushed it too far. As it was, with almost three thousand miles between him and his prey, it made him a little giddy.

"I'm not paying you a dime until I have proof that you have it, Malcolm."

"You'll get proof," Malcolm said. "I just thought I'd give you a chance to start liquidating some of your substantial assets." He took a puff of his cigar. "It's a bitch being in the Forbes 500, isn't it, Richard? More money, more problems, isn't that what they say?"

There was a quiet click in his ear and Malcolm flipped the phone shut. Richard Daly might be smart and successful, but once again, he was making the mistake of underestimating Malcolm. Just like when they were kids.

He really had no idea what he was dealing with.

Malcolm got up from the bed and stepped over the broken plate, then opened the side door and inhaled. Fresh pine. Not bad. Through the trees, he could see the lake, its surface glimmering in the full moonlight. Mick might have lacked vision, but he had a fine piece of land here. He thought for a moment that it might be fun to burn it to the ground, but…no. He had to rein in his sense of drama, at least for now. Once Nikkie had served her purpose and the plate was found, though, he could do whatever he wanted.

He looked forward to that.

Malcolm took one last puff of his crap cigar and dumped it into the cheap glass of whiskey.

It wouldn't be long now before he'd be enjoying the good stuff.

CHAPTER NINE

FREYA'S EYES fluttered open and she raised her head from the warm space where it had been resting.

On Nate's shoulder.

She took in a deep breath, trying to get her bearings. Sun was still streaming in from the window, so it couldn't be that late. Still, she'd fallen asleep.

In his arms.

After sex.

Not good.

She was half naked, lying practically on top of Nate, who was also half naked. And kinda snoring a little. At some point he had pulled the afghan over them and it had been very comfortable. It would be so easy to just close her eyes and go back to sleep, snuggle her head in the crook of his neck, let the rhythms of his breathing lull her back to—

No. The problem was, she was wedged between his body and the back of the couch. How the hell was she going to get out?

Good thing I was always an ace at Twister, she thought as she reached over him, bracing one hand on the edge of the couch, and then slowly shifting herself from its back. *Okay. This could work.* She lifted herself over him, getting extra stability by placing the toes of her right foot on the edge of the couch by his knees. Okay. Now she was hovering over him, careful to keep her body from touching his and waking him up. She balanced there for a minute, thinking over her next move. She couldn't put her hand on the floor, because her body would definitely touch his, and then he'd wake up, and she'd have to explain why she was performing silent acrobatics to escape. But her foot would almost definitely make a thunk sound, in which case he'd wake up and she'd have to explain—

"Hey."

She looked down to find him smiling up at her.

"Guess we fell asleep, huh?" he said.

"Yep."

She hovered there, frozen, and he raised one eyebrow.

"What are you doing?"

"I needed to get up," she said. "Didn't want to wake you." She thunked her foot to the ground, then pushed off him in an awkward movement that involved some arm flailing before she got her balance. She snatched the afghan and wrapped it around her shoulders, leaving him exposed, but he was a man. They loved being exposed.

"Sorry," she said.

"Nothing to be sorry about." He swung his feet over the side of the couch, grabbed his pants and boxers, and padded over to the bathroom. Freya took a second to put her hand to her forehead and curse to herself, then made quick work of slipping back into her clothes. She heard the water in the sink running and then a few seconds later Nate was standing before her, fully dressed and watching her with those eyes that saw everything. Jeez, couldn't he just leave?

"What's the matter?" he asked.

"Nothing," she said.

"You're freaked out."

"Pffft. Am not."

"What is it?"

"Nothing."

He reached out, put his hand under her chin, and gently angled her face until her eyes met his.

"You're lying. Out with it."

"Okay, fine." She took his hand from her face, letting his fingers hold on to hers even though it felt weird. "I don't sleep with people."

He raised an eyebrow in surprise. "Now that I wouldn't have guessed."

"I mean . . . you know what I mean. I have *sex*. I don't *sleep*. I'm not a cuddler. I don't—" She motioned toward the couch with their entwined hands.

Nate laughed.

"Shut up, Captain Cleft Chin." She pulled her hand from his. "I don't hold hands, either."

He watched her for a second, then said, "Oh. I get it."

"Get what?"

"Actually, this explains a lot."

"Explains what?"

"Nothing. Just, you know, you're all tough and in charge, but being naked with someone when not in the active pursuit of an orgasm makes you feel like you're making a promise you can't keep. I get it."

"You do?"

"Yeah," he said. "I'm a guy, I get it. But don't worry

about it. It's been a tough couple of days for both of us and that sex was..." He trailed off, his eyes on the couch, and released a quick breath. "Well, you were there."

She smiled, her heart rate increasing at the memory. "Yeah."

"So, we were tired and fell asleep. Together. And we cuddled. A little. Accidentally. It happens." He leaned over and gave her a quick kiss on the forehead, and her legs wobbled. Great. She had sex legs.

She should have stretched first.

"Hey," he said, reading her expression. "Don't worry about it. I'm not gonna worry about it. We're friends, right?"

"Barely even that," Freya said, a little too loudly and a little too quickly, and she caught a slight flash of surprise in Nate's eyes. She reached out and grabbed his hand. "I mean, yeah. We're friends. Definitely friends."

He glanced down at her hand holding his and raised his eyes to hers. "I thought you didn't do that."

She released him, surprised a bit by her own instinct to touch him. "I don't."

"Right." He checked his watch. "I'm late. Nikkie's coming up to the house for dinner with Ruby and Piper."

"Oh, hey," Freya said. "Then you should go. See you."

"Yeah." He started toward the door, then paused and turned back to face her. "The thing is...this is going to be hard on Piper. Before we"—he motioned toward the couch—"had all the great sex, I was going to ask you to come, you know, to be a friend, a neutral party. For Piper. And now I feel a little weird about it, but it really is for her. I'm not trying to make this into something it's not, I promise you."

He met her eyes and held them for a moment, and her stomach went all crazy with the butterflies.

Great. She had sex legs *and* butterflies. This was not going according to plan.

He cleared his throat. "You don't have to go, but I really am asking for Piper."

She watched him for a moment, and the butterflies went away. This really wasn't about her, it was about Piper, and an external focus suddenly relieved her awkwardness. "What time?"

His expression brightened. "Six-thirty?"

She glanced at her watch. "That gives me an hour to get cleaned up." She smiled up at him. "I can do that."

"Great. Thanks. I'll see you then." He gave a tiny wave and left, shutting the door quietly behind him. The second the door was closed, the butterflies started up again.

"Oh, shut up," Freya said to her stomach, then headed off to start her bath.

Nate had just pulled the roasted asparagus spears out of the oven when he heard the front door open and the sound of heels clicking on the floor. He smiled to himself, thinking, *Freya,* but when he closed the oven door and straightened, he found himself face to face with Nikkie.

"Oh, it's you," he said. "Don't worry, Nik. No need to knock or anything."

"Please don't look so happy to see me. You know how that kind of thing can go to a girl's head."

He leaned back against the kitchen counter, crossing his arms over his chest. "I should know better than to even ask, but just to be clear, you don't have any expectations of starting anything up between us again, do you?"

She cringed physically at the suggestion, which, while not flattering, was a comfort. "Fuck no, Nate. We should never have gotten married in the first place. I wouldn't do that again if you paid me."

Nate relaxed a bit. She seemed to mean it, although he'd never been that great at telling when Nikkie was lying. He'd found it worked in his favor to just assume everything she said was a lie—the odds worked for him there—but on this one he decided to break with tradition and believe her. His life was complicated enough right now without adding Nikkie into the mix as a romantic combatant.

"Okay," he said, then turned back to the stove. He flipped the lamb over in the skillet and checked the time, then turned to find Nikkie going through the cupboards.

"What are you doing?" he asked.

She pulled out one of the dinner plates and turned it over in her hand. "These are blue, right. Not purple?"

"They're blue," Nate said. "Something wrong?"

"No," she said, snorting out an odd laugh, and then put the plate back. "I was going to set the table, and you know what they say. Always serve pork on purple plates."

"We're having lamb, and who says that?"

She shut the cupboard and looked around. "Are those the only plates you have?"

"Yes," a firm voice came from behind them, and Nate turned to see Ruby standing there, watching Nikkie with a look of severe distrust. A well-earned look, Nate thought, and didn't bother trying to protect Nikkie from Ruby. He ducked into the fridge to get his chicken stock for the sauce, keeping an eye on the two of them in case he needed to jump in and referee.

"You're a guest," Ruby said, taking the plate from Nikkie's hands. "Sit."

"I just wanted to help," Nikkie said, her voice as steely as Ruby's smile.

"Thanks so much for the offer," Ruby said, "but if you touch anything else in my kitchen, you might just lose a hand."

"This isn't your kitchen," Nikkie said. "It's not your house. It's Nate's. He inherited everything."

Nate stopped what he was doing to look at Nikkie. "How do you know that?"

"It said in Mick's obituary," she said. "It said he was unmarried, that he had one son and one granddaughter surviving. She's not even your real stepmother. She's just Mick's tired afternoon delight."

"Let me tell you something, you little—" Ruby started.

"All right, that's enough," Nate said, stepping between them. "Nikkie, Ruby's family, and the next time you insult her, she'll take your head off and stick it on a pike outside, and I won't stop her. You get one warning. This is her house as much as mine, and you'll respect everyone in it, or you'll go. We clear?"

Nikkie's lips pursed, but she nodded. "Where's Piper?"

"She's in her room," Ruby said, "and she'll come down when she's good and ready. You leave her alone."

Nikkie raised her hands in a gesture of aggravated peace. "All right. Fine. May I use your bathroom?"

"What for?" Ruby asked.

"I'm gonna knit a tea cozy." Nikkie laid cold eyes on Ruby. "What do you think I need to use the bathroom for? The usual."

Nate motioned out toward the living room. "Go down the hallway, second door on your right."

Nikkie smoothed her hands over her skirt, nodded, and turned on her heel.

"I've counted all the fancy soaps!" Ruby called after her.

Nate watched her for a moment. Ruby had a lot of rough edges, but she loved the hell out of Piper, and Nate had never realized until that moment what that had meant to him all these months.

Ruby looked up at him, eyebrows raising. "What?"

Nate shook his head. "Nothing."

He walked back to the oven and checked on the lamb. Ruby followed, her voice low but insistent.

"She can't be trusted," Ruby said, eyeing the plate in her hand. "She's up to something."

"Yeah, probably," Nate said. "We'll keep an eye on her, but she's Piper's mother, so we need to be civil. For Piper."

Ruby huffed and muttered an unflattering suggestion under her breath. Nate patted her on the shoulder. "I'm glad you're on my side, I'll tell you that."

The doorbell rang. *Freya.*

Nate handed Ruby a wooden spoon. "Can you add the stock and the wine and reduce that sauce for me?"

Ruby nodded and took the spoon, then said, "Can't ever just make a simple gravy, can you?"

"No," he said, then ducked out of the kitchen and through the living room. When he opened the front door, Freya was fresh and beautiful in a navy blue pantsuit that made her body look almost as amazing clothed as it did naked. He smiled at her, and she held out the bag of Idaho Snowman Poop to him.

"I didn't have time to get a proper host gift," she said. "Hope you like feces."

He laughed and took it, then met her eye and said, "Thanks."

She smiled. "What smells so great?"

"Lamb," he said.

"Mmmmm," she said, a light smile playing on her lips. He stared at them, pink and plump and kissable, and wanted nothing more than to push her up against the wall and—

"Freya!"

He turned to see Piper at the base of the stairs, her face lighting up as she looked at Freya. She scooted around Nate and threw herself into Freya's arms for a hug. Freya glanced up at Nate and their eyes met briefly as they shared a thought.

So much for Piper not getting attached.

But then Freya closed her eyes and hugged Piper hard, and Nate felt gratitude surge through him. He couldn't protect Piper from everything, and he understood that now. For the moment, Freya was making a huge difference in Piper's life, and the only thing Nate could do was not to be too stupid to appreciate it.

"Hello, Piper."

Freya released Piper and they all looked at the hallway entrance into the living room where Nikkie stood stiffly, her eyes not on Piper, but on Freya.

"Hi, Nikkie," Piper said.

There was a long moment of taut silence, and then Ruby's voice called out from the kitchen. "Piper, come help get the table set, baby."

"Coming!" Piper called, then glanced around before heading into the kitchen.

"Why don't I help you?" Nikkie said, following close behind. He couldn't recall Nikkie ever volunteering to help the whole time they were together. Maybe she had changed.

A hand slid into his and he turned to see Freya looking at him, a slight expression of concern on her face.

"You okay?" she asked softly.

He smiled, squeezed her fingers, and released them.

"I'm great," he said. "Let's eat."

Ruby didn't care that Nikkie Cooper was Piper's mother; the woman was trouble. Nate knew it, Ruby could tell that Freya knew it, and it seemed from Piper's reserved behavior at dinner that she knew it, too. So why the hell didn't Nate toss that little bitch out on her ass?

Of course, Ruby knew why. Nikkie was his daughter's mother, and that was that.

Damn honorable men. Didn't know what was good for them.

"Well, that was great," Nikkie said, putting her napkin down on the table and sighing. "Excuse me. I'm just going to use your bathroom."

Ruby watched as Nikkie slid out from the table, keeping her eye on the woman until she was out of sight. "She sure goes to the bathroom a lot," she muttered.

"Yeah. Some women have a lot of sh—" Freya glanced at Piper. "Stuff to clear out."

Ruby met eyes with Freya and they shared a small smile. Now, *Freya* was a woman she could get behind.

Freya stood up and started gathering plates, and Nate was right behind her, taking the dishes from her hand.

"Um, *hey*!" Freya said.

Nate grinned at her like a big goof. "You're a guest. Guests don't clean up."

Freya put one hand on her hip. "Well, you're the cook. Cooks don't clean. I trump you. Ha!" And she took the dishes back.

"Fine," Nate said, gathering up the wineglasses. "We'll just have to clean up together, then."

Ruby looked at Piper, and they both smiled. She didn't know who those two thought they were fooling, but even the kid could tell what was going on.

But that was a secondary concern right now. Ruby stood up and walked over behind Piper, glancing down the hallway where Nikkie had gone.

"Help clean up, Piper. I'm gonna be right back."

"Okay." Piper rose and gathered her plate, then paused and said, "Hey, Ruby?"

Ruby turned around, trying to hide her impatience. "Mmmm? What, baby?"

"What did you wish for?" she asked. "You know. With the coin?"

Ruby blinked and turned her full focus on Piper. "Why do you want to know?"

Piper shrugged and scuffed a toe on the ground. "I'm just wondering if, you know, if it turned out the way you wanted."

Well. Isn't that an interesting question?

"It did." She watched the girl for a reaction, but Piper's face was unreadable. "Why do you ask?"

"Nothing," she said. "Have you ever unwished a wish?"

"No," Ruby said. "But then, I only used it twice. Like I said, you have to have a special kind of want in order for it to work in the first place." Ruby glanced down the hall-way. Nikkie sure was taking a long time in that bathroom. Ruby turned back to Piper and put one hand on her arm. "Baby, can we talk about this later?"

Piper nodded. "Oh. Sure."

"That's a girl. I'll be right back." Ruby turned and hur-ried out, just about to pass the stairwell to check on the downstairs bathroom when she heard the click-click of high-heel shoes on the stairs.

Son of a bitch. Ruby took three steps back and looked up, and wasn't there Nikkie Goddamn Cooper coming down the steps?

"Something wrong with the downstairs bathroom?" Ruby asked, not bothering to mask her tone.

Nikkie paused on the last step and laid cold eyes on Ruby.

"Yeah. I already stole all the fancy soaps out of that one." Nikkie stepped down on the last step, called out, "Thanks for dinner!" and started toward the front door. Ruby grabbed her by the elbow and Nikkie's eyes widened.

"I don't know why you're here or what you're after," Ruby said, "but you're gonna go say good night to your girl."

Nikkie wrenched her elbow out of Ruby's grip and seemed about to bash that elbow into Ruby's face—oh, how Ruby would have loved for her to try—when Piper hurried out, the plate she was drying still in her hand.

"You're going?" she asked.

Nikkie shot a glance at Ruby, then nodded. "Yeah. I'm wiped out. Jet lag. Gonna go get some sleep."

"Oh. Okay." Piper seemed about to take a step forward,

then didn't. Ruby began seriously contemplating Nate's head-on-a-pike idea. "Well, good night, Nikkie."

"Good night."

Nikkie was gone two seconds later. Nate poked his head out and gave Ruby a questioning glance. Ruby motioned toward the door, and Nate nodded. He was, after all, fairly used to getting a fleeting glimpse of that bitch's backside. He put a hand on Piper's shoulder.

"Come on," he said. "Let's finish up and we'll play Monopoly or something."

Piper nodded and went into the kitchen, and Nate looked at Ruby. "You up for some Monopoly?"

"Yeah." Ruby glanced up the stairs. "I just need to go check on something first."

Nate gave her a brief nod and retreated into the kitchen. Ruby headed up the stairs, her eyes scanning every inch she passed for something out of place. There wasn't anything of real value for Nikkie to steal.

Except…

Ruby's eyes flew to her own bedroom door; it was slightly ajar. Had she closed it before coming to dinner? Hell, she had no idea. She was too fucking old to waste precious brain space with those kinds of details. She pushed it open, went inside, and slid the rug out. She stepped on the edge of the floorboard to dislodge it, then pulled it up and sighed with relief.

The tackle box was still there. She was just about to reach for it when she heard footsteps on the stairs. She hustled to replace everything and had just scurried to her bedside drawer when Piper poked her head into her bedroom.

"Dad's gonna take the shoe if you don't hurry," Piper

said. Now that her mother had left, the tension in her face had ebbed considerably. Poor kid.

"The hell he is." Ruby pulled a bottle of Tums out of her bedside drawer and popped two into her mouth. "No one takes my shoe without a fight."

"It's not in the house," Nikkie's voice whined through Malcolm's cell phone. "I looked."

"It's in the house," Malcolm said. "I've already looked everywhere else."

There was a pause on the line. "I thought you said you couldn't come here."

Don't try to look for holes in my story, Nikkie, Malcolm thought. *You're untrained. You could hurt yourself.*

"Go back and look again. It's there somewhere."

"Where are you?" Nikkie said.

Malcolm smiled. He could just picture her glancing over her shoulder in her cabin, wondering if he'd been there.

Which, of course, he had.

"I'm nearby," he said. "And I'm watching."

"You know what? Fuck this, Malcolm. You're just as batshit crazy now as you were when I married Nate, and that's a lot of batshit. I'm outta here."

Malcolm sighed and leaned back in his lounge chair, looking up at the stars. "I think you may be underestimating my determination, Nikkie."

"I think you may be underestimating my 'fuck you,' Malcolm."

He could hear the distinct sound of a suitcase zipper in the background.

"Stop packing," he said.

The zipping stopped.

"Good. I think it's important that you understand something. I don't care about Nate, I don't care about Piper, and I certainly don't care about you. What I do care about is that plate. Now, you can get back in that house and find it for me, or you can run the risk that my batshit crazy might get on your daughter. Is that a risk you want to run, Nikkie?"

There was a cold silence. Good. He liked that. It meant that for once in her life, Nikkie Cooper was listening to someone.

"Piper was very pretty in that blue shirt with the cat on it tonight, wasn't she? She looked so innocent and sweet. Gosh, I'd hate for anything to happen that might mar that innocence. Wouldn't you?"

"Where the fuck are you, Malcolm?"

"It won't matter where I am," Malcolm said, "if you keep up your end of our deal."

She sighed heavily. "It's not there. I don't know what happened. Maybe Mick had it buried with him, I don't know. Give it up. It's done."

"It's done when I say it's done." Malcolm pressed his fingertips to his temples. The woman was thick as hell. "And just in case my threat was a little too veiled, let me make sure you understand. I don't *want* to hurt Piper. It's just that I *will*. The good news is, you have total control over that. Find me that plate, and I will pay you, and you can leave secure that your little girl will continue in her life without ever knowing I exist. I'm a man of my word."

"You're a deluded asshole," Nikkie said. "That's what you are."

"Fine. I'm a deluded asshole of my word. I'm not going to quibble over semantics. The point is, it's time someone took me seriously, Nikkie, and I really think that someone should be you."

There was another long silence, but she didn't hang up on him, which was a good sign. Malcolm sat forward in his lounge chair, staring out into the blackness of the small lake at night.

He heard Nikkie take a drag on her cigarette. "I can call the police, you know, let them deal with your crazy ass."

"I'd think twice about that, Nikkie. You're not the only one who can call the police."

"What the hell are you talking about?" she said, but there was tension in her voice.

Good.

"Identity theft is a federal offense, Nikkie, whereas my little threat against your daughter is really just your word against mine."

There was a long silence. Finally. She was taking him seriously.

"Right. And how exactly are you going to get your precious plate if I'm in prison, Malcolm?"

Or not. Malcolm tightened his grip on his phone, imagining it was her bony little chicken neck. "Is this a game you really want to play, Nikkie?"

"Nate won't let you get within two feet of Piper," she said. "And I have three passports and a burning desire to see South America. I'll be out of here before the authorities so much as have their paperwork filed. So I think I'm standing by my original 'fuck you.'"

And she hung up.

She *hung up.*

Malcolm stood up, staring at the phone in his hand, squeezing it tight in his fist.

This was maddening. He'd told Richard Daly he had the plate, and the man had practically laughed. He'd threatened Nikkie's daughter *and* her freedom, and she swatted him away like a fly. All those years of being a useless drunk had done his image more damage than he had realized, perhaps.

"Fucking hell," he said, getting up from his lounge chair. "What does a villain have to do to be taken seriously these days?"

Of course, he knew exactly what he had to do. He had to take action. He patted his pocket for the box of matches; they were still there. Then he walked around to the back of the RV and grabbed the two two-gallon gas containers he'd filled the day before.

It was time to send a message to them all.

Way past time.

CHAPTER TEN

FREYA TOOK the first step on her cabin porch and turned to face Nate, their eyes level. The full moon cast him in a sexy blue glow that made her want to throw him to the ground and have her way with him on top of the pine needles.

But her condoms were inside the cabin.

"Thanks for walking me home."

"Thanks for coming to dinner." He moved a little closer. "It meant a lot to Piper."

"Yeah," she said. "Piper."

He smiled. "Piper. Yeah."

He put one hand on her hip, sending waves of heat shooting through her, and she raised a brow at him.

"So, it's like this now, is it?" She moved a little closer to him, to the point where she was close enough to feel his breath on her, but not so close their bodies were actually touching.

Man, this was fun. She'd forgotten how much fun this could be.

"You have an objection?" He slid his hand around her

waist and pulled her close, pressing the small of her back as their bodies finally touched. *Whoa.*

"No," she said, her voice barely registering as the blood rushed in her ears. "No objection."

He angled his face toward her, almost kissed her lips, but then grazed her neck lightly with his lips, running his tongue in a light little circle over her skin, sending tingles down her back.

"I'm especially not objecting to that," she breathed.

"Good to know." He worked his way up her neck to her jawline, placing light, teasing kisses in a path until he got to her lips. Then he pulled her lower lip gently between his teeth and suckled it, then let it go.

You're definitely coming inside, Cap'n.

She put her hand on his chest, slowly unbuttoning the top button. "We're clear, right? It's just sex. No commitment. No honorable behavior allowed."

"Right." He leaned in and exhaled behind her ear, sending tickling rays of warmth down her neck with his breath. "It means absolutely nothing."

"Mmmm," she said, closing her eyes as his hands ran down her lower back. "Good man."

"Put it back in your pants, Brody, we need to talk."

Nate stiffened and stepped back and there, of course, was Nikkie, stalking toward them in the moonlight.

"Go to bed, Nikkie," Nate said. "We'll talk tomorrow."

"No," she said. "We'll talk *now*. It's important." She took a drag on her cigarette, and Freya caught herself staring at the brightly glowing red ember on the end.

She'd forgotten how pretty lit cigarettes were at night.

"Nikkie," Nate started, but Freya touched him on the shoulder.

"It's okay," she said.

He turned to her. "No. It's really not."

"If it's about Piper. You should go." Freya knew it was the right thing to say, but she hated it. *This is what I get for having mommy issues.*

He looked at her, an expression of disappointed helplessness crossing his face before he accepted his sexless fate. "All right. Fine."

Nikkie took another long drag on her cigarette. Freya inhaled deeply, taking in as much of the secondhand smoke as she could.

Hello, old friend.

"Let's go to the house," Nikkie said, shooting the world's least subtle glance at Freya. "I want you to be able to concentrate."

Nate sighed. "Fine. Let's go."

"Hang on," Freya said, then walked down the steps to Nikkie and held her hand out, palm up. "Gimme."

Nikkie looked at her like she was crazy, but Freya raised her open palm higher.

"Smoker's code," she said. "Unless you're down to the lucky in that pack, you know you have to."

Nikkie sighed, pulled the pack out of her purse, and opened it. It was almost full. Freya plucked a cigarette out and placed it between her index and middle finger.

It was like coming home.

"You smoke?" Nate said.

"No. I quit." She put the cigarette between her lips and raised an eyebrow at Nikkie, who sighed and flicked her lighter. Freya leaned in, touched the tip to the flame, and inhaled.

Ahhhhh.

She pulled the cigarette from her mouth, exhaled blue smoke into the moonlight, and took a few moments before noticing Nate's expression of severe disapproval.

"I only smoke now when I'm frustrated," she said, hitting *frustrated* hard so he didn't miss her meaning.

He didn't. "It's bad for you."

"I know that." She took a drag. Ohhhhh, that was good. She exhaled. "That's why I quit."

"Don't bother explaining," Nikkie said, taking another drag on her own cigarette. "He'll never understand."

"Of course he won't," Freya said, giving Nate a wicked smile. "He's Captain Cleft Chin."

Nikkie laughed. "That's good. I'm gonna have to use that."

Nate put one hand on Nikkie's elbow. "No, you're not."

"Whatever you say, Cap'n," Freya said, and both she and Nikkie giggled.

"All right, that's enough," Nate said, guiding Nikkie away. "The last thing I need is you two bonding. Good night, Freya."

"Night," Freya said, waving with one hand as the man she wanted desperately between her thighs strode off with his ex-wife. She sighed, took another drag off the smoke, and tossed it to the ground, crushing it under her shoe.

It wasn't helping.

But, she thought, remembering the shower head in the bath, *perhaps something else will.*

She headed inside, kicking the door shut and stripping down to her underwear. She picked up her cell phone and turned the power on; there were four messages waiting. She checked the call log quickly—two calls from Flynn's house; she guessed one was from Flynn worrying about her, the other from Jake with the results of his inquiry. Then there were two from her father, neither of which she cared to hear at the moment. She powered the phone down again, grabbed her MP3 player, turned it on full blast, and stuck the earbuds in her ears, then went into the bathroom and shut the door and locked it.

Who needs a man? she thought, looking at the hand-held shower head as she started the hot water running. She slipped out of her underwear and stepped into the tub, lowering herself in gently. She closed her eyes and imagined Nate settling into the bath with her.

Nate placed a mug of black coffee in front of his ex-wife, then sat down across from her at the table.

"You want to talk, let's talk," he said. "What is it?"

She sat back, crossing her arms over her stomach like a petulant teenager. "All right, let's cut to the chase, because I'm out of time. Where's the plate?"

"What?"

She widened her eyes at him, not even trying to hide her annoyance and frustration. "The plate. I need the plate."

"Okay," Nate said. "Fine."

He walked to the cupboard, got a saucer and placed it under her mug. She looked down at the saucer, then back up at him.

"What the hell are you doing?"

"You asked for a plate," he said, trying to keep the edge out of his voice. "I gave you a plate. It's getting late, Nikkie, so if you want to talk about Piper—"

She pushed herself up from the table. "Knock it off, Nate. I'm not fucking around here. Just give it to me and

I'll be out of here by daybreak, never to darken your door again."

Nate stared at her. "What the hell are you talking about?"

She watched him for a moment, her eyes narrowed. "You *do* know about the plate, right? Tell me you know about the plate, Nathan, because if you don't, my pretty pink brains are going to explode all over your nice wall."

"I don't know anything about a plate," Nate said, "but now I know for sure that you're not here for Piper. Goddamnit, Nikkie. If you wanted money or something, you could have just asked me. Why'd you have to drag her into it?"

"It's a plate." She held her hands out, about twelve inches apart. "It's got some kind of gold inlay. Scalloped edges. Some kind of bird in the middle. Purple rim. Where is it?"

Nate froze, flashing on his last conversation with his father. "Purple?"

Her eyes brightened and she put her hand on his arm. "*Yes.* You know it. Where is it? Nate, I can't tell you why, but I need it. Now."

He leaned back against the wall, taking a moment to absorb this information. "Christ. It's a plate?"

"Um, *yeah.* And quit playing dumb. I saw the look on your face. I know you know what I'm talking about."

"No, I..." He sighed and ran one hand through his hair, trying to gather his thoughts. He was pretty damn sure he hadn't seen anything matching that description in his searches of the grounds. He'd handled every plate in that house over the last six months; there wasn't a purple-rimmed one in the bunch. He looked up at Nikkie. "How did you know about it?"

Nikkie shrugged. "It's not important. But I'm telling you, I need that plate, like *now*, so just hand it over, and this whole thing will be done."

He shook his head. "Not a chance. How did you know? Did Mick tell you about it? Have you been in touch with him?"

She sighed, then sat down in the chair next to his, leaning over the table, her eyes pleading.

"Nate," she said, "this is really serious. If I don't get that plate, something could happen to Piper."

The air in the room went still, and he stared at her. "What?"

"It's complicated," she said, unable to meet his eye. "I just... all you have to do is give it to me, and it'll all be over. She'll be safe, I'll be gone, and you can go back to fucking your snow bunny—"

He shot over to her, grabbing both her arms in his and practically lifting her off her feet.

"Jesus, Nate," she said, her eyes widening in surprise as she glanced down at his hands clamped on her arms. "What the hell's wrong with you?"

"What the fuck did you do, Nikkie?" he asked, his heart pounding with a primal fury. "Did someone threaten Piper? Because I'm telling you right now, if one of your fuckups so much as touches her, I'll kill you myself, do you understand?"

"Ow," she said, squirming in his grip. "Nate. You're *hurting* me."

He realized what he was doing and let go.

"Wow," she said, laughing bitterly as she rubbed her arms. "I didn't think you had it in you to hurt a girl, Nate."

"You don't count," he said. "Tell me what's going on, Nikkie, because so help me God, if anything happens to Piper, you'll find out exactly what I've got in me."

Nikkie's eyes flashed with surprise and, Nate was satisfied to see, a little bit of fear. She stepped back from him and ran her hands through her hair.

"Just give me a minute," she said, closing her eyes. "I need a minute to think."

"You'd better think fast, or—"

There was a crashing sound from upstairs, and Piper called out, "Dad!"

Nate met Nikkie's panicked eyes for a second, then charged through the house, taking the stairs three at a time until he burst through Piper's door to find her leaning over the desk by her window, peering out, her desk lamp lying sideways on the floor at her feet. He ran across the room and pulled her into his arms, then released her and knelt before her, his hands running over her arms, her face.

She was fine.

"Jesus, Pipes, you scared me," he said. "You okay?"

"Dad, look," she said, pointing out the window. Nate ran his eyes over her once more to be sure she was okay, then looked in the direction where she pointed. In the distance, bright orange flickers laid angry, dancing shadows on the trees surrounding the cabin area. He stared for a moment, calculating exactly which cabin they were coming from, and then his body went cold.

"Ruby!" he shouted, dragging Piper out to the hallway.

"Dad, is that Freya's cabin?" Piper asked, her voice trembling, but he just put her hand in Ruby's as the older woman came out of her bedroom.

"What's going on?" Ruby asked, all business.

"Number Four's on fire," he said. "Call 911, and don't let Piper out of your sight."

Ruby nodded. "Done. Go."

Nate pushed Nikkie out of his way and flew down the stairs and out of the house, running toward the cabins as fast as he could, whipping down the path through the trees, his lungs screaming for oxygen as he pushed harder, faster. The crackling of the flames got louder as he approached, and he felt the heat from the fire on his face even before he ran up the porch steps.

"Freya!" he yelled. He put his hand on the doorknob and the heat seared his skin, so he stood back and kicked at it, coughing as his already starved lungs took in the acrid smoke pouring out of the cabin. He stepped inside.

"Freya!"

There was no answer.

I can't believe this is how I'm gonna die, Freya thought as she dunked a towel in the bathwater and placed it over her head.

She lay curled on the floor of the cabin's bathroom, having already exhausted all the elementary school fire tips she could remember. When she'd first smelled the smoke, she'd thrown her MP3 player to the floor, jumped out of the tub, and felt the door, which was searing hot. Bad news, that. Then she looked at the bathroom window — high and small, too small for her to get through. Plus, she thought she remembered something about extra oxygen feeding the fire, so she didn't want to open it unless she was sure she could get out. By the time the bright orange flames had started licking under the door, she had nothing left but to douse the robe in the water, wrap it around herself, wet a towel to put over her head, and hunker down in the corner.

To die a horrible death.

The smoke was coming down to her level as the fire licked up the door, sucking greedily at what oxygen there was in the room, and she pressed her cheek against the floor, trying to breathe as well as she could through the wet towel. Panic shot ice cold through her, and her body began to shake and calm in sputtering waves.

Stupid, stupid, so stupid, she thought, remembering the cigarette she'd tossed aside so casually underneath an old wooden cabin. She'd always expected smoking to kill her, but she thought it would be cancer, or a car accident while she searched for a lighter under the driver's seat.

That's what you get for not having imagination, she thought, then laughed a panicked laugh and coughed as the smoke seared her lungs.

Ohgodohgodohgod. Her body calmed as her breathing became more ragged. She closed her eyes and saw Flynn crying at her funeral and hot tears slid from her eyes. *Jake will take care of her, Jake will take care of her.* Her father's face flashed through her mind, disappointed at her stupid, stupid end. *I'm sorry, Daddy.* All those years wasted, trying to make him proud of her, and she went and died like this without ever getting over the need for approval from Daddy. She'd always thought she'd have time to work that crap out.

Stupid, stupid. She should have quit that job years ago and done something that actually mattered, that made her happy. Like Flynn. Of course, then she would have been broke like Flynn, and she wasn't that strong.

Stupid, stupid. Her body felt like it was whirling in an ever-faster circle on the floor.

It's the lack of oxygen, she heard her father's rational voice saying. *Won't be long now. Just go to sleep, Freya. It'll be easier.*

She felt her body sinking into a comfortable blackness, but then heard Nate's voice calling her name, and her heart seized as the realization hit her with a clarity she'd never known before.

He's the one.

Her consciousness rose from the black and she tried to laugh but her lungs could only manage to choke and sob. Here, she'd finally met the man she was sure didn't exist, and she was gonna die before she could enjoy him.

Stupid, stupid.

There was a crash behind her and her insides screamed even though her lungs couldn't. It occurred to her that maybe it was the door, maybe she could get out, but her body felt too heavy to move. She tried to raise her head, but then the world seemed to flip under her, and she felt as if she was clinging to the ceiling, and if she tried to move, she'd fall, fall, fall into nothing but fire.

It's the lack of oxygen, her father's voice said. *Go to sleep, Freya.*

And then everything went black.

"Freya!" Nate held her body, wet and heavy in his arms, against his chest as he ran out of the blaze. He coughed and stumbled down onto the ground with her, weakened from his own body's lack of oxygen. He pulled her into his arms and wiped the hair out of her face. Her skin was hot, but she didn't seem singed at all. The wet towels had at least saved her from that.

"Freya." He leaned his ear against her chest, but couldn't hear anything over the crackling flame from the cabin.

"Goddamnit, I can't hear." He pulled back and put his fingers by her nose and mouth. He thought he felt some air moving, but whether it was her breath or a breeze, he couldn't tell.

"Goddamnit," he said again, the panic racing through him. Somewhere in the distance, sirens were getting louder, and the ground seemed to tremble under him, but inside the small bubble of his focus, it was just him and Freya. He pressed his face next to hers, put his lips next to her ear, and spoke the one thing he knew to be true.

"We're not done," he said. "There's more."

He pulled back and looked at her face, focusing on how beautiful she was, remembering her smile. *We're not done,* he thought, staring helplessly down at her.

There's more.

And then she coughed.

"*Christ,*" he said, pulling her into his arms and rocking her as she sputtered and gasped. Her arms came up suddenly as if to fight him off, but he held her still against him until she calmed.

"You're okay," he said. "I've got you. You're okay." He pulled back and put one hand on her face, his eyes locking on hers, which were wide and glassy and panicked. "You're okay."

She coughed again, spasms wracking her body, and he hoped to God he was right. She was alive, though, and that was what mattered. He pulled her to him and held her as the coughs gave way to sobs and she clutched at him. She started to say something, but was only able to hack and gasp for air.

He smoothed her hair away from her face. "Don't talk, okay? Just breathe slow and even."

"Is anyone else in there?"

Nate started at the voice, and suddenly the tiny bubble that held only him and Freya burst. Everything got loud—the sirens, the yelling, the vehicles screaming into the campground, and then one of the voices came through.

"Sir!" Nate looked up to see a fireman shouting at him over the din around them. "Is anyone else in the cabin?"

"No," Nate tried to shout, but his lungs felt as if they were filled with hot pokers, and he just coughed and shook his head. Someone tried to take Freya from him, but he wouldn't let her go, and then there were arms under his, pulling him to his feet, but he still held on to her. She was holding on to him, too, her arms working as they clamped strongly around his neck, her lungs breathing even as she coughed and sputtered.

It seemed more like the ambulance just appeared before him than that he'd walked there, and the world started to spin a bit. The paramedics pulled a gurney out of the ambulance and he set Freya down on it, gripping its side to keep his own balance. Freya's eyes flickered shut, and a male paramedic slid an oxygen mask over her face.

"Is she going to be okay?" Nate said as loudly as he could manage, but the guy didn't seem to hear him. He felt a hand on his shoulder and turned to see a female paramedic at his side. He glanced at the patch on her jacket: *Lucy.*

"Sir, I need to give you oxygen," she said, putting one of his arms over her shoulder and leading him toward an SUV that read "Kemp County Emergency Services" across the back.

The dizziness ebbed, and he turned back toward the ambulance. "Is she going to be okay?"

Lucy glanced past Nate at one of the paramedics tending to Freya. He made some kind of motion with his hand, and Lucy nodded.

"She needs to go to the emergency room," she said. "And right now you need oxygen."

"I'm fine," Nate said, coughing. "I need to go with her."

"You want to help her?" Lucy said, firmly pulling him toward the SUV. "Stay out of the way."

Nate swallowed hard as two paramedics slid Freya into the ambulance and hopped in after her, shutting the doors efficiently behind them. The lights came on and the ambulance sped out.

They'd take care of her. She was going to be fine. He closed his eyes and repeated it in his head, trying to believe. *She'll be fine, she'll be fine.*

Lucy pulled an oxygen tank out from the back of the SUV and slid a plastic mask over his nose and mouth.

"Breathe slowly," she said. "Breathe as deep as you can."

Lucy leaned him against the SUV, then ducked in the back of it and pulled out a folding camping chair. He tried to take in a deep breath, and his lungs seized and he doubled over against the SUV, hacking and coughing until black spots clouded his vision.

"All right," she said when he was able to stand up straight again. "Just sit down here—"

"Daddy!"

Nate looked up and saw Piper running toward him, Ruby close behind. Piper threw herself into his arms and he held her tight against him.

"Honey, your dad needs to sit down," Lucy said, then put her hands on Nate's shoulders and guided him down into the camping chair. She pulled the oxygen mask's straps until it was snug on his face and said, "Breathe. Slow and deep."

Piper settled on the ground at his side and rested her head on his knee. He ran his hand over her hair and looked at the smoking cabin. He could still see some orange flames inside, but the firemen were dousing it down, and mostly, there was smoke.

He took a deep breath, and this time his lungs didn't protest quite so much. He looked up to see Ruby, a cardigan thrown over her flannel nightgown, watching him from a few feet away, her arms crossed sharply over her midsection. Her face was taut, and he could see the deep concern in her eyes. He held out his hand, and she stepped forward, taking it in both of hers, which were shaking slightly.

"You're all right?" she asked, her voice strong.

He nodded. She patted the back of his hand and tightened her grip on him, nodding toward the cabin. "And Freya?"

He pulled the mask down with his free hand. "She's alive. They took her to the emergency room."

"Alive is good," Ruby said. "She'll be fine." She released his hand and stood closer, putting her arm around his shoulder. "She'll be *fine*. Now put the goddamn mask back on," she said. "There's been enough heroics from you for one night."

Nate put the mask back on, but only had it on for half a second before a thought hit him and he lowered it again. He glanced down at Piper, who was still resting her head on his knee, watching the fire. He turned to Ruby, and their eyes met, and her lips pursed as she understood his question.

"Gone," she said, nodding toward Number Two, where Nikkie's rental car was suspiciously absent. "Ran out right after you did. Big shock."

Nate put the mask back on and touched Ruby's hand on his shoulder, then rested it on the back of Piper's head. He'd deal with Nikkie later.

Right now, he had more important things to think about.

CHAPTER ELEVEN

OW, FREYA THOUGHT. Everything was black, but her head was pounding, and her body felt too heavy to move. She opened her eyes, giving them a moment to adjust to the shadows in the room. The first thing she was able to focus on was the square white ceiling panels over her head. Somewhere behind her, something cast a soft blue glow into the darkness. Cool air shot into her nose through tubes that were strapped over her cheeks.

Oxygen.

Not heaven. Not hell.

Hospital.

She'd take it.

She lay still for a moment. Aside from the pounding in her head, everything seemed okay. She wiggled the toes on her right foot, then her left. No pain. She pulled her right hand into a clumsy fist; no pain. Then she tried to move her left hand, and something on the back of it pinched. Plus, there seemed to be something warm lying on her fingers.

She looked down. It was another hand. A strong, warm, slightly charred hand.

She angled her head a bit and saw him. His face had been washed hastily, there were still blackened smudges near his hair- and jawlines, and his usually blond hair was dark with soot and a bit singed on one side. His chin rested on his chest, which rose and fell slowly with his sleeping breath, and his arm stretched over onto the side of her bed, where his fingers rested on hers.

The glass door to her room slid open and a short, pudgy nurse stepped in, navigating deftly around Nate's sleeping form to check the computer screen over his head. She jotted some numbers down, then walked around to the other side of Freya's bed, where she pulled an empty bag of clear fluid off the IV hook before noticing that Freya was awake.

"Hey," the nurse said softly. "How are you feeling?"

"Headache," Freya said. Her throat scratched a bit, but she could talk. That had to be a good sign.

"I'm not surprised. You were pretty dehydrated." The nurse gave one of those well-practiced, comforting nurse smiles. "Tell you what. I'll check with the doctor and see if I can't get a little something-something for you."

"Thank you," Freya said. "That'd be great."

The hand on hers twitched, and when she turned her head, Nate had jerked awake, his eyes focused on the nurse.

"How's she doing?" he asked, his voice low and raw and scratchy.

The nurse quirked her head toward Freya. "Ask her yourself."

Nate blinked a few times then looked at Freya. Their eyes met and a slow smile spread over his face, warming her.

"Hey, there," he said, his voice soft and yet still strong. It was the kind of voice a girl could lean on. "How are you?"

Freya tried to answer with something light and flip, but she was too tired to block how happy it made her to see him, and ended up only being able to squeak as the stupid tears tracked down her cheeks.

His smile faded. "Oh, hey." He grabbed a tissue from the box on the tray at the end of the bed and leaned over her, dabbing at her face. "It's all over. You're okay. Everything's fine."

"I know," she said, sniffling. "It's just that I have this stupid eye condition..."

The crinkles at the corners of his eyes were enhanced by the soot as his face broke out in a smile. "Right. I forgot."

The nurse touched Freya lightly on the shoulder. "I'm going to check on those painkillers." She leaned over the bed a bit, shot Nate a teasing glance, and then spoke out of the side of her mouth to Freya. "In the meantime, so I don't get in trouble for letting him violate visiting hours, he's your husband for as long as you're in this hospital, okay?"

"Um. Okay."

The nurse straightened up. "Good girl."

As the nurse padded out, Freya raised an eyebrow at Nate, who shrugged.

"It was her idea."

"I knew you'd try to marry me," Freya said.

"Yeah." He took her hand in his. "Well. Old habits die hard."

He reached up with his free hand and pushed a lock

of hair away from her forehead, and the comfort she felt in his presence was almost overwhelming. She allowed herself to relax for a moment, but then a rush of panic hit her before she could name it, and she tightened her grip on his hand.

"What?" he asked, leaning closer. "You okay?"

"Piper," she said. "Ruby."

"Everyone else is fine." He ran his hand over her hair, keeping his eyes solidly on hers. "Don't worry about it."

Freya relaxed a little, but on the edges of her consciousness, something was still troubling her. She flashed on the cigarette she'd tossed away, and it all came rushing back.

"Oh, my God," she said. "Nate. Your cabin."

He reached up and moved her hair away from her face. "Hey. Don't worry about that."

"I wasn't thinking. I thought I stamped the cigarette out, but I guess I didn't." She swallowed, and the tears filled her eyes again. "I'm so sorry."

He gave her a confused look, and then realization struck. "You think you started that fire?"

Freya's mind went blank looking for other possibilities. "I didn't?"

Nate shook his head. "No. They're still investigating, but it pretty much had to be arson for it to move that fast." He swallowed, and she could see the tension and anger in his eyes for a second, but only for a second, then his strong, lean-on-me expression returned and he smiled down at her. "You don't need to worry about that, though."

"Right." *Someone tried to kill me. No need to worry.*

"Freya?"

She angled her head to look at him.

"I haven't called your family," he said. "If you give

me some names and numbers, I can let them know what happened."

Freya's entire body went tense at the thought. "No."

Nate paused for a moment. "But...your sister, your dad..."

"They don't need to know," Freya said. "I'm fine. Why worry them?"

"Why...?" Nate seemed stunned. "They're your family, Freya. If something like this happened to Piper—"

"Piper's a kid."

"That doesn't matter," he said. "If she was hurt, I'd want to know."

"That's not how it works with us," Freya said. "I'm the one who worries. I'm the one who rushes out and fixes things. Flynn's the one who screws up at work and almost gets killed by crazy people. I'm the one who—"

Doesn't need anyone. She knew it sounded bad, so she stopped. She was too tired to explain why it made perfect sense, so she just closed her eyes and took a deep breath. She felt movement at her side, and Nate's soft lips pressed against her forehead and she wanted to cry for the sheer relief she felt having him there. When she looked up, he was smiling down at her.

"Okay," he said. "I won't bring it up again. Just rest and try not to worry about anything, okay?"

"Sure. Your cabin burned down and someone tried to kill me." Freya laid her head back on the pillow, the exhaustion catching up with her. "Nothing to worry about."

"Right." He sat back down in the chair, and she could see how tired he was.

"You should go home," she said. "Get some sleep. It's been a long day."

She felt his hand on hers, and she turned her head to look at him. He looked beat up, his eyes red and his body blackened by soot, but when he smiled at her, it pushed all the bad stuff away like so many fallen leaves under a strong wind.

"I'm fine right here," he said.

She closed her eyes, tightening her fingers around his. "Whatever you say, Cap'n."

Ruby had been dreaming about living in a hotel with forty-four cats when the light knock on her bedroom door woke her up. She pulled her head up from the pillow, instantly awake, and checked on Piper, who was sleeping like a stone next to her, a baby snore emanating from her slightly opened mouth.

Kid could sleep through anything. Ruby envied that. She pulled her robe up off the floor and slid it over her shoulders, tying the knot quickly before opening the door to find Nate standing there, looking like he'd literally been to hell and back.

"You need a shower," Ruby said.

"Yeah," Nate said, his eyes bleary. "Probably do."

She stood on her toes and tried to assess the damage to his hair. "And probably a buzz cut."

"Thanks, Ruby," Nate said.

She settled back on her heels and looked at him. "How's Freya?"

"Good. They let me bring her home. She's sleeping in my bed."

Ruby raised an eyebrow, and Nate followed that quickly with, "I'll be on the couch."

"Right."

He glanced past Ruby through the crack in her door.

"Piper's okay?" he asked.

"She's fine," Ruby said. "She was a little scared last night, so she crawled into bed with me. And she brought the fire extinguisher."

Nate's eyebrows raised up. "You're kidding."

"I think it might be her new security blanket. We'll have to get another one for the kitchen."

"I'll put it on my to-do," he said.

Ruby glanced behind her. Piper was still sleeping, but just to be safe, she shut the door and lowered her voice.

"What have you heard?"

Nate shook his head. "Nothing new. They suspect it was gasoline, but we have to wait for the investigators to run some tests and analyze the evidence they got last night." His face went hard. "I'd just like to know how the fuck she did it."

Ruby felt cold tendrils squeeze her stomach. "You think Nikkie did this?"

"Well…yeah. She pulls me away from Freya right before the fire, then takes off right after? I don't know why she would do something like that. She was a mess before, but…I don't know. She must have gotten worse." He took a deep breath and ran his hand over the top of his head, then looked at Ruby. "Ruby, did Dad have a…this is going to sound crazy. Did he have a special plate or something?"

Ruby kept her poker face on. "What kind of plate?"

"I don't know. When Nikkie pulled me in here, she said that she needed a plate with a purple rim. She said someone was going to hurt Piper."

Ruby's fight-or-flight went straight to fight, and her whole body stiffened. "Who's gonna hurt Piper?"

"I don't know. It doesn't make any sense. Maybe it was just some kind of decoy to keep me busy while the cabin burned down. I don't know. It just..." He ran his hands through his hair, visibly exhausted. "You haven't seen anything like that, have you?"

Ruby put her hand on his arm. "Take a shower. Get some sleep. We'll talk about it later."

He ran his hand over his face. "Yeah. I don't think I can sleep, though. I'll get cleaned up and make breakfast. How do you feel about pancakes?"

Ruby smiled. "Nothing fancy this time. I come down there and see you lighting bananas on fire, we're gonna have a talk."

Nate smiled and nodded. "Fine. Nothing fancy."

"Good boy." Ruby turned to go back to her room, but stopped and turned when Nate said her name. "Yeah?"

"Thank you," he said. "I know I'm not your son and Piper's not your granddaughter. You don't have to do what you do for us. But, uh..." He sighed heavily. "I appreciate it."

Ruby nodded, then blinked hard and cleared her throat. "Well. You go on and get cleaned up."

He headed down the hallway into the bathroom. Ruby watched him go, then quietly opened the door to her room. She stepped inside and closed the door behind her, leaning against it, releasing a breath she felt like she'd been holding for six months.

It was time.

"Ruby?"

Ruby smiled and looked at her bed, where Piper sat up and rubbed her eyes. "What time is it?"

Ruby glanced at the bedside clock. "About nine."

"Oh." She blinked again. "I'm not going to school today?"

"No, but that doesn't mean you get to lie in bed all day. Go to your room and get dressed. Your dad's gonna make pancakes after he's done with his shower."

"Okay." Piper slid out of bed, picked up the fire extinguisher, and carried it with her as she shuffled toward the door. She paused at the door and looked at Ruby, one eye half squinting. "He's not going to light the bananas on fire again, is he?"

Ruby laughed. "No, baby. Not this time."

"Good." Piper nodded and left, the fire extinguisher dragging along behind her like a wayward teddy bear. Ruby watched her leave, the smile on her lips fading as she did.

She was gonna miss that kid.

CHAPTER TWELVE

*F*REYA SAT on the edge of Nate's bed, staring down at the hospital-blue pair of scrubs the nurses had given her to go home in, trying to wrap her mind around the fact that this outfit was her entire wardrobe at the moment. It was almost like being naked. No cell phone in her purse, no laptop slung over her shoulder in a bag matching her outfit, no three-inch stiletto heels to spear the competition with.

It was almost like being free.

There was a light knock at the door.

"Come on in," she said, pushing herself up off the bed. Her limbs were still a little achy, but considering the fact that she could be fried up good and crisp right now, she was okay with it.

The door opened slowly, tentatively, and Piper stuck her head in, her little brown eyes wide with uncertainty.

"You're awake?"

"Yep," Freya said, smoothing the covers on Nate's bed. "I was just about to come down." She raised an eyebrow at Piper. "I heard tell of pancakes."

"Yeah, Dad's cooking them now. He sent me to check on you and see if you were hungry."

"Starving," Freya said. "Especially if your dad's cooking."

"I'm glad you're okay," Piper said suddenly. The kid had a way of taking a conversation on a hairpin turn.

"Me, too," Freya said. "You were here, right? You were safe?"

"Yeah." Piper nodded, settling on the edge of her father's bed. "I was scared, though. It's freaky. You hear about fires happening like that, but you never think it'll happen to you."

Freya watched her for a minute, wondering how much Piper knew about the gasoline and the arson, then decided nothing. "Right. Freaky."

Freya stood still for a moment, watching Piper, who sat with her legs kicking out in random circles. A sign, Freya had learned, that she had something she wanted to talk about. Freya sat on the bed a few feet away from Piper and waited.

"Are you going to go home now?" she said finally.

"I don't know what I'm going to do," Freya said truthfully. "I haven't really had much time to think about it."

Piper raised her eyes to Freya's. "Are you in love with my dad?"

Well, hello, hairpin. Freya sat up straight. "What makes you ask a question like that?"

Piper fought a smile and looked away, her cheeks blushing. "Just because I'm a kid doesn't mean I can't tell when stuff is going on."

"Well," Freya started, then stopped when she realized she had no idea what to say to the kid. What was she supposed to say? *I'm not in love with your dad, but I've sure enjoyed the hell out of his penis recently?* "Well."

"He's happy around you," Piper said. "Even when he was angry at my mom, you'd walk in a room and he'd be happy again."

Freya laughed. "Not to toot my own horn, but I have that effect on a lot of people. It's what happens with girls like us, Piper. We just bring happiness wherever we go. It's completely out of our control."

Piper lowered her eyes. "I'm not like that."

"The hell you're not," Freya said. "Don't get down on yourself, kid. If you let that shit in your head now, you'll never get rid of it."

Piper angled her head to look up at Freya, and a slight smile graced the edge of her lips. "He makes you happy, too. I can tell."

Freya pushed herself up off the bed. "Those pancakes are gonna get cold if we don't hurry."

Piper stood up as well and bumped her shoulder into Freya as she passed. "You like him. You think he's cute."

"Shut up," Freya said, laughing.

"You *love* him," she said, in a teasing sing-song. "You want to *marry* him."

"Do not!" They walked out into the hallway and she put her arm around Piper's shoulders. "And you're gonna keep your big mouth shut around your dad or I'm gonna tell him all about Matt Hartley."

Piper gasped and grabbed Freya's arm. "No! No!"

Freya cleared her throat and called down the stairs. "Hey, Nate! I've got something to tell you!"

"No! Nononononononono!" Piper pleaded, pulling on her arm and laughing.

Freya held up a warning index finger at Piper. "Are we at a détente?"

Piper blinked. "What's that?"

"You shut up, I shut up."

"Oh!" Piper jumped up and down. "Yes, yes, yes! A *total* détente!"

"What's going on up there?"

Freya looked down to see Nate at the bottom of the stairs, a kitchen towel draped over his shoulder, watching them with a suspicious look.

"Oh...nothing," Freya said, then held her hand out to Piper, who shook it. "We're just heading down for pancakes."

She motioned for Piper to go first, and the kid practically bolted down the stairs past her father, who watched her and then turned questioning eyes to Freya, who took a more leisurely pace down the stairs.

"What are you two up to?" he asked, a smile playing on his lips.

"Oh, nothing. You showered." She hit the bottom of the steps and reached up to touch the singed patch of hair on the side of his head. "You need a haircut."

"Great," he said. "I risk my life saving you, and all I get is criticism on my hair?"

"Play your cards right," Freya said under her breath, "and you'll get more than that."

She looked up at him, feeling playful and giggly, but something in the way he looked back at her made her catch her breath, and for the first time it occurred to her that maybe they weren't playing anymore.

"Well," she said. "I'm starving."

He nodded toward the kitchen. "Let's get you fed, then."

They walked into the kitchen together. Nate pulled out a chair for Freya and settled her in, then went to finish up on the pancakes. Freya slid her napkin into her lap, noticing Piper watching her with a smirk on her face. She glanced around to make sure no one was watching, then stuck her tongue out at Piper.

At least there was one person in that house she always knew how to behave around.

Ruby was quiet through most of breakfast, watching Nate and Freya flirt, and Freya and Piper tease each other. Much as she liked Freya, Ruby thought things were moving a bit fast with her and this family. There was too much going on, too much unresolved, and Piper was too vulnerable. Nate could take care of himself — and it seemed he was doing just that — but Piper was not in a good place to be getting too attached to someone like Freya. There was also the business about the plate that needed clearing up, and soon, and she needed to get the timing right on that so it didn't make anything worse.

Freya was a good woman, but she complicated everything, and they couldn't afford more complications right now.

"So, Freya," Ruby said finally while Nate was occupied doing the dishes. "How are you feeling?"

Freya smiled. "Better, thanks."

"Wasn't your return flight today?"

Freya met Ruby's eyes. "No. It was open-ended. I was hoping to go back today, but —"

"You're not going, right?" Piper said.

Freya shifted her focus slowly from Ruby to Piper. "I'm not sure what's going to happen yet."

Piper grinned. "Then you can stay!"

The sink turned off and Nate walked back to the table,

so Ruby leaned back in her chair and went silent. There would be time to broach the topic again later.

"Piper," Nate said, "don't you have some homework to do?"

"Nope," Piper said. "You made me do it Friday afternoon, remember?"

"Well, go on up to your room and play for a while," he said. He raised his eyebrows at her, and seemed anxious for her to get gone.

Piper hopped up. "Okay." She turned to Freya. "Wanna play Playstation?"

Freya smiled and seemed about to take the kid up on it when Nate said, "No, Pipes. I need to talk to both Freya and Ruby about something. Grown-up stuff."

Both of us? Ruby thought, then looked at Freya, who shot an equally questioning glance back at Ruby.

"So you're getting rid of me?" Piper shrugged. "Jeez. Just say so."

She shared a look with Freya and headed out. Nate stood with his hands resting on the back of his chair, listening. He waited until the sound of Piper's door shutting came from upstairs, and then he sat down and looked back and forth from Ruby to Freya.

"I've made some decisions," he said. "And I wanted to talk to you two about them."

"This sounds like a family thing," Freya said, starting to get up from the table. "Don't include me to be polite. I can—"

"No," he said, putting one hand on hers. "This affects you, too."

Their eyes locked for a second, some silent communication going on between them, then she nodded and sat down. Ruby took a sip of her coffee and waited to react until she knew what she was reacting to.

Nate sat back and rested his hands in front of him on the table, staring at them as he spoke. "I got a call from my partners at the restaurant. Lulu"—he looked at Freya—"she was my sous chef, and she took over when I left. Anyway, Lulu's gonna walk if they don't make her permanent."

Freya sat forward. "Well, they can't do that. It's your restaurant. You're the chef."

"I've been gone six months. Lulu's made changes to the menu. Things seem to be working, and a good head chef isn't easy to find." He cupped his hands together and stared at them on the table.

"So," Freya said, "you're going back, then?"

Ruby felt her back go stiff. Nate hesitated for a moment, then shook his head, "They offered to buy me out of the restaurant. I'm taking the offer."

Ruby's stomach flipped in her gut. "Nate, why would you do that?"

Nate raised guilty eyes to hers, which was almost laughable, considering her deception.

Of course, he didn't know about her deception yet.

"Look," he said, "I know you wanted to move out to Oregon to live near your sisters, and the money from the sale of this place would have made that possible for you. But I can still do that for you. They've made me a generous offer." He reached out and patted her hand. "Don't worry. I'll take care of you."

She pulled her hand away. "That restaurant means everything to you. Can't they hang on for a little while longer?"

"It's been six months," Nate said. "If I don't go back

right now, they're gonna be without a chef, and that could kill the restaurant. And I can't leave. I mean, this whole thing with Nikkie, the fire...I can't put Piper through fifteen-hour days right now. The nanny I had has gone on to another family, so that means someone new with her all the time and it's just not fair to her." He shrugged, although his face didn't look relieved at all. "And it takes the pressure off. Now I've got time to find this plate or whatever it is, and the money from the restaurant will give me some starting capital to fix this place up." He glanced around, looking as though the walls were closing in around him. "I'll make it work. Which means..." He turned to Freya. "I'm sorry. I won't be selling the land."

Freya looked confused. "What plate?"

He ran his hand over his face. "Right before she took off, Nikkie said something about a plate with a purple rim, and it fit the description of the thing Dad wanted me to find but...I don't even care about that right now. I just want to do right by Piper." He paused for a moment, looking at Freya. "Sorry. I know this deal was important to you."

"What deal?" Ruby asked.

Freya took a moment to pull her eyes from Nate, then looked at Ruby. "My father sent me out here to buy the place. That's why I'm here."

Ruby turned to Nate. "You didn't tell me about that."

Freya lifted her coffee cup and mumbled into it, "Probably because he didn't want to tell you he'd turned down two million dollars."

Ruby slapped her hand down on the table. "*Two million dollars?* You turned down two million dollars for this place? Are you out of your mind?"

"That's debatable," Freya said.

"Yeah, it is." Nate turned to Ruby and opened his mouth to speak but she held her hand up.

"Don't tell me you turned it down to keep your word to your father. I just ate."

Nate closed his mouth, and Ruby put her hand to her head.

Freya put her coffee cup down, her eyebrows knit again. "This doesn't make any sense."

"No kidding." Ruby reached out and hit Nate on the arm. "*Two million dollars!*"

Nate shrugged, and Freya shook her head. "No, I mean, why in the world would his dad want him to find a plate?"

Ruby sat back. This was all so much worse than she'd thought it would ever get. She looked at Nate.

"You're not giving up your restaurant."

Nate looked resolved. "I think this is what's best for Piper. I can open a restaurant again later, but she's only going to be a kid now. So, that's it. Stop arguing with me. It's done. I've already called and told them I'm taking the offer."

Ruby's stomach churned. There weren't enough Tums in the world. "You *what*?"

Nate sighed. "I called them this morning. It's done."

"No," Ruby said. "Call them back."

"A plate with a purple rim," Freya said, in her own world at the other end of the table. "That's just weird. Did Nikkie say anything else about it?"

Nate ran a hand over his forehead. Ruby understood; she'd have a migraine, too, if she'd just turned down two million dollars.

"It's, um, gold at the edges," he said, "and it's got some kind of bird in the middle."

"An eagle," Ruby muttered.

Nate turned to her. "Look, I'll keep my word to you, Ruby. I'll get you the money to move out to Oregon. It'll just be a little while, couple weeks. There will be lawyers and paperwork, I'll probably have to take a trip out to Cincinnati—"

"Oh, for fuck's sake." Ruby couldn't take it anymore. To hell with just the right time. She needed to tell him about the plate *now*. She threw her napkin down on the table and stood up. "Follow me."

Nate exchanged a glance with Freya and then looked back at Ruby. "Why?"

Ruby rolled her eyes and stalked out. "Just come on."

She stalked up the stairs, stopping by Piper's door and sticking her head in. Piper sat on her floor, engrossed in whatever she was playing on her game console.

"You stay in here," Ruby said, and Piper said, "Yeah, later," as if she hadn't even heard.

Good kid.

Ruby shut the door, then glanced behind her at Nate and Freya, who were watching her, waiting. Ruby crossed the hall to her bedroom door and opened it, holding it open for them before stepping in and shutting it behind them. She stepped past Nate and Freya and shoved the rug aside, then removed the floorboard. Ruby knelt, reached into the empty space in the floor, and pulled out the tackle box.

"I found it about two weeks after you and Piper got here," she said, keeping her eyes on the box as she spoke. She couldn't look at Nate. "I hid it because I didn't want you to leave just yet. And then the longer I hid it, the more I didn't want you to go, so I never said anything." She held the box out to Nate and steeled herself to meet his eye. "And I apologize."

She stepped back and sat on the edge of the bed. Nothing to do now but wait.

Nate looked at her, then looked at the box in his hands. "My father wanted me to find a big, purple ladies' tackle box?"

Freya nudged him with her elbow and leaned her head over toward his shoulder, speaking in low tones.

"Maybe open it," she said.

"Oh. Right." Nate flicked the catch on the box and flipped the top open. "Okay."

Ruby kept her eyes on the floor. "So, there you go, Nate. Now you can keep your word to your father, and go back to your restaurant." She heard the sound of the box shutting, and swallowed hard, then pushed up off the bed. "I'll just start packing my things."

"Wait," Nate said. "What the hell are you talking about, Ruby?"

Good God. She knew he'd had a rough night and probably hadn't slept much, but Nate was being pretty slow on the uptake this morning.

"The *plate*," she said, and as the words came out of her mouth, it hit her how light the box had seemed when she'd lifted it out of the floor. She snatched the box out of his hands and opened it, then—just to be sure—turned it upside down and shook it.

The plate was gone.

"Son of a bitch," she said.

CHAPTER THIRTEEN

$\mathcal{N}$ATE SAT on the couch, staring at the patterns in the wood floor under his feet. His mind was going off in a million directions.

Ruby had lied to him.

He'd been searching for a plate.

He'd lost his restaurant.

He was stuck in Idaho.

Nikkie'd been telling the truth.

Someone had threatened Piper, and that someone was probably going to be back for that plate, whatever the hell it was.

*Where*ever the hell it was.

And he was right back where he started—searching for an item he neither wanted nor understood. Only this time, instead of his career being at stake, it was Piper who was at risk.

"Son of a bitch," he said, rubbing his eyes. There were footsteps on the stairway, but he didn't remove his hands from his face until Freya had settled on the couch next to him.

"How are you doing?" she asked.

"Great." He put one hand on her knee. "How are you? You feeling okay?"

"I'm fine," she said. "And quit it."

"What?"

She cut her eyes at him. "Worrying about me. I'm *fine*." She pushed up off the couch. "Now, come on."

He stared at her. "What?"

"You haven't slept in two days. You're going to bed."

He shook his head. "Can't. I have to think."

She reached down and took his hand. "Think in bed."

He got up, too tired to fight her. "But Piper—"

"Piper will be fine," Freya said, leading him to the stairs. "Ruby and I will be here."

"Christ," he muttered. "Ruby." He guessed he should have expected surprises from Ruby—the woman had lived with his father for eight years—but still. He'd never expected her to lie like that.

But he couldn't think about that now. He couldn't think about anything. He followed Freya up the stairs dutifully, letting his mind go blank. Freya opened the door to his bedroom and stepped aside for him to go through. He walked in, made it to the bed, and collapsed into it. Hell, it was good to lie down. He felt tugging on the bed behind him and turned to see Freya lifting the covers from the other side of the bed and settling them over him. He rolled onto his back and watched her.

"You're amazing," he said.

She rolled her eyes at him. "Well, that settles it. The exhaustion has officially made you delirious."

"Maybe," he said. "Stay here with me."

She quirked an eyebrow at him. "You've got to be kidding me."

He laughed. "Not for sex. Just..." He stared at her, trying to put into words what he was feeling. He couldn't explain it, he couldn't rationalize it, and he couldn't defend it. All he knew was that if she walked out that door, he felt sure that part of him would die. His need for her at that moment was beyond sex, beyond words. It just *was*, and he hoped to God she'd understand without his having to explain it, because he couldn't.

She watched him, her brain working behind those blue eyes, and then she simply nodded and crawled into the bed next to him. She rested her head on his chest and he put his arm around her, the two of them fitting together so perfectly that he wondered how he'd gone his whole life without realizing she was missing from it.

Of course that didn't make any sense, but he didn't care. She was with him, and at that moment, that was all that mattered.

Freya raised her head from Nate's chest and angled herself to look at his face. He was out cold. His arm had drifted from her waist and fallen dead to the mattress over an hour before. She'd known for a while that she needed to get up, start things moving, but the idea of pulling herself away from him required more energy than she had.

But still. It needed to be done.

Carefully, she slipped away from him and sneaked out of the bed. She put her hand on the doorknob and quietly turned it, but then hesitated, taking another moment to watch him sleep before she finally got up the strength to leave him there.

It wasn't until she was out in the hallway that it occurred to her how weird it was to *want* to watch a man sleep. What the hell was happening to her? Didn't matter much, though. She could worry about that later. At the moment, there was work to be done. She crossed the hall to Ruby's room and knocked lightly on the door.

"Come in," Ruby's rough voice called out.

Freya stepped in. Ruby sat at the far edge of the bed. Her eyes were slightly reddened, but aside from that, there were no signs that the woman was experiencing any real emotion at all. Damn, but that lady was tough.

Freya liked her.

"How is he?" Ruby asked.

"Sleeping," Freya said.

Ruby nodded. Freya leaned against the wall, tapped her nails against it a few times, and then sighed.

"Look," she said. "Most women, a situation like this, they'd sit down and have a heart to heart and talk it all out well into the next day. There'd be chocolate and tea and possibly shopping."

Ruby's eyes closed heavily, as if she was fighting off a headache. Freya took a step forward, bracing both hands on the edge of the bed as she leaned over until her eyes were level with Ruby's.

"You and I both know, we're not most women, so let's just skip that shit and fix this and maybe later we can get drunk on some good single malt. What do you say?"

Ruby opened her eyes and locked them with Freya's. Freya thought she saw her mouth twitch up a bit in something that might have been a smile, but she couldn't be sure.

"What do you need?" Ruby asked.

"A phone with long distance and a decent Internet connection," she said.

Ruby pushed herself up off the bed. "Let's go."

Malcolm sat outside on his lounge chair, enjoying the midday sun. Idaho in June was really quite lovely. He didn't know why more people didn't take advantage of it. The RV part of the campground was nearly empty. Apparently, his nephew had the same weak head for business that his brother had had. Of course, at the moment, that was working in Malcolm's favor, but still.

It was a damn shame.

His cell phone rang. He waited two, three rings, then picked it up. "Yes?"

"Malcolm, you stupid piece of shit, what the fuck do you think you're doing?"

"Nikkie," he said. "Always a pleasure to hear from you."

"What the hell are you thinking?" Nikkie said. "You almost killed the snow bunny."

"The snow bunny?" Malcolm said, then got it. "Oh, you mean Freya Daly. So, she survived, did she?" Malcolm had had a hell of a time deciding if Richard would move faster with his daughter dead or not, and had decided to leave it up to fate. "That'll work."

"Jesus," she breathed, and Malcolm heard the deep inhalation of a cigarette from the other end, followed by a shaky exhalation. "Nate almost died pulling her out of there. Do I seem like the kind of woman who does single mother to you?"

"Are you taking me seriously now, Nikkie?" he asked, keeping his voice cool.

There was a pause. "What the fuck is that supposed to mean?"

"It *means*," he said, his teeth clenched; the woman was tragically thick. "Do you have my plate?"

"I should smash it over your fucking head," she grumbled.

"So you have it?" he asked again.

"Yes," she said. "I have it."

Malcolm smiled. Finally, things were looking up for him. "Good girl. Now nothing untoward needs to happen to your daughter. Well done, Nikkie. I'll meet you at the diner in an hour."

"I can't," she said. "I'm already back in L.A."

Malcolm closed his eyes and counted to five before saying, "What?" through clenched teeth.

"What did you expect me to do?" she said. "You were burning the place down like some kind of maniac. I got on the next plane. The plate and me, we're in L.A. If you want your stupid plate, you're going to have to come out here and get it, because I sure as fuck am not going back."

"Has anyone ever talked to you about your language?" Malcolm asked. "It seems quite the oversight that no one taught you how a lady should speak. That said, you've got twenty-four hours to get back here and give me my plate, or I'm gonna burn this whole fucking place down with your daughter in it, you fucking cunt."

There was silence on the line, and then Nikkie said, "Tomorrow. Eleven A.M. I'll text you the location where I'll be. And then, this is over."

"I'll tell you when it's—" Malcolm started, but there was a click in his ear.

She had hung up.

People really needed to stop doing that to him.

Freya's eyes grazed over the screen in front of her, making sure all her information was right. She thought it was. Now there was just one more thing to check.

"Hey," she called to Ruby, who was standing by the front window of the office, staring out. Freya didn't blame her, the woman obviously had a lot to think about, but right now Freya needed her.

Ruby turned and walked over, and Freya angled the computer screen to face her.

"This the plate?" Freya asked.

Ruby leaned in a bit and squinted, then nodded. "Yep. That's it. What is it?"

Freya released a breath. "It belonged to Abraham Lincoln."

Ruby's eyebrows shot up. "No shit."

"No shit." Freya tip-tapped into the computer. "Limoges china, created for the White House in 1861 from Haviland in France." She shook her head. "Except here's what I don't get. It's worth, on the outside, fifteen grand. And that's if you go through traditional auction-house channels with full provenance. On the black market, you're talking maybe five grand." She swiveled in the chair to face Ruby. "Who's gonna threaten to hurt a little girl for five grand?"

Ruby looked down at Freya. "Well. There's more."

"More?" Freya tapped her nails on the desk as she looked up at the older woman. "You're kinda like a jack-in-the-box. I never know what's gonna pop up. What else?"

"The plate was wrapped in Saran Wrap, and it had a note taped to it that said to take it to the Boise police."

"Boise?" Freya went stiff. "That's . . . interesting." She went quiet for a minute, thinking. "Mick's handwriting?"

Ruby nodded.

"When did he write it?"

Ruby shrugged. "Beats the hell out of me. It was torn from a yellow legal pad, but it was pretty dusty and faded. Could be ten years, could be thirty."

Huh. "Is there any reason you didn't mention this before?"

Ruby met Freya's eyes solidly. "Because Nate's been through enough over this whole thing. We can deal with all that when we find it."

Freya swiveled back to the computer. "*If* we find it. For all we know, Nikkie might have gotten it and delivered it to whoever's threatening Piper."

"Maybe, but I don't think so," Ruby said. "Things were crazy, but I don't think Nikkie's smart enough to sneak it out under my nose like that. She didn't have time to get the plate after Nate ran out to pull you from that cabin, and if she had it before that, then she would have taken off without saying a word."

"Know Nikkie well, do you?" Freya asked.

"Know the type," Ruby said.

There were a few moments of silence while Freya concentrated on her search, and then Ruby asked, "Why are you still here?"

Freya stopped typing and looked up at Ruby. "What?"

"Well, you came out here to buy the place, right?"

Freya nodded. "Right."

"And Nate's not selling. He's already turned you down. Plus, someone set a cabin on fire with you in it. If I were you, I'd be on a plane back home right now."

Freya took a deep breath. It was the same question she'd been avoiding asking herself. "Someone tried to kill me. I want to know who, and why."

Ruby nodded, her sharp eyes evaluating Freya. "You're not a great liar."

"Excuse me?" Freya said. "I'm in real estate development. I am a fabulous liar."

"No," Ruby said. "You have a tell. Your right eyebrow raises a bit at the edge when you lie."

"That's ridic—" Still, Freya's hand went up to her eyebrow. Did she really have a tell?

"What's going on between you and Nate?" Ruby asked.

Freya lowered her hand and met the older woman's eyes. "That's none of your business."

"My business is taking care of my family, and Nate and Piper are as close to family as I've ever had. I may be out of line, but it's damn sure my business if I see someone in my family in danger."

"Are you kidding me?" Freya said. "Who's in danger here? I was the one who was almost fried extra crispy because of you people and your stupid plate."

"Nate's a grown man and can take care of himself," Ruby said, "but Piper's just a little girl who wants her mother, and her mother is useless. She's bonding with you, and when you leave, it's gonna be hard on her."

Freya went quiet. She couldn't argue with that. The idea of leaving Piper didn't sit too well with her, either. As for leaving Nate...

Well. That was just complicated. And she had other things on her mind at the moment.

"Can I make a private phone call?" she asked.

Ruby eyed her for a moment, then nodded. "I'll head back over to the house. Take care of whatever you need to take care of."

Like a plane ticket, Freya thought, watching Ruby's retreating back. Once she was gone from the office, Freya picked up the phone and dialed.

"Goodhouse Arms, Flynn Daly speaking."

"Hell, you almost sound like a real professional," Freya said. Her sister had been running the place for almost a year, and Freya still couldn't get used to Flynn's professional voice.

"Well, it's about time you called me back. I've called you five times since last night."

"Yeah, my cell phone's..." *melted and fused to my hair dryer.* "Broken."

"You're gonna be broken. You hired Tucker and didn't tell me? Why do you need a private detective? What's going on?"

"You ever gonna call Jake by his first name?"

"That's a weak deflection." As usual, her sister wasn't one to be easily distracted. "So what's up?"

"Flynn, I need a few favors, and I need you to not freak out on me. I also need to talk to Jake."

"He's right here; I'll put him on speakerphone."

There was a click on the line followed by the fuzzy hum of speakerphone.

"Hey there, Freya," Jake said.

"Hey, Jake. Okay, Flynn, the cabin I was staying in burned down—"

"Wait, *what?*"

"—and I need you to send me some things—"

"What the hell is going on out there? Are you okay?"

"I'm fine," Freya said. "But I lost all my stuff—my laptop, my purse, my cell phone, my clothes. I need you to overnight me some emergency cash and clothes, and then call Suzanne at my office and tell her to take care of everything else. But tell her she's under strict orders not to say a word to Dad."

"Wait," Flynn said. "You're not telling Dad? You tell Dad everything."

"Not this. And don't you tell him, either. He's got me working on something out here that's getting a little complicated, and I don't want to deal with him until I have to deal with him."

"The complications don't have anything to do with Nikkie Cooper?" Jake asked. "Because I ran a check on her and it ain't pretty."

Freya tensed up, thinking of Piper. "What'd you find?"

"Mostly fraud, identity theft, that sort of thing. She's wanted on a federal warrant."

"Well, that makes sense," Freya said. "Actually, Jake, I need you to look into something else for me. I need to know the connection between Boise, Idaho, and a Haviland Limoges china plate commissioned for the Lincoln administration." She waited a moment, tense that Flynn might make the same connection she had, but when Flynn said nothing, she relaxed and went on. "I think it might have been stolen, and probably a while back." If she was to guess, she'd say somewhere around thirty-five years ago, but she kept that to herself.

"Um...okay." Through the line, she could hear him scratching on a pad. "Anything else?"

"That should be enough. Let me give you my contact

information." She read off the address, and phone and fax numbers. "Call me at the house if you find out anything. And send me a bill, Jake."

"Sure, you bet," Jake said flatly.

"Freya," Flynn's voice cut in, "what the hell is going on? Do you want me to fly out there?"

"No," Freya said. "I'm fine. I'll give you a call when I get home and tell you all about it then." *Well, most of it.*

There was a hesitation, and then Flynn said, "Okay."

Freya relaxed. "Thanks. Love you."

"Love you, too," Flynn said, and then disconnected the call. Freya stared at the computer, then typed in the URL for Daly Developers, Inc. Three clicks, and she was on her father's bio. She scrolled down until she got to the education section.

Richard Daly got his MBA at Harvard Business School after graduating with a bachelor's degree in business administration from Idaho State University.

Of course, it could just be a coincidence that her father was willing to pay an outrageous price for a craphole in the middle of nowhere that just happened to feature possible evidence of a possible crime that possibly took place in the same town where he went to college.

And that might be easier to swallow if Freya believed in coincidence.

CHAPTER FOURTEEN

*N*ATE WANDERED downstairs to find Ruby sitting at the kitchen table, staring down into a mug of coffee. The way she was staring, he half suspected that it had gone cold already.

"Hey," he said quietly.

She looked up, seeming almost surprised to see him there. "Hey."

There was a strained moment of silence, reminding Nate of those first few awkward days when he'd arrived to find his father dying and living with this woman he'd never heard of, let alone met. It hadn't taken long for him and Ruby to get used to each other and become friends, but now they were back at square one again. Or square minus one.

He stood in the entryway to the kitchen and tucked his hands in his pockets.

"Where's Freya?" he asked.

"She had some things to take care of in the office." Ruby raised her eyes to his, and while her expression was as tough as always, he could tell she was feeling bad, and he felt a slight tinge of guilt for still being so angry with her. He knew she never meant any harm. He knew she'd only wanted to keep them with her, for just a little while longer.

Still, knowing that didn't take the edge off his anger. Ruby had put Piper in danger and almost gotten Freya killed, and whether she meant any harm or not, she'd caused it, and he wasn't ready to forget that yet.

"I'm gonna go check on her," he said. "Piper's up in her room. Can you keep a sharp eye on her? I don't want her to be alone until we've got this whole thing figured out."

Ruby pushed up from the table. "What are we gonna do about school?"

Nate bristled at the *we*. "I haven't decided yet. Right now, I'm just worrying about today, so if you could keep an eye on her—"

"Of course." Ruby poured her coffee into the sink and set the mug in it, then turned to face Nate. "I think you should ask Freya to leave."

The simmering anger in Nate's gut kicked up a notch. "That's not your call."

"I'm not making a call," she said. "I'm making a suggestion. Up till now, you've been okay with me making a suggestion."

"Up till now, I didn't know that you'd lied to me. Up till now, I thought Piper was safe and that I could trust you. Up till now, I still had a life to go back to if I wanted."

Ruby nodded. "I see."

"All these months, Ruby. I thought I could trust you, and you lied to me. What the hell is that about?"

She raised her eyes to his. "You think that makes me just like your father?"

"Don't make this about him. This is about you."

"Is it?"

"Yes."

"Okay."

"Okay." He turned again and almost made it to the door this time before spinning around and heading back into the kitchen. "What? What? What do you see?"

She allowed a small smile as she looked up at him. "Your father was a first-rate son of a bitch, and I know it. I lived with him eight years, and he made every one a nightmare in one way or another."

Nate felt his stomach drop. It was the one thing he'd wanted to know since day one, and the one question he hadn't gotten up the nerve to ask. But now, politeness and appropriateness were out the window anyway, so he looked at Ruby and finally let himself ask. "Did he hit you?"

Ruby was quiet for a long time, which answered the question. Nate pulled a chair out from the kitchen table and sat down.

"Why'd you stay with him?"

"Probably the same reason your mother stayed."

Nate sat back and met Ruby's eyes. "I never asked her."

Ruby nodded and settled down into the chair across from Nate. "You get comfortable with what you're used to."

"He killed her," Nate said. "You knew that?"

Ruby's brows knit. "I thought she had a brain aneurysm."

"Getting knocked in the head can aggravate that," Nate said.

"Well," Ruby said. "I guess maybe it can."

There was a long silence, and Nate stared down at the kitchen floor.

"I know you want to believe that maybe he changed

in the time you two weren't talking," Ruby said after a while, "and I'm sorry to tell you — if he did, it wasn't for the better."

Nate ran his hands over his eyes, suddenly feeling tired again despite the long nap he just took.

"I'm sorry your father was who he was, Nate. But it doesn't matter, because you're a good man. The plate doesn't matter, this place doesn't matter, and that restaurant doesn't matter."

Nate felt a surge of anger and looked up to find Ruby looking back, defiant.

"Yes, I said it. It doesn't matter. You think you can't build another place where you can cook? You can do that anywhere, even here. If you really wanted that restaurant bad enough, you could have gone back, to hell with your father's last wishes. You didn't stay here because of that damn plate. You stayed because you wanted to discover that there was something honorable in your father after all, that his last breath was spent on something that meant something." She raised an eyebrow. "And what does it really matter anyway?"

Nate felt taken aback by her insight. "It matters. Of course it matters."

"Why?" she said. "He's dead."

Nate glanced into the living room. "Why do I feel like I should be lying on a couch for this?"

Ruby sat back in her chair. "Stop making your entire life about not being him. You're not him. So now grow the hell up and be you."

Nate looked up at her. "Has anyone ever told you you suck at apologizing?"

Ruby went still, her eyes on the tabletop. "Apologies

are just so much talk. You show you're sorry by changing what you do."

"Right." Nate sat there for a while, feeling drained.

"So," Ruby said finally, "are you ready to listen to what I have to say about Freya now?"

Nate had to laugh at that. "Does it matter if I'm ready?"

She shrugged. "It was a courtesy." She folded her hands in front of her. "It's not that I don't like Freya, because I do. But Piper's got some serious shit in her head because of her mother right now, and Freya complicates that. I'm the last person to say you should live like a monk for Piper's sake, but right now..." She shook her head. "I think Freya complicates a lot of things."

Nate nodded, but didn't say anything. Ruby was right, and he knew it, but Freya's leaving wasn't something he could talk about. Not now. Not yet.

Ruby sighed and pushed herself up from the table.

"I'm going to go up and check on Piper," she said. "Damn kid keeps beating me at Super Monkeyball, but I think today's gonna be my lucky day."

She shot him a small smile, then went upstairs. Nate stared at his hands on the table for a while, trying to figure out what to do next. When he left for the office, he still wasn't sure.

Freya drummed her fingers on the desk while she waited for her father to answer his office phone.

"Richard Daly."

"Hey, Dad," she said.

"Freya." His voice sounded tense. "How is that deal coming along?"

"It's not," she said. "He's not going to sell."

There was a long pause, then, "Offer him more."

She picked up a pencil from the desktop. "Why? Why do you want this property so badly, Dad?"

"I told you," he said, and he went on about the expansion of the business, blah blah blah. She reached across the desk and put the pencil into the electronic sharpener while he was still talking. It was louder than she'd expected, and when she pulled the pencil out she heard her father on the other end of the line saying, "What the hell was that?"

"Pencil sharpener." She reached across and sharpened it some more, then blew the sawdust off the tip of the pencil.

Perfect.

"Freya, what are you doing?"

"I'm thinking." She leaned back in the chair, looked up at the textured ceiling panel. "I'm wondering why all of a sudden, you want this property so bad. And expansion of the business just isn't a good enough answer for me, Dad, mostly because it smells like a tremendous heap of bullshit, you know what I mean?"

Richard sighed. "Freya, I really don't have time for games right now."

"I thought you were making me jump through hoops. To get the promotion. But now, I'm thinking I was just sent out here to do your dirty work." She pointed the pencil upward, practicing her trajectory with the angle of her hand. "But you know, it doesn't matter. Nate's not going to sell. All the men in the world you had to send me to do a deal with, and you pick the one guy who can't be bought."

"I have no patience for theatrics, Freya. You know that. Perhaps you should call your sister and the two of you can get it all out of your systems together."

"Oh, hell," Freya said. "Is that how we've been talking to Flynn all these years? We're really a couple of assholes, aren't we, Dad?"

"Have you been drinking?"

"No, Dad. I said I've been *thinking*. Thhhhh. *Thinking*. And you know what I think?"

"I'm very busy—"

"I think that there's nothing wrong with my eyes," she said, allowing her eyes to tear as she said the words, allowing her voice to crack. Goddamn, it felt good to just *allow* it. "I think that I've been shutting my emotions down for so long that they're just leaking out around the edges and you know what? I don't think that gives you the fucking right to tell me there's something wrong with me. That's what I think."

She heard her father shuffling papers in the background. "I have a meeting in three minutes."

She exhaled and gathered herself. Time for business. "Okay, then let's make this quick," she said. "I'm giving you one chance to tell me why you really want this property."

There was a short silence, and then her father said, "Is this an ultimatim?"

"No," she said. "Well, yes. But no. I'm going to resign anyway, I just thought..." *That we were the same. That you trusted me. That I knew you.* "All these years I thought we were close, and we were just...I don't know." She swiped at her eyes. "Nearby."

"If you're going to resign, Freya," her father said, his voice taut, "then I suggest you get on with it."

"I'm right, though, aren't I? There's something to tell, isn't there? A reason why you're willing to pay so much for this land?"

"Freya, honestly—"

"It has something to do with a plate, right? From the Lincoln administration?"

Total silence, which was as good as a confirmation, because talking about a plate from the Lincoln administration was just nuts, and Richard Daly never hesitated to express himself when he thought one of his daughters was nuts.

But now, he hesitated.

"Do you have it?" he asked.

Freya closed her eyes. "Are you going to tell me why it's worth two million dollars to you?"

"That's none of your business, Freya. I asked you a question. Do you have it?"

"None of my business? How can you—?" And she stopped. He didn't know that this plate business had almost gotten her killed. He didn't know that it had lost Nate his restaurant. He didn't know that it had put Piper in danger.

And he probably wouldn't care if he did.

"I faxed my resignation letter to Suzanne a few minutes ago," she said. "She's going to come into your office in a minute or two and ask you what to do about it. I suggest you just accept it."

And she hung up before her father could say another word.

Wow, she thought as she stared up at the ceiling. *I'm unemployed.*

She angled the pencil toward the ceiling and shot it upward. It bounced off the ceiling and shot back down at her, the sharp tip nearly stabbing her in the shoulder.

"How do all the slackers do that?" she muttered.

"It's an acquired skill."

She looked up and there was Nate, standing outside the screen door, the sun glinting off his hair. He was beautiful, and seeing him right at the moment her life was ripping apart at the seams was exactly what she needed. He opened the screen, stepped inside, and shut both doors behind him, then walked over and sat on the edge of the desk facing her.

"How are you doing?" he asked.

"Super," she said. "You?"

"Me? Great." He sat there in silence, one leg kicking out a bit from the desk. Freya smiled; like father, like daughter.

"What's on your mind?" she asked.

"Ruby thinks you should leave."

"Yeah. She expressed that to me."

"And I agree."

Their eyes met, and Freya saw that he meant it, and a hot spike of pain cut through her, and the muscles in her legs went weak. She wanted to cry and she wanted to run and it didn't make sense that she should feel this way just at the thought of leaving him. She'd worked her whole life to avoid this very situation, and here it had sneaked up on her when she wasn't paying attention.

She needed him.

"Okay," she said, once she caught her breath. "You know, I think maybe she's right. Maybe it's a good idea."

She started to walk past him toward the door, but he

grabbed her wrist. He didn't grab hard, but pain shot up her entire arm, weakening her even more.

"I don't want you to go," he said quietly, and she froze where she was, her heart beating, panic rushing through her, her mind screaming, *Get out, get out, get out.*

But instead, she looked at him, wanting to throw herself into his arms and let him carry her through all this. Except she didn't *want* him to carry her, she *needed* him to carry her, and that was a whole 'nother kettle of fish.

What the hell have I gotten myself into?

"Look," he said finally, "Piper's already attached to you, and you've got your job and your life in Boston. I mean, it's not like you're staying forever. It wouldn't be fair for me to expect something like that of you. We've only known each other a few days."

Freya lowered her eyes. This made sense, perfect sense. His fingers loosened on her wrist and traveled down her hand until they were entwined with her own.

"And I don't know what's going on with everything here," he said, staring down at their hands. "I don't want you getting hurt again. Not when you've got a nice, safe life somewhere else."

"Right," she said, every beat of her heart blasting pain through her chest. *This is good, this is right. You don't need him. You can walk away, on your own, just like always.*

"But..." He raised his eyes to hers. "I don't want you to go. I don't want you to go so bad that I think I'd stand in the path of your car if you tried."

They stared at each other for a long moment, and what strength Freya had left seeped out of her.

"I don't want to go," she said.

He smiled lightly, his eyes trailing down her cheeks, stopping on her lips. She took in her breath, waiting for him to pull her to him, to kiss her, to touch her, but all he did was run his fingers over hers.

"I'm a little lost here," he said, his voice low and rough. "It's not right, me asking you to stay."

"Then don't ask," she said softly, taking his hand and putting it on her waist. He pulled her closer to him until he'd drawn her into his arms. She rested her cheek on his shoulder as he held her, feeling the heat building between them.

I need him, she thought. She pulled back a bit and moved her face next to his, closing her eyes as her lips found his. He lifted her up and she wrapped her legs around him on the desk. Things clattered to the floor around them and she didn't care. He picked her up and spun around until she was beneath him on the desk and she pressed herself against him, the fabric of the scrubs she was wearing allowing her to feel how strongly he wanted her. She reached out and unbuttoned his jeans, then put both hands on his face and said, "Tell me you have a condom, or I'm going to have to kill you."

He smiled and reached into his back pocket, flicking the package onto the desktop next to her.

"That's my Boy Scout," she said, pulling him to her again. He hooked his thumbs under the waist of her scrubs and slid them off, running his hands up her thighs, finally cupping her bottom and pressing her against him. She kissed him, her left hand grappling on the desk until she found the condom and pressed it to his chest. A few moments later, he was inside her, moving slowly, as they savored the feeling of being together. Nothing had to make sense now, nothing had to be done, all she had to do was live in this moment. She wrapped her legs around his hips and arched back until the motion hit all the right spots inside, and her mind was wiped blissfully clean of everything but Nate.

And he was all she needed.

CHAPTER FIFTEEN

$\mathcal{R}$ UBY STOOD at the kitchen counter, staring at the toaster, listening to the coffee maker gurgle as Piper chatted away.

"...and the Hello Kitty toaster burns little Hello Kitty faces actually into the toast, it's so cool. We totally need to get one, it's so much better than our boring old toaster. They done yet?"

Ruby yawned. "Not yet."

"So, I'm not going to school again today?" Piper said. "Why not?"

"You have pneumonia." The Pop Tarts popped up, and she whipped a paper towel off the roller. "If anyone from the school calls, cough."

Ruby brought the Pop Tarts over to Piper and set them on the table. Piper picked at the edge of one tart and looked up at Ruby. "Is anyone going to ever tell me what's going on?"

Ruby riffled her hair. "Kid, the joy of childhood is not needing to know what's going on. Trust me."

Piper grumbled and took a bite of her tart. Ruby walked over to the coffee maker and poured herself a cup of coffee. When she turned around, she saw Freya shuffle into the kitchen through the entryway.

"Morning, Piper," Freya said.

Piper turned in her seat. "Hey, Freya. You missed dinner last night."

Freya shot a look at Ruby, then looked away. "Yeah. Sorry. I was tired. Just passed out."

In Nate's bed. And Ruby had noticed he was not on the couch that morning. Which was fine. She'd given her counsel, and Nate had made his decision. She just hoped it was the right one. She pulled another mug out of the cabinet and looked at Freya. "Cream and sugar?"

"Black," Freya said, and walked over to get her mug. "Thank you."

"You're welcome," Ruby said. She followed Freya back to the table, where they sat down opposite each other and sipped their coffee.

And with that, Ruby knew that everything between them was good. And she had to admit, whether Freya was gonna complicate things for Nate and Piper or not, there was one thing about her that Ruby liked. She didn't need to talk things to death, and she didn't hold a grudge.

With Ruby, those two traits counted for a lot.

Malcolm flipped open his cell phone, checking the text Nikkie had sent him, to be sure he was in the right place. Bear Paw Motel, 1381 S. Main Street, Room 223.

It was the right place. He smiled to himself as he raised his hand to knock. Over thirty years, he'd been waiting to chance across the instrument of Richard Daly's destruction, and now it was just on the other side of this door.

"Who is it?" Nikkie's voice came from inside.

Malcolm glanced to his left, then his right, then leaned into the door.

"You know who it is," he said. "Now open up."

He listened as she unleashed the chain and turned the deadbolt, then pulled the door open.

"You look as lovely as ever," Malcolm said, although if he was being truthful, the trenchcoat she was wearing made her look a little bulky. "May I come in?"

She stepped back, allowing him passage. He walked in, surveying the meager surroundings.

"Well," he said. "Times are tough now, love, but you're going to be back on your feet in no time." He turned to face her. "Where's my plate?"

"Where's my money?"

Malcolm smoothed his hand down over his tie. "I told you. You'll get it. But I need the plate to get it, so if you'd be so kind—"

"Oh, of course," she said, and reached inside the coat, then proceeded to withdraw not a plate, but a gun.

"For fuck's sake," he muttered. This was what happened when you tried to deal honorably with treacherous bitches.

"I don't know what made you think I'd let you threaten my kid," Nikkie said, her gun hand shaking slightly, "but you seriously underestimated my maternal instincts, you crazy fuck."

"Nikkie, you're about to kill me. Let's not play games. You have no maternal instincts."

"Oh, no?" She raised the gun. "I've got a good instinct to pull this trigger."

"And then what?" Malcolm tsked at her. "Shots are fired, and the people in the room next door call the police, and they run your fingerprints, and then you're in a hell of a pickle, aren't you?"

"I don't care," Nikkie said, but her trembling hand showed that she cared very much, if not for the life she was threatening to take, then for the freedom she would surely lose as a result. "I only have one way to make sure that you don't hurt Piper, and that's to kill you right this minute."

There was a long silence. Malcolm raised his eyebrows at her. "If you don't shoot soon, I'm going to request a newspaper and a cup of coffee for the wait."

"Just . . . shut up! Give me a minute." She put her other hand underneath her gun hand, but it only shook more.

"Nikkie, I think we both know you're not a murderer," Malcolm said. "You're hardly a lady or even much of a human being, but there are certain lines your type won't cross, just from pure cowardice, and one of those lines is taking another life. Now just give me my plate and let me be off. I promise, Piper will come to no harm."

Nikkie rolled her eyes. "I don't have your stupid plate, you dumbass. I just told you that to get you here so I could shoot you."

"Hell," Malcolm said. "I was afraid of that." Then he stepped forward and backhanded her hard across the face. She crumpled to the floor with barely a sound, and the gun slid out of her hand and across the room, hitting the wall with an innocuous plunk.

"Treacherous bitch," he said, stepping over her body to get to the bedside phone. He picked it up, dialed 911, and when they answered said in a wimpy, breathless American accent, "Hi. I'm in room 221 at the Bear Paw on Route 8. I hear fighting in the room next to mine. Somebody said something about identity fraud and some woman said she was going to kill him. I think maybe you guys should come check it out." Then he hung up, picked up the gun, and clicked on the safety catch before tucking it in the waistband of his pants and slipping out the door. Although it would have given him endless pleasure to have shot the bitch, handing her over to the police had a certain poetry to it. And if she mentioned his name, that was fine. The police weren't going to act quickly to find him on the word of a forger. And if it got back to Nate that his uncle Malcolm was back in town, the timing on that would work just fine. Nate had always been a good, reasonable boy. He wouldn't refuse him one simple memento of his useless brother. It was just a plate, after all, to everyone but Malcolm and Richard Daly.

Nate would take him seriously.

He was almost sure of it.

Nate watched as the sheriff's deputy brought Nikkie into the interrogation room. She was wearing an inmate orange jumpsuit, her hair was flat on one side and shooting out on the other, and she sported a light bruise on her right cheek. He lowered his eyes, keeping his focus on the wood veneer table until Nikkie was seated across from him.

"You have ten minutes," the deputy said, and left the room.

Nate raised his eyes to look at her. Her expression was hard. Too hard to read. Too hard to crack. The lines on her face, which had been light back at the campground, now seemed etched and immutable. It was like everything that Nikkie had tried to be had been stripped from her, and what was left was the shriveled core of who she could have been.

And she looked so much like Piper that it almost killed him just looking at her.

"It was Malcolm," she said, her voice quiet and spent, but still carrying her signature undercurrent of anger. "He's the one who wants the plate. I don't know why, but he offered me a lot of money to get it for him. He also did this"—she motioned to her bruised right cheek with her cuffed hands—"and called the police to come get me while I was knocked out." She closed her eyes heavily, as though warding off a headache long in coming. "Should have shot the fucker."

Nate sat back, trying to take in this information. "Malcolm? Malcolm Brody? My uncle? The drunk?"

She opened her eyes. "Try to keep up, Nate. We've only got ten minutes."

"I didn't think he and my dad were even talking," Nate said. "Ruby said she never even knew Dad had a brother. How would he even know about the plate?"

Nikkie leaned forward. "Who gives a shit how? He's here and he wants the plate. So...just...wherever you've got it, or whatever, just give it to him, okay? Just give it to him and he'll go away." She sat back. "Although it would have saved me a lot of trouble if you'd just given it to me when I'd asked."

"I don't have it," Nate said. "It's gone."

"Gone?" Nikkie stared at him. "It's a plate, not a dog. Where the fuck did it go?"

"I'll take care of it," Nate said. "Where's Malcolm staying?"

Nikkie shrugged. "Beats the hell out of me. All I have

is a phone number." She rattled it off, and Nate punched the numbers into the contacts list in his cell phone. "Call it and tell that fake Irish fucker that in five to ten years, I'm gonna kill him for real."

"Little advice," Nate said, tucking his phone into his back pocket. "No murder threats while you're in the county jail, okay?"

She rolled her eyes. "Whatever. Look, Malcolm is not the same guy who got drunk at our wedding and drove the catering van into the gift table, okay? The years have not been good to him and he's gotten both mean and crazy. He almost burned down your girlfriend, for crying out loud."

Nate's body tensed. "What?"

"This is what I'm telling you," she said. "It's all Malcolm. He's batshit crazy and he's gonna try to get you through Piper. That's what he did to me, and you see how that ended up." She raised her cuffed hands and lowered them. "And now he's got my gun."

Nate leaned forward. "Your *gun*? Christ, Nikkie. Identity theft, guns, what the hell happened to you?"

She eyed him. "I got pregnant at nineteen and married the wrong guy. Pretty much been all downhill from there."

"Right." Nate sat back. "I haven't seen you in ten years, Nik. Eventually, the statute of limitations is gonna be up on your problems being my fault."

Nikkie met his eyes and held them, and for a moment, he thought he saw something genuine in them, but then she looked away. "Piper...she's a good kid." She shifted uncomfortably in her seat. "You did a good job. Better than I ever would have done. So...thanks."

"You're welcome," he said. He'd never loved Nikkie, but he felt protective of her, wanted things to turn out well for her, and not just for Piper's sake. She had given him the thing he loved most in the world, and that had earned her a certain status with him. And knowing she'd gotten herself thrown in jail to protect Piper only elevated her. He was trying to figure out how to say that to her when she interrupted his thoughts.

"Look," she said, "just keep an eye out. I already told the police about Malcolm but in their eyes all he did was turn in a chick wanted on a federal warrant so my word that he's a crazy fucker isn't shooting him to the top spot on their to-arrest list." She raised her eyes to his, and nibbled her lip. "Keep her safe."

"I will." There was a long silence, and then he said, "Is there anything else you need? A lawyer, or something?"

"No," she said, stiffening. "I've got that all taken care of. I just wanted to warn you about Malcolm. They say they're gonna transport me to a federal facility tomorrow, so ... I'll see you when I see you."

Nikkie code for *never*.

"Right." Nate pushed up from the table. "I'll talk to the police about Malcolm."

"Do that," Nikkie said. She held his eyes for a moment, then pushed back from her seat and yelled, "Done here!"

And they were.

Freya pulled the towel off her head and tossed it into the hamper in Nate's room. Flynn had overnighted her a suitcase full of clothes containing T-shirts, jeans, light sweaters, and the simple cotton camisole and flannel lounge pants Freya was wearing at the moment. The rental company had sent her a new set of keys, her bank was rushing her a replacement debit card, and life should be okay.

Well, it would be okay if her hand would stop shaking. She guessed it made sense; in the course of a few days, she'd started a whirlwind affair with a man she hardly knew, had nearly gotten herself killed in a fire, and had fought with her father for the first time in her life and quit her job. Who wouldn't be shook up after a few days like that?

"Not to mention I'm wearing flannel," she muttered, staring at herself in the mirror, not recognizing the woman who stared back at her. She took a deep breath in, exhaled slowly, and lifted her hand.

It was still shaking.

The door opened behind her, and she turned quickly to see Nate stepping in, looking wiped out. Then his eyes locked on her and his face brightened, and the shaking moved from her hand to the muscles in her lower arm.

"Well, hello," he said. "My name is Nate. Have we met?"

"I don't think so," Freya said, looking down at the lounge pants. "My sister sent it. I think she's trying to tell me something." She looked back up at him and shrugged. "At least it's not hospital scrubs."

"I liked the hospital scrubs," he said, closing the space between them and taking her in his arms. "I liked the silk. And I like this. I like you."

He leaned down and kissed her and she pulled him into a hug, feeling awkward. She was suddenly unsure about her elbows — she'd never noticed them before when she put her arms around him, had never thought about anything but him, but now they felt weird, sticking out at weird angles, and she pulled her arms in and tucked them between them, her palms flat on his chest. That was weird, too.

He pulled back and looked at her. "Is everything okay?"

"What? Me? Sure," she said, stepping back. She rested her hands on her hips and then at her sides. Stupid elbows. *Focus on him.* "How'd it go with Nikkie?"

"As well as could be expected, I guess." He sat down on the edge of the bed, and Freya sat next to him. "They're moving her to a federal prison tomorrow afternoon."

"Wow," Freya said. "Are you going to help her?"

"She didn't ask. Said she had it covered. She wanted to warn me."

"Warn you?" Freya crossed her legs, but that felt weird in flannel, so she uncrossed them, which also felt weird. Luckily, Nate was rubbing his eyes and didn't notice.

"Apparently, the evil mastermind here is my uncle Malcolm, who, according to Nikkie, has sobered up and become a sociopath. She thinks he started the fire the other night, and the police are looking into it." He pulled his hand down from his face and smiled at her. "I'm a hell of a catch, huh? I've got a forger ex-wife, a father who beat women, and an insane arsonist uncle who tried to kill you."

"None of that is your fault," Freya said, reaching for his hand. Finally, a motion that felt natural.

He nodded, but didn't seem to believe her. "I can't believe we're going through all this for a fucking plate."

Freya released his hand. "And there's my cue." She reached for the file folder she'd set on the end table and handed it to him. "It's not just any fucking plate. You might want to do a shot of something before you read this."

"What is this?" he asked, taking it from her.

"I have a private detective in the family," she said. "So I told him what I knew and he came back with...this."

Nate flipped open the folder to the first pages that she had printed off the Internet.

"You're kidding. Abraham Lincoln?" He raised his head. "*This* is the plate?"

Freya nodded. "According to Ruby, that's it."

He shook his head. "I don't understand. All this for...what? A collector's item?"

She flipped to the next page in the stack, bringing them to the fax she'd received from Jake a few hours before. Nate gave her a confused look, then bent his head and read through the report. When he was finished, he looked up at her, his face grave.

"What does this mean?" he said. "The plate was stolen from a museum?"

"Thirty-five years ago," she said. "Along with fifty grand worth of goods, most of it sold on the black market and recovered over time, but they never caught the guys who did it."

Nate stared down at the documents in his hands, his expression tightening. "And that security guard..." He tossed the paperwork on the nightstand. "Just when I thought my pedigree couldn't get any better, my father's a killer."

"Not necessarily," Freya said, feeling oddly detached as she said the words. "I'm pretty sure my father was involved, too."

Nate looked at her. "I don't understand."

"I thought he sent me out here to jump through another hoop, but as it turned out, he'd already recommended someone else to take over for him."

Nate's expression went hard. "Your father gave away your promotion?"

"Well," she said, shrugging it off, "he had some solid points. I've been unreliable. You know..." She closed her eyes against the embarrassment. "...with the crying. My performance has been spotty, and that's my responsibility. He was right to name Charlie instead."

"But...still. He's your father."

"Yes, but that doesn't mean he owes me a promotion I haven't earned. And it doesn't matter anyway, because I quit in a big, emotional huff."

"Good for you. You should have quit, he..." He trailed off, and she could feel his eyes on her, but couldn't look at him. Then he reached for her and she stood up before he could touch her.

"Freya? Are you okay?"

"I'm fine. Really." She forced a smile, hoped it was convincing. "The point is, my father was in Boise thirty-five years ago, and it's a hell of a coincidence that he's offering two million dollars for this place right when murder evidence starts to come to light. Whatever your father did, I don't think he did it alone."

Nate sat up straight, watching her, then shook his head. "I don't know. That's a hell of a jump. Did you ask him about it?"

"Yes. He didn't deny it, didn't ask me what the hell I was talking about, but he wouldn't tell me what happened, either."

"Christ." He got up and walked over to her, pulling her into his arms. Freya wanted to lean her head against his chest, to lean into him, but she couldn't. He pulled back a bit and looked down at her. "What's going on?"

She shrugged, and he loosened his hold on her.

"Nothing," she said. "I mean, everything. It's just . . . I'm sorry. I think I'm freaking out."

"Well, yeah. You find this out about your father, quit your job, I mean—"

"It's not just that." She looked up at him, tried to brace herself to say what she had to say, then decided to just get it out. "I think I need to leave."

He let her go entirely. "Um. Okay." He paused for a second, then sat back down on the bed and looked up at her. "But . . . I thought we talked about this. I thought you didn't want to leave yet."

"I didn't. I don't." She sighed. "But I think I have to."

"Oh." He nodded. "Okay."

She sat down next to him. "This? Here? Between us? It's only going to work for so long. I think we both know that."

He didn't look at her, didn't seem to be hearing her, just stared down at the floor. God, this was hard. Her eyes started to tear and she threw herself back on the bed in frustration. "Agh!"

Nate angled to look at her. "You okay?"

"No," she said, staring at the ceiling. "I'm a wreck." Her eyes filled and she let it happen, let the tears track down her face. What was the point in fighting it anymore? All her Tic-Tacs had burned up in the fire, anyway. "I don't have a condition. I know that. I'm just a mess, and my entire life has imploded, and I don't know how to do this. I buy and sell property, Nate. I'm cold and professional and . . . well, I was. But now I'm unemployed and feeling all these emotions and I don't have any Tic-Tacs." A fresh wave of tears rolled down her cheek, and she bit her lip, tried to batten down the emotion enough to keep some control. "I'm scared, and I don't know what I'm doing, and I just want to put my feet down somewhere and know who I am again."

She let out a stuttered sigh, her eyes locked on the ceiling even as she felt Nate lie back next to her, not touching her, just lying on his side, watching her.

"Hey," he said, his voice so quiet, she almost didn't hear him. As a matter of fact, she pretended not to hear him, just stared straight ahead, because the idea of looking at him physically hurt—

"*Hey.*" He touched her chin and angled her face until she had to meet his eyes, and seeing them looking at her, so loving, so kind, made her want to throw herself into his arms and never leave. And it was just that kind of thinking that had gotten her into this mess in the first place.

"Put your feet down wherever you have to," he said, gently wiping a tear from her cheek with his thumb. "If that's what you need, I won't stop you. But do me a favor?"

Freya smiled. "What? You want me to cry all over the place and get your bed all soggy? Done."

He laughed, but then his face went serious. "No. I'm just hoping you don't have to leave tonight."

He looked at her, his expression so tired, so vulnerable, and Freya reached up and touched his face, running her fingers down his cheek, to his lips.

"I don't have to leave tonight," she said, and pushed herself up to kiss him, her body relaxing as he responded, pulling her in closer to him. They made love quietly, gently, slowly. Freya closed her eyes and forgot everything except how good it felt to be with him.

The rest of it she'd think about tomorrow.

CHAPTER SIXTEEN

$\mathcal{M}$ALCOLM WOKE up the next morning, treated yet again to an unobstructed view of the low, cheap ceiling in his crap RV, and he knew that it was time. He'd tried to play nice, tried to be a gentleman, but these people had no appreciation for refinement.

It was time to take the gloves off.

He made himself a pot of coffee and two fried eggs, tried to enjoy the sunrise through the tiny window by his kitchenette, but the skies were a little cloudy, and the window was grimy as hell.

But that was okay. Soon he'd have money, he'd have vengeance, and he'd be able to drink whatever he wanted, whenever he wanted it.

Life was just about to get good.

The alarm on his watch went off and he hit the button, silencing it. It was officially 9:00 A.M. Eastern time. He pulled out his cell phone and dialed Richard Daly's office for what he hoped would be the last time. When Richard answered, he said, "I'm done farting around, Daly."

"What a coincidence," Richard said. "So am I. Take the plate to the police, do what you want. I'm out of it."

Malcolm took a moment to absorb this, then said, "What?"

"I don't believe you have it," Richard said, "but if you do, do whatever you will with it. I didn't kill that guard, and all that plate does is place me at the scene. Which is fine. I have the money to hire lawyers and public relations people, and to be honest, I would rather pay them millions than give you a single penny. So go ahead, Malcolm. Do your worst."

Malcolm closed his eyes, a red fury building inside him until he felt like a volcano about to erupt. What the *fuck* did a guy have to do to be taken seriously by these people? A little *fucking respect*, that was all he wanted, and—

Click.

"No."

He held the phone out and stared at it.

Richard Daly had hung up on him.

What the hell was *wrong* with these people?

That was it. The absolute last straw. He punched the redial button with his thumb and held the phone up to his ear.

"Richard Daly."

"You're going to want to listen to me this time, you dumb fuck," Malcolm growled, the faux Irish accent making way for the backroads Midwest that he'd been born to, "because I'm not talking about the plate anymore."

There was a slight pause, then, "I'm a busy man. Get to the point fast."

"Your daughter is very pretty," Malcolm said. "She looks so much like Veronica. Hell, I thought it was Veronica when I first saw her. But then I realized, no, Veronica's dead."

Silence. Malcolm held his breath, just waiting for Richard to hang up again. He almost wanted him to hang up. At that moment, he would take any excuse to unleash his fury, but to be able to unleash it all over Richard Daly's precious daughter...now that would be poetic.

"I'm just a short walk from her," Malcolm said. "I can get to her in twenty minutes. How far are you?"

"Go sleep it off, Malcolm," Richard said. "You and I both know you're not capable—"

"You have no idea what I'm capable of," Malcolm said. "All these years, Mick thought you killed that security guard, and you thought he did it, both of you too stupid to figure out what really happened," Malcolm said, his voice cold. "But now, I think it's time to let those old ghosts out for a run."

He let Richard absorb this for a moment, go through those etched memories of that day and see if he could put the pieces together that pointed to Malcolm. The fact that neither Richard nor Mick had figured it out before now spoke to their old enmity, but really, it wouldn't take a genius to put two and two together, and Richard Daly was no genius.

"Son of a bitch," Richard breathed.

"There we go," Malcolm said. "I knew you'd catch on eventually."

"So, what's to stop me from calling the police right now and telling them everything?"

"Go ahead," Malcolm said, but he knew Richard would do no such thing. You don't get as far in business as Richard Daly had without having a keen sense of self-preservation. But, just for insurance, he added, "But that'll certainly leave you with some messy questions to answer, won't it?"

"I've got lawyers who will handle that for me."

"Can they bring your daughter back to life, these miracle lawyers of yours? I'm just curious. I hear there are a lot of fascinating things going on in the law these days.

My nephew managed to save her when I set her cabin on fire. I wonder what your lawyers could do if I put a bullet through her head?"

"What the hell are you talking about?" Richard said, his voice tight. "What cabin?"

This took a moment to absorb, and then Malcolm realized—the daughter hadn't told Richard about the fire. Malcolm raised his eyes to heaven. *A little help here?*

"You should call your girl and ask her about it, Richard. Ask her how it felt to fry on the bathroom floor before my nephew broke in to save her. But maybe don't waste a lot of time. You've got some errands to run."

"What do you want?"

"That's more like it," Malcolm said. "I'm gonna text you an account number. You're going to move two million into it. Meanwhile, your daughter and I are gonna spend some quality time together."

"It takes time to get those kinds of resources together," Richard said. "I can't just—"

"Despite all evidence to the contrary, Richard," Malcolm said, "I think you're a smart man. Smart enough to figure out how to transfer large amounts of cash to an off-shore account, anyway. And you'd better get on that. I'll be waiting here for your arrival, with your daughter. Then you'll charter the three of us to a destination of my choice and then . . . well. We'll just play it by ear."

"If you touch her, I will put every resource I have into making you pay," Richard said. "And since you've done your research, you should know the kind of resources I have."

"If you do as you're told, I won't have to touch her," Malcolm said. "But if you don't, you'll have the rest of your life to know it was all your fault for not taking me seriously from the start."

And this time, it was Malcolm who hung up.

It felt pretty damn good, he had to admit.

Freya sat on the porch swing on the front deck of Nate's house, staring out over the horizon. The peaks of evergreens reached into the sky, cutting into gray clouds turned warm at the edges by what little of the morning sun they'd let through. The air was crisp and fresh, smelling of pine and fresh-mown grass, and she breathed in deeply, exhausted but at peace.

Well. Sorta at peace.

At three in the morning, she'd given up on the idea of getting to sleep and had slipped downstairs to make coffee and think, and that was when the idea had hit her, so obvious, and yet, she hadn't seen it until right then. She quietly got the laptop Flynn had sent her out of the bedroom and padded downstairs to work. By six, she'd had a business plan all set out for him, complete with luxury cabins and a golf course where the RV park was and all the media contacts Nate would need to get the word out that the latest and greatest in luxury getaways was nestled away in these quiet Idaho woods.

And, the best part of all, the whole place would revolve around a swank restaurant that would have people driving from hours around just to taste Nate's food. All she needed was to copy the files to Nate's computer and print them out. Then, when she left, she'd know that she had left something helpful behind, which would make it a lot easier to go.

At least, she hoped so.

"Morning."

Freya turned to see Piper standing in the doorway, squinting in the morning light.

"Do I still have pneumonia?" she asked.

"Whooping cough." Freya took another sip of her coffee. "Do kids your age get whooping cough?"

Piper sat down on the swing next to Freya. "What's whooping cough?"

"I have no idea," Freya said, "but it sounds more fun than pneumonia."

Piper nodded, staring at her feet. They weren't kicking out from the swing, just hanging.

Wow, Freya thought, *that's not good.*

"My mom's in jail, right?" Piper said, angling her head to look at Freya.

Freya had to take a moment. Where the hell was Nate when you needed him? Yeesh.

"Ye-esss," she said finally, watching Piper carefully for her reaction. The kid's eyes were still big and brown and pretty, but they were tinged with a distinct sadness that made her look much like she'd aged five years in just the past few days.

"I overheard Dad talking on the phone. Something about stealing people's identities or something." Piper sat up straight. "What does that mean?"

"It's complicated," Freya said.

"Did she...hurt people?"

"Oh, no. No. I mean, yes, but in a stressful, money way, not in a beat-you-up way." *If you exclude trying to kill your great-uncle, which I personally give her a pass on.*

"I'm never going to see her again, am I?" Piper asked. Freya's heart tugged in her chest, and her eyes started to water as she watched this sweet little girl wrestle with the fallout that came from being born to Nikkie Cooper.

"I don't know," Freya said. "But there's always a chance."

"She doesn't love me, does she?" Piper asked, her chin trembling.

"That's not true," Freya said. "She does."

"No." Piper wiped her face on her sleeve. "She was only here for a day, and then she ran off and she didn't even say good-bye."

"I know," Freya said, "but it's complicated, you know?" She hesitated for a moment, not sure what Nate wanted Piper to know, but to hell with him. This was what happened when you slept in.

Freya put her arm around Piper. "You know that night of the fire?"

Piper sniffled. "Yeah."

"Well, someone set that fire. And your mom, she thought that person was going to hurt you, so she ran off to stop him. That's how the police got her. So your mom knew that protecting you could mean going to jail for a long time, and she chose to protect you anyway. That's love, honey. It's screwed-up love, but it's real."

Piper's chin trembled even more, and then she burst out into hard sobs.

"Oh, no," Freya said, pulling her arm back and patting Piper on the knee. "Oh, god, I'm so bad at this."

"I didn't even get a chance to say good-bye," Piper squeaked.

"I know, honey," Freya said. "I know."

Piper leaned her head against Freya's shoulder, and for a moment, Freya wasn't sure what to do. Then she tightened her hold on the girl and smoothed her hair and let her cry. It was such a simple act, holding a child while she wept for her lost mother, and yet something about it calmed Freya inside. She kissed the top of Piper's head and inhaled. Piper's hair smelled of strawberry shampoo, and for that moment, it seemed like the most wonderful scent in the world.

"I believe that your mother loves you," Freya said quietly, "because you're her daughter, and it's natural. But even if she didn't, even if she'd just met you for the first time a few days ago, she would love you, because you're an amazing kid. I want you to remember that always, okay? You're too great not to feel loved every minute of your life."

Piper pulled back and looked up at Freya. "Okay."

Freya smiled. "Good."

Piper hesitated for a moment, nibbling her lip. "Do you think Dad would take me to see her? You know, to say good-bye?"

Freya thought on this for a second, then said, "Tell you what. Go on upstairs. Get dressed and cleaned up, and then ask him. If he says no, send him to me, and I'll argue your case for you."

"Okay." Piper started toward the front door, then stopped and looked at Freya. "Would you come, too?"

"Oh, honey, I can't, I have to—" Freya cut herself off before she said "pack." The kid had enough to think about right now. "I think it's best if it's just you and your dad on this one."

Piper nodded, then ran into the house. Freya sat outside staring at the horizon, swinging gently on the porch swing. In a few minutes, she was going to have to call on her old self, shut herself down long enough to do what had to be done. She could pack while they were gone to see Nikkie, then have a quick good-bye and get on the road before nightfall. She knew it was what she needed to do in order to get her head on straight, and she knew it was probably the best thing for Nate and Piper as well. She was resigned to it; the decision had been made, and now it was just a matter of seeing it through. But for a few more minutes, she could sit and look at the beautiful landscape, and remember what it felt like to wake up in Nate's arms, to sniff the clean strawberry scent of a little girl's hair.

So that's exactly what she did.

"So," Nate said, glancing at Piper in the passenger seat. "How are you doing?"

He'd waited for her to start the conversation for almost the entire drive back, but she'd stayed quiet, just staring out the window. She'd spent less than five minutes with Nikkie, and from what Nate could see through the one-way glass, hadn't said much at all.

"Pipes?" he said.

She turned her head and looked at him. "Sorry. What?"

"Talk to me," he said. "Tell me how you're doing?"

"I'm fine," she said simply.

"You don't seem fine," he said. "You're pretty quiet."

"I'm just thinking."

"About what?"

"I wished for my mom to come back," she said. "On this magic Irish coin that Ruby gave me. And at first I thought it had gone all wrong, that I'd done it wrong, because she didn't come back the way I wanted her to come back. But now I think it's good." She went quiet for a moment, then nodded. "I'm sorry she's going to jail. She said she'd write me, though."

"Yeah?" Nate pulled up to the gate, reached out his window, and punched in his code. "So, you're doing okay?"

Piper smiled at him. "Yeah. I'm okay."

The gate lifted and Nate drove down the dirt path toward their house, enjoying a momentary sense of peace until he saw Freya's rental car, the trunk open just enough for him to see the packed bags inside. He pulled up quietly next to the rental in the driveway, and Piper had her seatbelt off before he came to a full stop.

"I'm gonna go play Playstation, okay?"

"Yeah," Nate said, still staring at Freya's car. After a few minutes, he pulled the keys out and headed up to his room to face reality.

She was going.

He found Freya sitting on the edge of his bed, dressed in jeans and a light sweater, her rental keys in her hands and a flight pass printout sitting next to her on the bed. Nate stepped closer, angled his head to read it.

American Flight 2928, to Boston. Leaving in eight hours.

"Right," he said.

"Nate —"

He looked at her. "It's okay. I just thought…"

"What? That I would change my mind?"

He looked at her and realized yes, that was exactly what he'd thought. Dejected, he sat down on the bed next to her. "I thought there'd be more time."

"Oh," she said, and he reached for her hand. She didn't look at him, or even squeeze his fingers back. She just…allowed it.

"I did want to talk to you," he said after a moment, "before you went. Figure out what you wanted to do about this whole thing with Malcolm and your dad."

"There isn't anything to talk about." She pulled her hand from his and stood up, her expression oddly unemotional and businesslike. "Call the police, hand this whole mess over to them."

"I can't," he said. "Not yet."

"Why not?"

"Because..." He stared at her, not sure how to process the sudden coldness coming off her. "If your father is involved... I mean, it's your *father*. I can't just hand everything over to the police, not without talking with you about it first, knowing how it's going to affect you."

She shrugged. "Whatever he did is his responsibility. It's not my problem. But Malcolm, out there on the loose, that's a problem. Just call the police, give them the information Jake got for us, and if anyone needs to talk to me—" She grabbed a business card out of her purse, jotted something on the back. "The office number isn't good anymore, but I put my home number and address on the back for you."

He flipped the card over, then looked up at her. "Okay."

She shifted her eyes toward the door. "I also, um, I had some ideas about what you might want to do with the place. You know, to make it profitable. I left a folder for you in your office, on the desk. If you have any questions, please feel free to call me."

"Feel free to...?" He stood up and stepped into her line of vision, forcing her to look at him. If she had to leave, fine, but he was damned if he was going to let her leave like this. "Freya, what the hell is wrong with you?"

"Nothing." She reached behind him and picked up her boarding pass from the bed. "I have a flight to catch, and it's two and a half hours to Spokane, so..."

She put her hand on his shoulder, kissed him awkwardly on the cheek, and then started toward the door, but he grabbed her hand and she stopped, her eyes on the floor.

"Nate..." she said, almost in a whisper.

"I'm not going to stop you," he said. "I'm a man of my word. But you could at least look at me when you say good-bye."

He watched her, waiting, and finally she raised her eyes to his. They were tired, cold, and dry. She squeezed his hand and let go.

"Good-bye."

"Dad, I think my stupid controller is broken," Piper said, pushing the door to the room open. Freya turned and looked at Piper, who stared back at her.

"What's the matter?" Piper's eyes went to the boarding pass in Freya's hand, then back up to Freya. "You're leaving?"

"Yes," Freya said. "I was just coming to get you to say good-bye."

"But...I thought you two..." She looked at Nate. "You didn't tell me she was leaving."

"Piper," he said quietly, "Freya needs to get going, so it's best to get your good-bye in now."

Piper's eyes went cold and she looked at Freya. "Fine. Bye."

And she left the room, her feet pounding down the stairs.

CHAPTER SEVENTEEN

*F*REYA STOOD where she was, between Nate and the open door, feeling sick and weak and almost out of the cold, professional resolve she'd spent most of her morning working up. Across the hall, Ruby's door opened, and she poked her head into Nate's room and looked at Freya.

"You told her?" Ruby asked.

"Yes, she—" Freya began, but then the front door slammed shut.

"Piper!" Nate shouted, but Ruby said, "I got it," and started for the stairs.

"Ruby," Freya called, running down the steps after her, finally catching up at the front door. "Let me."

Ruby took a moment, then nodded. Freya went out the front door, tossed her purse and boarding pass into the open front window of her car, and watched as Piper grabbed her bike next to the office.

"Piper!" she called, but Piper either didn't hear her or ignored her. Freya ran to the office, grabbed the other bike, and made chase through the woods, gaining on Piper until they reached the lake. Piper threw her bike down on the ground and stamped out to the end of the dock. Freya leaned her bike against the shed and followed, settling down on the dock behind her.

"Piper?" she said. "We need to get you back to the house, babe."

"I'm fine out here," Piper said. "And don't you have a plane to catch?"

Freya sighed. "I don't live here, Piper. I live in Boston."

"So?" Piper picked up a pebble on the dock and threw it into the water, where it skipped across the dark gray surface, mirroring the clouding sky. "You could move. People move."

"It's not that simple," Freya said.

"What about Dad?" Piper shifted to look at Freya. "He loves you."

"He does not," Freya said, lowering her eyes. "He just met me."

"So?" Piper said again. "I know my dad. He's never looked at anyone the way he looks at you. He loves you, and you're just going to leave."

"Look, Piper...your dad is amazing. He's kind and smart and honorable, and he cares so much about you. You're his world, and you're lucky to have him. And this is hard to explain but..." She took a deep breath and looked at Piper. "Between the two of us, I don't want to leave."

Piper shifted around, hope on her face. "Then why are you?"

Freya went quiet for a long moment, staring out at the water. "People...people are made certain ways, okay? Like your mom, you know? Just...people are flawed. And they need to understand their flaws before they can inflict them on other people." Freya shook her head and let out a heavy breath. "Okay. See, it's like this—"

"You don't even know why you're leaving," Piper said.

"No, I do. I know why. I just...it's complicated, and hard to explain."

Piper shot her a cold look over her shoulder. "If you had a good reason, it wouldn't be that hard to explain."

"It's...complicated," Freya said lamely.

They sat in silence for a while, then Freya caught a shadow moving in the woods and she tensed, her heart pounding as she thought of Malcolm. She was about to grab Piper's arm and make a run for it when Ruby emerged from the path, and Freya relaxed. Piper looked up, following Freya's eyeline, and sighed. "I'm in trouble, aren't I?"

Freya shook her head.

"No," she said, "but I think you should go with Ruby." She scanned the rest of the woods surrounding the lake, and saw nothing, but she still felt on edge. If Malcolm was out there, she wasn't going to feel comfortable until Piper was safe at the house. "Go on."

"What about you?" Piper asked.

Freya stared out at the water. "I need to think for a minute."

"Are you still leaving?"

Freya stayed quiet, not wanting to answer. She just wasn't sure anymore, about anything. Which was part of the reason she wanted to go home, but now...

"Hey."

Freya looked up to see Piper reaching into her front pocket. She pulled out a small pullstring pouch. She held it in her hands for a moment, then opened it and took out a coin, which she handed to Freya.

Freya twirled it in her hand; it was an Irish half crown. "Where'd you get this?"

"It's a magic wishing coin," Piper said. "What you do is you face east—" she pointed across the lake "—and you close your eyes and hold it over your heart and you make a wish. But the wish has to be really good, something you want more than anything, not like money or that some stupid team wins the World Series. It has to be important. Then you put it back in the bag and keep it with you until it comes true."

"Wow," Freya said, handing it back to her. "That's pretty cool."

Piper didn't take it. "I want you to have it."

She held the little bag out for Freya. Freya took it carefully. "Are you sure? Magic coins don't come around every day."

Piper held Freya's eye. "Make a wish. See what happens."

Freya smiled, holding the coin in her hands. "Thanks."

At the path from the woods, Ruby stepped out, her arms crossed over her stomach, her stance protective and ready to pounce. Freya patted Piper on the knee.

"Go on with Ruby," Freya said.

Piper stood up. "You coming?"

Freya smiled. "In a minute."

"Okay." Piper got up and started down the dock. Freya watched as she joined Ruby and disappeared into the woods, which were getting darker by the minute as the clouds above darkened, matching her mood. She stared down at the coin in her hand, wondering...

The wish has to be really good, she heard Piper's voice saying. *It has to be important.*

What do I have to lose? She closed her eyes, put the coin over her heart, and made her wish.

"Talk about the luck of the Irish."

Freya's eyes flew open and she scurried to her feet to find a stocky, white-haired man standing behind her in a tweed coat with patches on the elbows, and a shot of fear coursed through her.

"You've got your mother's eyes," Malcolm said as he moved closer. "Did you know that?"

Nate watched from his bedroom window as Ruby walked back up the path with Piper in tow and breathed a sigh of relief as he heard the front door shut behind them downstairs. He kept his eye on the path from the lake; no Freya. He pulled back from the window.

She probably just wanted some time alone, and if that's what she needed, he was going to give it to her. Judging by the sky, it was going to rain soon; she'd be back before it did. He'd get a chance to talk to her again.

Just give her some space, he thought, but doing nothing was making him crazy, so after a few minutes of pacing, he went to Piper's door and knocked.

"Come in," she called.

He poked his head in to see her bent over her desk, head half hanging out the window, the sound of clanging metal suddenly reverberating through the room. "Piper?"

She pulled back in and looked at him, smiling, as the clanging quieted down. "Hey, Dad. Check it out."

He stepped in and looked at the window. Over the sill were the hooks of a metal fire escape ladder. He poked his head out and saw the dangling chains and rods still swinging by the side of the house. He pulled back in and smiled at her. "Smart kid."

"Ruby told me it wasn't safe for me to sleep with the

fire extinguisher, so she found these in the attic." She motioned to three boxes sitting next to the wall of her room. "There's another one for your room, and for Ruby's, and one for the bathroom."

"Good to know." Nate sat down on the bed next to his daughter. "So, how are you doing?"

"Okay. I wish she wasn't going, though."

"Yeah," Nate said. "Me, too."

"Do you think maybe we can go visit Freya in Boston?"

Nate stared down at his feet. "That'd be up to her." He looked at Piper and smiled. "But yeah. Sure."

"Good." She smiled back. Nate pushed up from the bed and went to the window.

"Do you love her?"

He turned around. "What?"

"Freya," Piper said. "I told her you loved her and she said you didn't and I think I'm right. Am I right?"

Nate took a breath. "It's complicated. I like her a lot. I don't want her to go."

"Well, maybe she won't go," Piper said. "Or maybe, if she does, she'll come back."

Nate stared out the window at the path from the woods, which was still quiet, with no sign of Freya. "That's what I'm hoping for, kid." He turned to her. "You think I should go down after her?"

Piper thought for a moment, angling her head to the side, then said, "Give her a little while. She has to come back for her car. You can talk to her then."

Nate smiled; he had raised a smart kid. And if Freya needed space, he needed to give it to her. Crowding her would only make her run faster.

"When did you get so smart, anyway?" he asked.

"I've always been smart," Piper said. "Duh."

"Get a load of this," Freya said, looking around the dank old RV as she stepped inside. "If it isn't Hell's Winnebago."

Behind her Malcolm pushed the gun into the center of her back and she stumbled inside and then turned on him.

"Watch it," she said.

Malcolm smirked, then checked his cheap digital watch. "I'm an hour early, but I could hardly pass up the opportunity, could I? Richard Daly's eldest, sitting out at the end of the dock, like ripe fruit just waiting to be plucked." He smiled at her. "Can I offer you a bit of Irish whiskey?"

Freya stared at him. On the one hand, drinking with the man who had almost killed her, and probably still wanted to, didn't seem like a great strategy. On the other hand...keep all negotiations friendly. And hostage situations, like real estate transactions, were just another negotiation.

"Jameson's?" she asked.

Malcolm pulled a bottle out from inside the tiny oven and held it out for her. "Tullamore Dew."

"Eh." She shrugged and sat down at the tiny kitchenette table. "What the hell, right?"

"That's what I say," Malcolm said. He grabbed two short-rocks glasses from a cabinet over the sink, set them down on the table, and poured two fingers of whiskey into hers. Then he went into the minifridge, pulled out a Coke, and poured that into his.

"You're not drinking?" Freya asked.

"Not yet." He held up his glass for a toast. "May we get what we want, may we get what we need—"

Freya raised her glass. "—but may we never get what we deserve."

They drank and Malcolm eyed her for a moment. "Your father teach you that one?"

"My name's Daly and I grew up in Boston," she said. "I learned that one doing Yoo Hoo shooters in nursery school."

Malcolm motioned toward the bottle. "Would you like another?"

Freya looked at him; maybe he'd be easier to handle if he had a few. "I would, but I don't like drinking alone. Are you sure you won't join me?"

"Sorry," he said. "Need to keep my head. But you're welcome to as much as you want. I have a feeling things are going to get rather unpleasant this afternoon." He refilled his glass with Coke. "Please, understand it's nothing personal. Not against you, anyway. You simply had the sad misfortune of being born to a right son of a bitch."

"It happens." Freya sat back. Malcolm was short, with a round face and ruddy, Irish cheeks. He had a bald spot and a bulb nose that had reddened, most likely, from years of drinking. He didn't look that dangerous, but he'd set her on fire, and as long as he had that gun, she guessed she'd best take him seriously.

"So, what's the plan here?" she asked. "You can't get the plate, so you're gonna use me to get money out of my father? Is that it?"

"Something like that," he said, the Irish lilt trailing out of his voice. "The plan has, of necessity, evolved."

A shot of ice went down Freya's spine at the sudden

hardness in Malcolm's eyes. "What do you mean, the plan has evolved?"

"I mean," he said, the anger suddenly showing in his taut face, "that he ruined my life, and now I'm going to ruin his."

Freya took in a breath, suddenly deathly curious to see her father from a new angle, even if it was a hostile, mentally unstable one. "Ruined your life? How, Malcolm?"

Malcolm held up one finger and closed his eyes. "Say my name again."

Freya glanced around the area, looking for something to hit him with while his eyes were closed, but the only potential weapon was the whiskey bottle, and he had his hand on the base, so she just sighed and said, "Malcolm."

"Ah." He opened his eyes, which had gone misty. "You even sound like her, you know? She had that same note of exasperation in her voice when she said my name."

Freya went still. "Who?"

"Why, your mother, of course." Malcolm's eyes trailed heavenward. "Veronica Jensen, the most beautiful girl I've ever known, before or since." He looked at Freya, a light, sad smile on his face. "I killed a man for her, you know."

Freya felt sick as the realization came to her. "The security guard?"

Malcolm's eyebrows raised in surprise. "Your father told you, did he?"

She leaned forward. "My mother was there?"

Malcolm nodded. "She found out the three of us were going to break into the exhibit. She came to stop Richard. She didn't give a good crap what happened to me, or Mick. It was Richard. Always Richard." He sighed. "When she showed up, she found me out idling the van, and she cried, begged me to get Richard out of there. And I thought my heart would break. A man can handle anything except the sight of the woman he loves in pain."

The woman he loves...Freya reached for her glass and downed the last drops.

Malcolm slowly, carefully twirled the whiskey bottle at its base, staring at it as he talked. "I sent her home and went in, but a security guard caught me, and asked about Veronica. He'd seen her." Malcolm raised his eyes to Freya's; they were red-rimmed and dreamy. "I had no choice, you see. It would have ruined her, being placed at the scene like that. So when the alarms went off—Mick denied it, but I know he tripped them, clumsy bastard—I shot him. For her." He lowered his eyes again. "And she repaid me by running off to Boston with your rat bastard father."

He opened the whiskey bottle and absently poured them both two fingers. Freya took hers and sipped it, while Malcolm just stared into his, sniffing it.

"I told her, you know," he said, more to his glass than to Freya, although she listened intently. "I told her I loved her and that I wanted to spend the rest of my life making her happy." He laughed bitterly. "And she told me that she loved Richard. So, I said some things that were maybe not so flattering to her, and she told me...I will always remember it...she said...." He closed his eyes again and Freya eyed the whiskey bottle in his hand. " 'Malcolm, if you ever thought there could be anything between us, you were deluding yourself, you crazy fuck.' " He opened his eyes, and Freya looked up to see that his cheeks were ruddy with laughter. "She had a mouth on her, your mother. I always loved that about her."

Freya leaned forward, fascinated despite herself. "Really? I don't think I ever heard her swear."

"Well, you wouldn't," Malcolm said, seeming offended at the idea. "You were just a child. Veronica was a lot of things, but she was always good around children."

Freya sat back and reached for her glass. As hungry as she was to hear stories of her mother, this woman he'd loved didn't sound like her mother at all. She sounded, honestly, more like Freya herself.

"All these years," Malcolm went on, stuck in his own reverie, "I've wanted revenge on your father for stealing Veronica from me. And then come to find, Mick had that plate with your father's precious prints on it, all these years." Malcolm laughed. "Can you believe that? He'd been saving it just in case the murder ever came to light, he could pin it on your father. And then your father made all that money and my brother got an idea." Malcolm held up one finger, then reached across the kitchenette and pulled open a drawer. He withdrew a stack of envelopes and dumped them on the table in front of Freya. "Five thousand a month. Pitiful. The man had no vision, I tell you."

Freya picked up an envelope; it was a bank statement under Mick's name, with a five-thousand-dollar direct deposit from Daly Developers, Inc., showing on the fifteenth of the month. She picked up another one. Same thing.

"Son of a bitch," she said.

"Yes, quite," Malcolm said, pushing up from the table. "Time to go."

"What?" Freya said. "Go where?"

"Up to the house," he said. "You're going to fetch me that plate."

The house. Piper. Freya pushed herself up from the kitchenette table. "No, I'm not."

He looked surprised and raised the gun. "Say that again?"

"What do you even need the plate for? You've got me."

"Yes," Malcolm said. "I do. But you won't ruin your father's reputation forever, now will you? My plans have evolved, they haven't changed entirely. I still want that plate, and you're going to give it to me."

"No," she said. "I'm not taking you to the house. I won't."

She got up and started toward the door, but stopped when she heard Malcolm's voice behind her, cold as ice, saying, "Maybe take a moment to think this through, girl."

She turned to find him standing, the gun pointed at her, and for the first time since he'd approached her on the dock, she felt stark fear.

He smiled coldly. "If I shoot you now, then the next best hostage for me to take would be the little girl, would it not?"

Freya took a step toward him. "You touch her, and I swear—"

"Your ability to protect her will be seriously limited," he said, "if you are dead." He paused for a long moment and when Freya didn't move away from him, he smiled. "That's my girl."

"I am not your girl, you miserable piece of shit," she said, and walked out in front of him.

Behind her, Malcolm chuckled.

"I see you got something else from your mother besides her eyes," he said.

CHAPTER EIGHTEEN

NATE SLAPPED the pile of cards in the middle of Piper's bed.

"Illegal slap!" Piper called, picking up his hand and going through the cards underneath.

"That was perfectly legal," he said, reaching into the card pile as well. "Look, seven of clubs on the six of hearts."

"No," she said, going through the cards. "That's wrong. I put down a three of spades after the six. They got mixed up."

"Looks right to me," Nate said. "Nobody likes a sore loser, Pipes."

"Nobody likes a big, fat cheaterpants, either!" she said, and plucked a card out of the pile. "Ha! The three!"

"Oh, sure!" he said, laughing. "Pulled from the middle of the pile!"

"It's not—" Piper stopped suddenly and went quiet. Nate listened, and heard the sound of the front door opening. They looked at each other, and Piper smiled.

"I bet it's Freya," she said, and patted Nate on the knee. "Go talk to her, and if it doesn't work, call me down and I'll cry."

"What?" Nate said, laughing.

"Go, go, go!" she said in a stage whisper, urging him on. He grinned and hopped up off the bed, just as the phone rang.

"Shit," he said. "I'm expecting a call from the guys at the restaurant." He looked at Piper. "You go down and keep her here until I get there, okay?"

Piper saluted and hopped off the bed. She ran out of the room and darted down the stairs, and Nate hurried into his bedroom to get the phone.

"This is Nate," he said when he picked up the phone.

A man's voice he didn't recognize said, "Nathan Brody?"

It wasn't either Clint or Eddie. "Yes?"

"This is Richard Daly. I need to speak to my daughter. Is she there?"

"I think she just came in," he said.

"I've been calling her cell phone all day," Daly said. "There's been no answer."

"Yeah, her cell phone burned up in the fire," Nate said.

There was a stark silence, then Daly said, "Your uncle Malcolm. Have you seen him?"

"Not in almost ten years," Nate said.

"You need to keep Freya with you at the house," Daly said. "Don't let your uncle in, under any circumstances. I'm about an hour away. I'll be able to deal with him when I get there."

"What's going on?"

"He's threatened Freya," Daly said. "He wants her to get to me."

Nate's body tensed. "Threatened how?"

"Is she there?" Daly said. "Put her on the phone."

Nate listened for the sounds of Piper and Freya talking downstairs; there was silence.

"I'll have her call you," Nate said, and hung up, then shot out of the room and down the stairs to see Uncle Malcolm leaning over Piper, pinching her cheek. Behind him stood Freya, looking tense and drained.

"Well, aren't you just the loveliest thing?" Malcolm said. "And how old are you now, girl?"

"Eleven," Piper said. "Gonna be twelve in August." She looked at Nate. "Dad, you never told me I had an Uncle Malcolm."

And then Malcolm stood up straight, and Nate saw the gun tucked into his waistband under his tweed jacket.

Freya's heart raced as she caught Nate's sharp look; he'd seen the gun. *Good.* He'd get Piper out of there; he'd think of something. She relaxed, slightly, as Nate moved closer to Piper.

"Piper," Nate said. "Come over here."

"Dad?" she said, looking curious.

"*Now.*"

Piper walked over to him and he stepped in front of her, blocking her from Malcolm. Freya released a breath, but then Malcolm put his arm around her, drawing her close, his other hand on his waistband, near the gun.

"And how are you, m'lad?" Malcolm said, and his eyes lit as he looked at Nate. "Been a long time."

"Piper," Nate said, not taking his eyes of his uncle. "Go to your room."

"Oh, no," Malcolm said, moving his hand a bit closer to the gun. "I just met the child. You can't cut the reunion short. I might get insulted."

Piper peeked out from behind Nate, looking confused, and Nate put his hand on her and gently pushed her back.

"Dad—" she started, but he said, "*Piper,*" and she went quiet. Just then, a door opened upstairs and Freya looked up to see Ruby coming down the steps.

Damnit.

"Who was that on the phone?" Ruby asked as she descended into the foyer, then raised a surprised eyebrow at Malcolm. "Hello, Mr. Bayheart. Everything okay on your lot?"

Then Ruby's eyes went to his waistband and his arm around Freya and she shifted over to stand next to Nate, blocking Piper.

"Go upstairs, Piper," Ruby said, and Freya held her breath, hoping against hope that Malcolm would let the rest go and just deal with her. It would be so much easier if it was just her.

"No one's going anywhere," Malcolm said. "It's a family reunion."

"You know what?" Freya said, turning slightly toward him. "I really don't think you need anyone but me, right, Malcolm?"

Malcolm opened his mouth to say something but Nate said, "No. Uncle Malcolm, I'll stay. Everyone else can go."

"No," Freya said, "*really.*"

Nate looked at her, his eyes hard and angry. "Knock it off, Freya."

"Nate," Freya said, trying to convey her conviction in her tone. "You don't understand what this is all about—"

"I don't care what it's about," Nate said, then looked to Malcolm. "Malcolm and I can settle this between us."

"No, Nathan, I think I'd like Freya to stay." He dug

his arm into Freya's back and side as he clutched her ever closer, and she winced.

"Malcolm," Nate said, his eyes on Freya as he closed in tighter to Ruby to block Piper. "Let her go."

"It's a simple problem with a simple solution," Malcolm said. "And the solution is, someone here has got to get me my goddamn plate."

First get them out, Nate thought. *Then kill him.*

"All right," Nate said, holding up one hand. "Just stay calm, okay?" He touched Ruby on the hand, keeping his eyes on Malcolm. "Ruby, take Piper up to her room and get the plate."

Ruby, God bless her poker face, simply nodded. Nate turned to Piper and gave her his I-mean-it look. "Piper, go show Ruby where the plate is."

"But how—?" she started, but Nate shushed her. If he could just get Ruby to the room with Piper, she'd see the fire ladder in the window and get them out. Then he could find a way to get Freya out.

And then he would deal with his uncle. But first things first.

He knelt in front of Piper and put both hands on her shoulders.

"Go up to your room," he said firmly, "and get the plate."

She lowered her eyes. "Okay."

Nate swallowed and stood up, turning to face Malcolm again. He touched Ruby's hand, and she turned toward the stairs and put one hand on Piper's shoulder.

"Just a minute," Malcolm said, and Nate felt Ruby stiffen next to him. "Since when does it take two people

to get a plate?" He looked at Piper through the crack
between Nate and Ruby's shielding bodies. "Go on, child.
Get me my plate."

"*Go*," Nate said forcefully, and Piper nodded and
retreated up the stairs. Nate closed his eyes. She was
smart. She'd go out the fire ladder. She'd be safe.

She'll be safe.

Now he just had to get Ruby and Freya up there...

Malcolm smiled, his eyes cold but clearer than Nate
had ever seen them before. "It's a shame to see you again
under these circumstances, Nathan. I've always liked
you, despite the fact that you came from my useless fuck
of a brother." He turned his eyes to Ruby. "And it's nice
to meet you as myself, Ruby. I apologize about the Mr.
Bayheart thing. The deception was a necessary evil, you
understand."

"Nice to meet you, Malcolm," Ruby said evenly. "You
hurt anyone in this family, and I'll kill you."

"He's after my father," Freya said, keeping her voice
low. "There's no need for him to hurt anyone in this family if you guys would *just go*."

Ruby kept her eyes on Malcolm. "That includes Freya."

"Look," Nate said, but then he heard the telltale tap of
little feet on the stairs. His heart sank, and he turned to
see Piper coming down the steps.

"Piper, I told you to go!"

Piper stepped into the foyer, a curious expression on
her face and a Saran-wrapped, purple-rimmed plate in her
hands.

"No, you didn't," she said, approaching slowly and
looking at Nate as though he'd gone nuts. "You said to get
the plate."

"Ha ha!" Malcolm said, releasing Freya and moving toward Piper. "That's a good—"

Nate stepped between them, grabbed the plate from Piper, and shoved it into Malcolm's chest. Malcolm straightened, took it, and stepped back, placing it on the hall table before putting his arm around Freya again. He grinned and winked at Piper.

"That's a good girl, Piper," Malcolm said. "Out of this entire family, you are my favorite."

Piper watched Malcolm suspiciously for a second, then raised guilty eyes to Nate. "I'm sorry, Dad. I found it in Ruby's room and I knew we'd go back to Cincinnati if you found it, so I hid it."

Nate looked at her and tried to smile encouragement. "It's okay, Pipes. I'm not mad." He looked at Malcolm. "You've got what you want. Now get out."

"I'm not going anywhere," Malcolm said.

"Fine," Nate said. "Then let them go, and you and I can talk."

Freya stamped her foot. "Would you *listen*? He doesn't want you, he wants—"

"Hush," Malcolm said, cutting her off with a sharp squeeze that made Nate want to kill him on the spot. Malcolm glanced from face to face, thought for a moment, then said, "I'm not unreasonable." He looked at Ruby and then nodded toward the door. "Take the child and go to the office, but if you call anyone…" He looked at Nate, and then back at Ruby, his eyes cold with the implied threat. "Are we clear?"

Ruby nodded, then took Piper's hand and nudged her toward the door, carefully keeping her body between Malcolm and Piper. She opened the door and nudged Piper out, then looked at Nate, her poker face dropping for a moment as he could see the wheels churning in her mind. Nate shook his head.

"Take her to the office," he said. "Play Slap, keep her occupied. I'll take care of things here."

Ruby nodded.

Nate turned back to Malcolm. "Freya goes, too."

"Oh, no," Malcolm said, pulling Freya closer. "This one stays. I've still got some business with her father."

Goddamnit. "Malcolm, there's no need—"

"Get going, you two," Malcolm said, nodding at Ruby and Piper. "Before I change my mind."

Ruby shot Nate one last look and then hurried out with Piper, shutting the door behind them. Nate watched through the living room window until they were safely away from the house, then locked his focus on his uncle.

"Let her go," he said, "or I swear, I will kill you myself."

"Stop it," Freya said. "I can handle this. If anyone goes, it should be you." She turned to Malcolm and gave him a professional smile, as if they were negotiating across a conference table. "Malcolm, consider your options here. You don't need him. You've got me. If you let him go—"

"That's sweet of you, girl," Malcolm interrupted, pulling the gun out of his belt and aiming it at her. "But Nate's got a dangerous look in his eye, and I have no intention of turning my back on him at the moment." Malcolm looked at Nate. "And she's not leaving my side until Daly gets here, so you can stop wasting your energy to that end."

It wasn't perfect, but at least Ruby and Piper were out. He could get Freya out, too, he was sure of it, but he'd need to placate his uncle a bit first.

"Fine," he said finally. "That was Daly on the phone before. He'll be here in an hour. We can wait in the kitchen."

Malcolm grabbed the plate from the hall table behind him, then smiled and motioned with the gun for Nate to go first. Nate led them to the table and Malcolm nudged Freya to take a seat next to him, opposite Nate, the gun aimed straight at her chest.

Fucking family reunions, Nate thought, and sat down across from them.

———

CHAPTER NINETEEN

$\mathcal{M}$ALCOLM TAPPED his foot on the floor, working out his nervous energy. He was so close, *so close,* to having everything he wanted. He was in charge, and as long as he kept the gun on Daly's daughter, Nate was taking him very seriously. A hero to the end, that boy was. It made Malcolm wonder whether Nate wasn't actually the mailman's son or something. Sure would explain a lot, considering the lazy coward Mick had been.

Malcolm's eyes went to the plate sitting in the middle of the table, all wrapped in Saran Wrap, ready for the police to analyze for Richard Daly's fingerprints, linking him with the security guard's death. Then, once Daly had commissioned a private plane to take the three of them to some nice South American country with white sandy beaches and sketchy extradition laws, he'd send them back.

Or kill the girl in front of Daly, then kill the rat bastard as well. That idea had merit, too.

Well, he could make that decision later. For the moment, there was nothing to do but wait.

"So, Nate," Malcolm said. "I heard you got your own fancy restaurant set up in Cincinnati. Good for you."

"I did," Nate said, his eyes locked on Daly's daughter. "I sold it."

"Ah, sorry to hear that," Malcolm said. "Did it fail?"

"No." Nate gave Malcolm a cold stare, and then his eyes went back to the girl again. Malcolm watched for a moment, noting the angry desperation in his nephew's expression, and began to rework his hero theory.

If he didn't know any better, he'd say that the boy was in love.

"Oh, no," Malcolm said, looking back and forth between them. "No, no, lad, say it isn't so."

Nate looked at him. "What?"

"You're *in love* with her?" he said, gesturing to Freya with the gun, and Nate dug his fingertips into the wood table so hard, they almost left claw marks. Malcolm sighed. "What are you, thick in the head, boy? Do you know who this is?"

Nate glared at him coldly. "That's enough, Malcolm."

"Oh, for crying out—" Malcolm leaned forward, moving the gun closer to the girl. "This is Veronica Jensen's daughter. *Veronica Jensen*, the woman who sliced my heart out of my chest, threw it on the cold ground, and speared it with the heel of her shoe. This is Richard Daly's daughter, a man with no personality to speak of and even less soul. What are you thinking?"

"That's *enough,* Malcolm," Nate said again, his voice low and serious.

"Tell me it's not true," Malcolm said, "because I'm thinking the best thing I can do for you is shoot her in the head right now before you get too far gone." Malcolm sat back, pulling the gun back a little, while still keeping it aimed at her chest. Shooting Daly's daughter in the head now wouldn't do him any good, and it would leave him without leverage for Daly later, but it would be the biggest favor he could do for his nephew.

"I'm going to ask you one last time," Nate said. "Let her go."

"I'm not sure you understand the balance of power here, young Nathan," Malcolm said, his own anger rising as his nephew looked about ready to throw himself across the table and take his chances with the gun.

"You got any alcohol, Nate?" the girl asked suddenly.

Nate's expression softened a bit as he looked at her, and then he nodded. "Yeah. I have some whiskey in the cabinet above the sink."

Daly's girl turned to Malcolm, her eyes calm and cold, just like Veronica's had been whenever she'd looked at him.

"Would you like some, Malcolm?" she asked.

He stared at her—*oh, so like Veronica*—and then a deep longing flickered to life in Malcolm's gut. He'd gone sixteen months without a drop. Sixteen months sober, and it had gotten him the ultimate prize—Richard Daly's total destruction. He was just minutes away from his vengeance. What could it hurt to indulge in a celebratory tipple?

He moved the gun closer to the girl and looked at his nephew. "Pour two. Do I need to tell you what'll happen if you try to pull anything on your old uncle?"

"No," Nate said, pushing up slowly from the table.

"*I* might pull something." Malcolm chuckled, a sudden giddiness overtaking him at the thought of how damn *close* he was. He looked at Daly's daughter, who was not even smiling. "Get it? Pull something? Like the trigger?"

"Tell me your jokes get better when you've had a few," the girl muttered.

"An Irishman is always funnier when he's had a few," Malcolm said.

"In that case, Nate," she said flatly, "pour him a double."

Malcolm watched as Nate looked up from where he was pouring and smiled at the girl, as if trying to comfort her, as if the only thing on his mind was this girl and her well-being.

Malcolm sighed. *Lord in Heaven.* Would the Brody men never learn?

Freya watched as Nate lifted his glass, his eyes locked on his crazy bastard of an uncle, and she couldn't help but be a little pissed off. If Nate had just played it cool and gotten out with Piper, she could have handled this situation. This was her thing, the one thing she knew how to do, and the threat of physical violence only made it slightly different from any other negotiation. All she had to do was leverage what she wanted against what Malcolm wanted and strike a deal. It would work, too, she knew it would, but Nate's presence there mucked it all up, breaking the cardinal rule of negotiation by putting something in play that she wasn't willing to risk losing.

Now, the only course she had left was getting Malcolm so drunk that he'd put the gun down or something. It was a weak strategy, she knew, but as Malcolm downed his double and asked for a refill, she felt a small blossom of hope.

It would take a while, though; the problem with drunks was, they had a hell of a tolerance.

"Let me tell you about Veronica," Malcolm said, his eyes still sharp and his speech still strong, even as he started in on the new glass. "Ah, now *that* was a woman. She was tough, and beautiful, and never took crap from anybody, even Richard. And when she danced..." Malcolm smiled down into his glass. "There was nothing in the world more beautiful than Veronica Jensen on a dance floor."

Freya lowered her eyes to her own glass, which remained untouched. She pictured her mother's face, remembering how lovely she had been, and refused to let Malcolm's memories taint her own. The woman Malcolm remembered was distorted by his demented ego; that woman was not her mother.

"Bitch," Malcolm said roughly, then lifted his glass and pointed his index finger at Nate. "Now you listen to me, young Nathan Brody. You have a chance to get out before it's too late, before she's made you sell your soul, only to run off with someone else while you crawl like a dog, begging her to..." Malcolm put his glass down, and his eyes were reddened, but deadly serious. "I tell you, the best thing I could do for you would be to kill her right now."

Freya took in a little breath, and Nate leaned forward.

"No," he said, his voice tight. "Don't. Don't do anything. Just...drink."

"She'll destroy you." He pulled on her arm, pulling her closer to the gun. "Do you think I don't know what I've become? Do you think I was always like this? I could have been more than this. I could have been a man who had the peace of knowing he'd never taken another human life. But I loved her, with all my heart, and it ruined everything. And this one will do the same to you, mark my words."

Malcolm gripped her upper arm tight, making her wince, and he moved the gun even closer.

"She's not going to destroy me," Nate said, keeping his eyes on Malcolm.

"She *will*," Malcolm said and Freya closed her eyes as the tip of his gun pressed against her chest. *Maybe getting him drunk wasn't such a good idea…*

"She can't. I don't love her."

Freya opened her eyes and looked at Nate, who didn't look back, just kept his gaze locked on his uncle.

"We've only known each other for a few days, Malcolm," Nate said. "I don't love her."

Freya swallowed hard and lowered her eyes. "It's true, Malcolm. We're friends. Barely even that. Practically strangers." Even as she said the words, her throat tightened around them. Nate was probably telling the truth, but she was lying through her teeth, and she knew it. *Nothing like having a gun aimed at you to make you realize that you're full of shit.*

"All right then," Malcolm said, relaxing a bit. "What if I told you you were free to go? Just leave her with me, and run off to safety with your daughter. Are you going to tell me you would go?"

Freya raised her head, hardly able to believe an opening had just fallen into her lap. "You know, that's actually a good idea—"

"Stop it, Freya," Nate said, cutting her off with a furious look.

"You'd stay because you love her, you idiot," Malcolm said.

"I'd stay because you've got a gun, Malcolm," Nate said, turning his eyes, cold and focused, on his uncle. "I'd stay because I'm not the kind of man who would leave a woman alone to die."

Freya looked up at that, glancing from Malcolm to Nate as they looked at each other. Some understanding flashed between them and she could see the pain under the anger in Nate's eyes, and then Malcolm raised his glass and said, "Here's to Mick, the miserable bastard." He drank and then turned to Freya. "Has he told you the story?"

Freya shook her head.

"Well," Malcolm said, "Mick went on a two-week bender while Nate's mom was complaining about headaches, and she died of a brain aneurysm. Nate found her, all alone. It was terrible. I would have come to the funeral, but no one in the family was talking to me at that point, so..."

Nate stared at the table as Malcolm trailed off into incoherent mutterings, and Freya wanted to reach out to him, to touch him, say something, but instead she stayed frozen where she was, powerless to do anything but sit.

After a long silence, Nate raised his head and looked at his uncle, his eyes hard.

"I'm staying because I have no intention of being the useless piece of shit my father was. It has nothing to do with Freya, so you can lower that gun and calm the fuck down."

Freya kept her eyes on Nate, whose own stare didn't stray from his uncle, and wished more than anything that she could tell him he was wrong, about her anyway, that she did love him. She wanted him to know it, just in case...

But it wasn't time for that. Not with Malcolm there, waving a gun around like a maniac. She ran her mind through all her rules of negotiation, most of which she'd already broken. Never get personal. *Too late.* Never get emotional. *Ha, funny.* Never negotiate with something you're not willing to lose. *Like the man I love.* Play to your advantage...

Play to your advantage. An idea struck her, and she rejected it at first, but looking at Malcolm, finally decided it was worth a shot.

Certainly couldn't make things worse.

"Need a refill?" she asked Malcolm quietly.

Malcolm glanced down at his empty glass.

"I guess I do at that," he said, and reached across the table for the bottle.

"Illegal slap again, Ruby," Piper said, her voice quiet from the other side of the office desk. Ruby lifted her eyes to the girl's and smiled.

"Damn," she said, pushing her reading glasses up on her nose. "Must need a stronger prescription."

Piper placed her hands down on the desk. "What's the matter? Are you feeling okay?"

Ruby raised her eyes, looking out the window over Piper's shoulder. She could just see the roof of the house over the trees.

She should have called the police.

She looked at Piper, knowing she couldn't live with herself if something she did left that child without her father.

Don't call the police.

She put her hand on her pile. "Okay. Let's keep going."

Piper nodded, but didn't flip a card.

"Piper?"

"I'm sorry I took the plate from your hiding spot," Piper said. "Is that why you're mad?"

"Oh, no," Ruby said. "No, honey, I'm not mad about that at all."

"I just wanted to stay," Piper said. "I wanted us to be a family, right here. All three of us."

Ruby nodded. "Me, too."

Just then, the gate buzzed and Ruby looked up at the monitors. A black Lincoln Town Car was at the gate.

"You wait here," Ruby said, pushing up from the desk. "And I mean it. *Wait here.* Do not go back to the house, do you understand?"

Piper's eyebrows knit a bit, and she said, "Ruby, what's going—?" and Ruby just said, "*Wait here,*" again, and Piper went still. Ruby gathered her old cardigan around her shoulders and left the office, walking around to the gate, where a tall man with silver hair and an expensive suit was stepping out of the Town Car.

"I'm looking for Freya Daly," he said. "I need to see her now."

Ruby cast a glance back toward the house, then turned and shook her head. "She's busy at the moment."

"I'm her father," the man said. "Malcolm is waiting for me."

Ruby stared at him for a moment. "Oh, he's waiting for *you*, is he? He's got them both at gunpoint in there right now. Your daughter and my boy. Said he'd shoot Nate if I called the police." She hesitated for a moment, then stamped her foot. "But it's been too long. I'm calling."

"No," Richard said. "Give me twenty minutes. I think

I can handle all this without it getting too bad. Where are they? In the house?"

"Yes." She eyed him, wondering if she wanted to trust this stranger to get Nate and Freya out safely. "Are you sure you can fix this?"

Richard looked down at her, then nodded, his expression appropriately dour. "He wants me. If he has that, I think he'll let them go."

Ruby watched him for a moment, then made a decision. "You have fifteen minutes, and if they're not out by then, I'm calling the cops. I hope you'll forgive me for not giving a good goddamn if Malcolm shoots you or not; I want the kids safe."

Daly nodded. "Okay."

"Get good with whatever God you believe in, Mr. Daly, because if anything happens to either of them, that gun will not be the scariest thing you'll face today."

Then she walked over to the gate and punched in the code.

CHAPTER TWENTY

$\mathcal{N}$ATE KEPT looking at her, but Freya wouldn't meet his eyes. She just stared at her empty glass, not seeming to listen anymore as Malcolm ranted on about her father, the plate, the murder of the security guard, her mother. She was so still that if her eyes hadn't been open, Nate would have thought she'd just gone to sleep.

"...am I right, or am I right?" Malcolm said, downing another glass and shoving it across the table to Nate to fill. Nate emptied the last of the bottle into it and shoved it back, and when he did, he noticed Malcolm's reflexes in reaching for it had slowed.

Good, he thought. *Drink so much that you pass out, asshole.*

He watched Freya, waiting for her to look up so he could see if she was okay, but her head stayed down. Only this time her eyes were closed.

Not good.

"Freya?" he said. "Are you okay?"

Freya raised her head, and tears were streaming down her face. Nate felt a stab in his chest and reached out toward her, but then the butt of Malcolm's gun came down hard on the table.

"No. Sudden. Moves!" he said, banging the gun on the table on each word.

And then the gun went off.

The popping sound made Ruby jerk her head up from the game, her heart in her throat. She listened carefully, but there was only the distant sound of the Town Car as it crunched down the gravel lane to the house.

"What?" Piper said, her eyes widening at Ruby's expression. "What's going on?"

"Tree branch," Ruby said, her eyes watching as the Town Car disappeared behind the trees. She'd promised Richard Daly fifteen minutes.

Fuck Richard Daly. She picked up the phone and dialed.

"Go to the bathroom, you look like you need to pee," she said to Piper as a woman said, "911, what's your emergency?" on the other end of the line. Piper got up and went down the hall and Ruby waited until she heard the door close before speaking.

"There's a man holding two people hostage at gunpoint at Brody's Camp and RV, out off Route 8," she said, her voice low. "He said he'd shoot them if I called the cops, so no sirens, but you get your asses here. Now."

"Okay, can you tell me—?"

"*Now,*" Ruby said as the bathroom door opened and Piper came back out. She hung up and settled down in her office chair.

"Ready for another round?" she asked, smiling brightly at Piper. She reached casually behind her and hit the remote button to open the gate for when the cops got there.

"Yeah. Okay." Piper sat down, her face grim as she eyed Ruby. She wasn't buying the "nothing's wrong" act, but she went along with it, and for that Ruby would always be grateful.

She was a hell of a kid, that Piper.

Nate kept his eyes on Freya, even as chunks of wall plaster fell to the floor behind him. Why wouldn't she look at him?

"Would you get a load of that?" Malcolm said, laughing and staring at the hole in the wall. "Damn thing works after all."

Nate wanted to lunge across the table and strangle his uncle, but the gun, now smoking from the tip, was once again pointed at Freya, who was still crying softly in her seat, her head bowed.

"*Freya*," he said, his voice firm, hoping the tone would get her attention. "Look at me."

She ignored him, just sniffled and swiped at her face.

"Come on, girl," Malcolm said, patting her on the shoulder with his free hand. "Stop all that crying, now."

"She can't help it," Nate said. "She has this condition—"

"Oh, *right*," Freya said, lifting her head. "It's a condition." She rolled her eyes. "Jesus. You just spent the last fifteen minutes telling your uncle how little I mean to you, and you want to blame my being upset on a *condition*?"

Nate felt like the floor had just dropped out from under him.

"Wait," he said. "Freya." He couldn't reassure her in front of Malcolm, who was crazy enough to shoot her if he knew how Nate really felt, but he didn't want to hurt her any more than he already had, so he just went silent, listening to her cry quietly in her chair.

"He was just using me, Malcolm," she said. "I can't believe it, but he was. How could I have been so stupid?"

"Freya—" Nate said, but then Malcolm slowly pointed the gun at him.

"Shut up and get the lady a tissue," Malcolm said, turning cold eyes on Nate. "You've done enough to the poor girl, don't you think?"

Nate stared at Malcolm, then let his eyes shift to Freya, who finally looked up.

And gave him a small wink before bursting out into even more dramatic tears.

She's playing him.

On the one hand, he was relieved he hadn't upset her like that. On the other, she was going to get herself shot.

"I said," Malcolm said, lifting the gun higher, "*get the lady a tissue.*"

"He doesn't *care*!" Freya said, wailing louder to get Malcolm's attention. "He never cared about me. It was all lies to get what he wanted. And I fell for it. I made a mistake, Malcolm. I made the biggest mistake of my life. Just like my mom." She sniffled and swiped at her face, tears falling from her eyes in fat drops.

Nate tensed, waiting for Malcolm to pick up on how obviously she was playing on his feelings for her mother. But Malcolm only watched her, his eyes softening.

Falling for it, hook, line, and sinker. Hell, watching her, knowing she was full of shit, Nate wanted to put his arms around her and comfort her, too.

She was good.

"Oh, no, shhhh," Malcolm said, putting his free hand around her shoulders, his grip loosening slightly on his gun hand. "You're only human. You made a mistake. You loved the wrong man. It can happen to anyone."

Nate watched Freya, wondering what, exactly, her endgame was. Was he supposed to dive for the gun while Malcolm was distracted? That was a crazy plan, and it was too risky for Freya. She was more calculating than that. No, it had to be something else.

Then Freya sniffled and looked up through wet lashes at Malcolm.

"I don't want him in my sight," she said. "Malcolm, can you just make him leave? Please? You don't need him. I'm the only one you really need."

Nate felt his stomach drop as he realized what she was doing. He stared at her as she looked at his uncle with pleading eyes.

No, he thought.

And then his uncle's gun hand rose, pointing at Nate.

"You heard the lady, Nathan," he said, his eyes turning coldly to Nate. "Get out."

Freya kept up the weeping routine, deliberately avoiding eye contact with Nate. He was going to hate the shit out of this idea, but it was the only way. He had to leave. She wasn't going to get anywhere with him there, not with Malcolm being so unpredictable and just as likely to shoot Nate as pour him another drink. Nate might not be in love with her, but she knew she loved him, and as long as she had something she wasn't willing to lose, she wouldn't be able to negotiate with Malcolm.

And she was done screwing up her negotiations.

"Fine." Nate stood up, and Freya breathed a sigh of relief. "Shoot me."

She raised her head in shock. He was staring down the barrel of Malcolm's gun like an idiot. A stupid, heroic, soon-to-be-dead idiot.

"Goddamnit, Nate," she said, slamming her hand on the table. "Just go!"

He looked at her, his face livid, and she knew his fury wasn't all for Malcolm. "No."

"I *will* shoot you, Nathan," Malcolm said. "I won't like it, but I'll do it. The lady asked for you to leave."

Panic overtook Freya and she pushed up from the table.

"Hey," Malcolm said, standing as well.

"Nate, go. You don't have to prove you're not your father, okay? We all know that. I don't need you to be a hero, I need you to leave."

"I'm not trying to prove anything," he said, "and I swear, I may kill you myself when this is all over, but I am not leaving you now."

"Nathan, the lady is upset, and she—" Malcolm stopped, looking at Freya, his eyes focusing slowly, but still focusing.

Crap.

"Those tears seem to have dried mighty fast," Malcolm said, grabbing Freya's upper arm so hard that pain shot all the way into her back. "You lied to me."

Freya tried to work up more tears, but her anger got the best of her. She glared and said, "Just make him go, and then you and I can talk."

"Veronica," Malcolm said, his voice low and soft, but with an unmistakable edge of rage roiling underneath.

"You are so like her, I can hardly tell the difference between you."

Nate moved closer. "Malcolm! Let her go."

Malcolm didn't seem to hear him, just stared at Freya. "Risking your life to save a man. Throwing everything away. Lying to me. Just like her. And I fell for it. Again." He yanked her around to face him, and she winced at the pain in her arm. "Look at me when I'm talking to you, you bitch!"

Freya looked at him, and he pointed the gun at her head. She stared at the gun, shock overcoming her.

He's really going to shoot me, she thought.

"No!" Nate darted between them, knocking Malcolm's grip on Freya's arm loose. Nate grabbed her away, then shoved her behind him so hard she fell to the floor. When she looked up, he was standing with Malcolm facing him, holding out the gun.

"You stupid little shit," Malcolm said.

"If you're gonna shoot, just fucking shoot," Nate said, staring his uncle down, "but I'm not gonna let you hurt her."

The seconds stretched, long and silent, as Malcolm, his eyes red and crazy from drink—*oh, hell was that ever a bad idea*—leveled the gun at Nate. Freya's brain whirled in panic and grief and fury, and she kicked out her legs at the backs of Nate's knees, bringing him down to the ground next to her, just as Malcolm pulled the trigger.

And it clicked.

"Son of a *bitch*," Nate said, grabbing the back of his knee and looking at Freya.

Malcolm pulled the gun down and stared at it, his eyes wide. He pointed the gun at the ceiling, pulled the trigger again, and it clicked again.

"That cheap bitch," he said, marveling at the gun. "She only put one bullet in."

"Oh, for Christ's sake," Nate muttered.

Freya pushed up from the floor and reached down to pull Nate up. He winced as he stood up, then shot Freya an angry glance, and Freya said, "Well, what did you expect? 'Just fucking shoot'? What the hell was that? Idiot."

Malcolm clicked the gun again, then held it up and popped out the empty magazine inside.

"Oh, *I'm* the idiot?" Nate said, his eyes furious and locked on Freya. "You're the one who wanted me to leave you alone with him!"

"Only because I couldn't negotiate with you in the room, you jerk! I could have had this thing over and done in a few minutes. God! I have half a mind to kick you again!"

"Bitch only put one bullet in," Malcolm said again.

Then the front door opened and her father's tall figure filled the doorway.

"Malcolm," Richard Daly said, stepping in. "This ends now."

Malcolm's expression shifted instantly from dismay to fury. He threw the gun to the floor, where it slid harmlessly until it hit the wall, and launched himself across the room at Richard Daly.

Nate pulled Freya out of Malcolm's path as he flew toward Richard, knocking the taller man out onto the porch with a thud. When Malcolm was out of the house, Nate realized he'd grabbed her by the same arm Malcolm had wrenched earlier.

"Shit, I'm sorry, are you okay?" he asked, his anger suddenly gone as he gently touched her good arm.

"I'm fine," she said, pulling away from him. "Your knee okay?"

"Yeah," he said, not sure what he wanted to do more, kiss her or yell at her. "Fine."

"Good." She motioned out the door, toward the ruckus on the porch. "Go break that crap up before one of them has a damn heart attack."

Out on the porch, there was a grunt and a series of thuds; they fell down the steps. Nate pointed a finger at Freya.

"Don't go anywhere," he said.

"I won't," she said, waving her hand at him. "Now, go."

He hesitated for a second, then headed outside, where Richard and Malcolm were grappling on the lawn, Malcolm on top, his hands going for Richard's neck. A crackle of thunder sounded in the distance, and fat drops of rain started to fall.

"Right," Nate muttered, and ran out. He grabbed Malcolm's shoulder, and his uncle looked up, surprised. Nate put all his anger into one solid punch, and the old man fell back next to Richard, unconscious. Nate held out his hand to Freya's dad, pulling him to his feet.

"Nathan Brody?" Richard said, somehow maintaining his dignified demeanor, despite the fact that he was caked in patches of grass and dirt that were turning to mud in the rain.

"Yeah," Nate said.

"Richard Daly," the older man said, and held out his hand. Nate almost laughed at the absurdity, but he was too pissed off, so he took the man's hand and shook.

Just then, two police cars flew onto the property, lights flashing. Behind them, from the office, Ruby came running out, with Piper close behind.

"Goddamnit," Ruby yelled, "would a little subtlety kill you people?" She slowed as she spotted Malcolm, knocked out on the lawn. "Never mind."

"Dad!" Piper scooted around Ruby and ran to Nate, throwing her arms around his neck. "Ruby wouldn't tell me what was happening, but it was bad, wasn't it? Uncle Malcolm is bad, isn't he? Is that why you hit him?"

Nate shot a look at Richard, who patted Nate on the shoulder and went toward the house. Nate glanced at the front window, but couldn't see Freya through it. Well, he'd deal with her in a bit. For the moment, he was happy to tighten his hold on his daughter, replacing his anger with the peaceful knowledge that she was safe.

"Don't worry about Uncle Malcolm." He kissed her cheek. "Everything's fine now."

Piper pulled back and looked around, her eyes wide. "Where's Freya?"

"She's in the house," Nate said. "She's okay."

Piper nodded and Nate set her down, holding her hand as the first police officer headed over, hand on the butt of his gun.

"We got a report about a hostage situation at this address," he said.

"Yeah, it's over." Nate nodded toward Malcolm, a second officer approaching his unconscious body carefully. "He's unarmed." Nate looked up and saw Ruby. "Ruby, can you...?"

Before he could finish, Ruby had taken Piper's hand from his. "Baby, let's go inside and get you into something dry, okay?" Ruby glanced at the officer. "Okay?"

The officer nodded. "Stay on the premises." He spoke

briefly into the walkie-talkie on his shoulder, then turned back to Nate.

"Ready to answer some questions?"

"Sure." Nate led him up toward the shelter of the porch as the rain started to fall in earnest. "Shoot."

Freya pulled the plate out of the hot, soapy water and rinsed it under the tap. Her hands were only shaking slightly now, which she thought was pretty damn good under the circumstances. The gold scalloped edges of the plate glistened under her fingers, and the purple on the rim seemed almost translucent. She rubbed the towel over the eagle in the center as she walked over to the table, then set it down again in the middle, angling her head to see if it maybe looked prettier from a different perspective.

Nope. That plate was always gonna be ugly.

"Freya?"

She looked up to see her father standing in the entryway to the kitchen, his immaculate gray suit wet and caked in mud and grass, his hair dirty and disheveled, and his lip starting to bruise at one edge. He looked down at the plate, and then at the towel in Freya's hands.

"What did you do?" he asked.

"I washed it," she said.

He took a step closer, his voice low. "Freya, you just tampered with evidence."

She laughed a little. She hadn't thought of it that way. "Oh. Right." She sighed. "I guess I thought I was protecting you. Think I'll be able to plead post-traumatic shock?"

Richard placed his hands on the back of a chair, as if leaning into it for strength. "I'm going to confess to everything. My lawyers are working on a deal right now and they think that if I put my resources into retrieving the remaining lost items, we can work out some kind of clemency."

Freya let out a stuttered laugh. "So I got dishpan hands for nothing? Is this what you're telling me?"

"I never meant for any of this to…" He stopped. Just…stopped. The way he always did before he'd let any emotion show, before any apology, any admission of wrongdoing, might sneak out. Thirty-four years, the man had never apologized for anything.

"That's not healthy, you know," Freya said, as her own eyes started to fill. "You hold in all that emotion and eventually, it explodes on you. Piper calls it emotional diarrhea."

And then she thought of Piper, and Nate, and Ruby, and everything that had actually happened that afternoon. The emotion cycloned within her, and her eyes teared up. She put her hands on the table, leaning forward, trying to ward off the breakdown she knew was coming, at least until her father wasn't around to see it.

She felt a cold, wet hand on her shoulder and looked up to see her father looking down at her. Slowly, he patted her shoulder, a little too hard and a little too fast, but he was trying. She had to give him credit for that, at least. She stood up straight and smiled at him through her tears.

"Thanks," she croaked. She wanted him to pull her into his arms, the way Nate did with Piper, to kiss her on the head and tell her he loved her and make everything okay again.

Instead, he pulled his hand away and stood there in silence for a while, then said, "I need to go speak to the police."

"Right," she said, and watched him walk away.

CHAPTER TWENTY-ONE

ATE KNOCKED twice on the door to his bedroom, and when he heard nothing from inside, he poked his head in. Freya sat on the bed, her back to him. Her hands rested in her lap as she stared out the window. Nate stepped in quietly and shut the door behind him.

"Everyone's gone," he said. "There's a judge in Boise who knew your dad in college, I guess, and they're working it out."

Freya nodded. "So, I'm not in trouble for washing the fingerprints off the plate?"

"It's a moot point, with your dad's confession and the evidence we gave about Malcolm regarding the security guard." He smiled, hoping she would smile back.

She didn't.

"Are you okay?" he asked.

She hesitated, then said, "Yeah. I'm fine. I've got... actually...a flight..."

Nate froze. "You're going? Tonight?"

"Yep. There's another flight out at eleven."

Damnit. He walked over and sat down next to her. "Any chance I could talk you into staying until tomorrow?

I'll sleep on the couch, it's not about sex, I just—" He took her hand in his and stared down at it. "I need more time to tell you how sorry I am."

She looked at him. "Sorry? For what?"

"For what? Christ, Freya. For almost getting you killed. For yelling at you. For... all that stuff with my uncle."

She smiled, but it was so small Nate barely caught it. "Well, I almost got you killed, too. And I yelled at you. And I kicked your knees out from under you." She cringed and looked at him. "How are your knees, by the way?"

Hurt like a son of a bitch. "Fine."

She went quiet for a long moment, and he watched her, wondering what was going on in her head. Then, finally, she spoke.

"When I went down to talk to Piper, on the dock, she gave me something."

She pulled a little cloth bag out of her pocket and handed it to Nate. He turned it upside down and a silver coin a bit larger than a quarter fell into his palm.

"It's an Irish wishing coin," she said. "Piper told me that I could make any wish I wanted on it. And you know what I wished for?"

Nate set it on the bed, then looked at her. "Nope."

"I wished for my old life back," she said. "My old, cold, empty, emotionless life." She turned to look at him, her eyes dry and exhausted. "And I meant it. That's what I want."

Nate straightened. "Freya... why? You weren't happy—"

"I was at peace. I knew who I was. I knew what I was dealing with, how to handle my life. I've been with you for a few days, and already, it's been too hard. I'm confused all the time and I'm worried about being hurt and hurting you or Piper and I'm just not made that way." She released a heavy breath, her eyes so sad Nate could hardly take looking at them. "Plus, it's too hard to love someone like that. At least I can save you from that."

"Save me from what? From loving you?" He tried to think of a better way to say what he wanted to tell her, but could only say, "You're too late."

She looked up at him, surprise on her face. "Don't say that. Please."

"Why not? It's true."

"It isn't. It can't be. We had great sex, you saved me from a fire, we were held hostage together. It's making us think there's something here that isn't really here and I can't—"

He leaned in and kissed her, as much to shut her up as to convince her that there was more here than she was willing to admit. She kissed him back, put her hand on his face, and he pulled her to him, trying to tell her everything he needed her to know, and she responded. *She knows it, too*, he thought. *She knows.*

When they pulled apart, she pressed her forehead to his and for a moment, he relaxed.

Then she kissed him on the cheek, whispered, "Good-bye," and pushed up from the bed.

"Freya, wait," he said, grabbing her wrist as he shot up after her.

"Nate, you're just making this harder," she said, and then he pulled her into his arms and kissed her again, putting everything he knew they had between them into it. Every laugh, every smile, every angry word, every quiet moment they'd shared, he put it all into that kiss. When he pulled back, he slid both hands up the sides of her face and forced her to look at him.

"We're not done," he said. "There's more."

"You really love me?" she said, looking up at him.

"Yes," he said. "This is what I'm trying to tell you."

"Then you need to let me go."

He stared down at her, unable to believe this was really happening. Was she crazy? Did she think this sort of thing happened every day? What the hell was she doing?

And still, while thinking all this, he watched her walk out of the room, and didn't move a muscle to stop her.

Freya paused in the middle of the stairway and wiped at her face. She didn't want to say good-bye to Ruby and Piper all teary and bawling.

A little strength, she said, raising her eyes heavenward. *All I'm asking is for just a little more. Enough to get me out the door.*

She got herself together and went down the rest of the stairs. She set her suitcase by the front door. Her purse and laptop were already in her rental car. From the kitchen, she could hear the sounds of Piper and Ruby playing Slap. She laughed to herself; those girls needed a new game.

I could leave now, she thought. *I could just go and send a letter later.*

But she couldn't, and she knew it. Ruby would understand, but Piper wouldn't.

She walked into the kitchen and leaned against the entryway. Ruby slapped at a pile and Piper's hand came down just a second too late.

"Ha!" Ruby said, doing a little victory shimmy in her

seat. "Think you can take advantage of an old lady. I've still got some tricks in me yet, kid."

Piper smiled and looked at Freya, and then her smile faded. "Freya? Are you okay?"

"I'm fine," she said, forcing a smile. "I was just leaving, though, and I wanted to say good-bye."

"What?" Piper said. "No."

"I have work," Freya said lamely. "My dad's gonna be out for a while. He needs me back at the office."

"I thought you quit," Ruby said, and Freya looked at her. The older woman shrugged, unapologetic. "What? You left your fax sitting right there in the garbage can."

Freya smiled. "Just when I think I don't have enough reasons to adore you, Ruby, you go and add one more."

Ruby shrugged and turned her attention back to the cards. Piper, however, kept her gaze locked on Freya.

"I thought you were going to stay," she said. "I thought you and Dad—"

"We're friends," Freya said. "All of us. And there's a standing offer for you guys to come to Boston." She met Ruby's eyes. "After a little while."

Ruby gave a brief, knowing nod.

Freya walked over to Piper and knelt in front of her. "You have to promise me you'll come to visit, okay?"

"Yeah," Piper said, her face sad. "Okay."

Freya pulled her in for a hug. "You are an amazing kid, you know that?"

Piper tightened her grip. "Duh."

Freya laughed, then released Piper and stood up. "I'm gonna be late for my plane."

Ruby pushed up from the table. "Let me see you out."

They walked in silence, side by side, to the door. Freya

pulled on her jacket. She held her rental keys in her hand and turned to Ruby.

"Well," she said.

"Yeah," Ruby said.

They paused for a moment.

"I'm not really a hugger," Ruby said.

"Yeah," Freya said. "I never used to be, either. Well..." Freya turned toward the door. Ruby pulled it open for her and Freya walked out to the porch. The rain beat down on the porch roof, and the sad pattering in the dark felt somehow fitting to Freya's mood.

"Hey," Ruby said, and Freya turned. "You ever change your mind, we'll be here. Okay?"

Freya smiled. "Thanks."

Ruby nodded and closed the door slowly, leaving Freya outside in the dark, in the rain, alone.

And, finally, it was over.

CHAPTER TWENTY-TWO

I CAN'T believe it." Flynn's wavy brown hair framed her dumbstruck expression as she put her glass down on the bar at the Goodhouse Arms. "Dad was a thief."

Freya patted her sister on the shoulder. "Yep. Kinda explains a lot about how we ended up the way we did."

"Wow," Flynn said. "And how long is he going to be in Iowa?"

"Idaho," Freya said. "About a week, I guess. Which means I need to be back in the office on Monday."

"No," Flynn said. "Tomorrow's Sunday, and you're not leaving yet. Not until I fully absorb the fact that Dad's a thief. That's gonna take at least another week."

"I've already been here four days," Freya said. "Someone has to run the office or all our holdings, including this one, will go bankrupt and die."

"How are you girls doing?" Jake said, approaching them from behind the bar.

"She's leaving tomorrow," Flynn said.

"Sorry, babe. Want me to pour you another one?" Jake said, throwing a bar rag over his shoulder and reaching for the bottle of Jameson's they'd been working on for the past hour.

"I resent that," Flynn said. "Are you suggesting that I turn to alcohol to deal with my problems?"

"I'll have another one," Freya said, sliding her glass toward Jake.

"Oh, hell," Flynn said, sliding hers across as well. Jake smiled and poured the drinks.

"Still not enough detective work to fill all his time?" Freya asked Flynn quietly.

"Are you kidding? In this town? Your plate was the most exciting thing that happened in months." Flynn shrugged. "But, I have to admit, I like him behind the bar when things are dull. Reminds me of when we met."

Jake put the bottle down, slid Freya's glass over to her, and held on to Flynn's.

"This is your last one for the night," he said. "I want you clear-headed when my shift ends."

Flynn put her hand on the glass over his. "Yeah. Good luck with that."

Freya watched as Jake leaned over and kissed her sister lightly before heading off to serve a guy at the other end of the bar.

"He is so crazy about you," Freya said.

"Yeah, poor son of a bitch," Flynn said, then lifted her glass. "To being held at gunpoint, may it never happen to either of us again."

Freya laughed and clinked the glass with her sister. "I'll drink to that."

They both sipped and put their glasses down, and then Flynn said, "So, tell me the rest."

Freya picked up a swizzle stick and stirred her drink

with it. "What do you mean? You heard the part about me being held at gunpoint, right? And Dad got in a fistfight on a muddy lawn? You think it gets any better than that?"

Flynn was quiet, and when Freya looked up, her sister's face was serious.

"You're depressed," she said.

"I'm not depressed," Freya said. "I'm fine."

"Whatever," Flynn said. "You know, when you started having those panic attacks last year, I thought it was a good thing."

"You did?"

"Yeah. Dad put way too much pressure on you to be just like him. You were long overdue for the panics."

"Great," Freya said.

"And then you started in with that crying thing, and that was weird but..." Flynn looked at her, shaking her head. "Now I'm worried."

"Oh, great," Freya said. "You're worried about me? It must be bad."

"It is," she said. "All that funky psychological weather was your subconscious telling you to change things. I thought you'd figure that out. But now, here you are, all set to go right back where you started."

"Of course I'm going back," Freya said. "My life is in Boston. Why wouldn't I go back?"

"Because of the guy," Flynn said simply.

Freya bristled. "What guy?"

"The guy who owned the place, the nephew of the crazy guy who almost killed Dad. What's-his-name. Dale."

"Nate," Freya said quietly, looking into her drink.

"Right," Flynn said. "Nate. You've hardly talked about him at all."

Freya shrugged. "That's because there's nothing to talk about."

"You really expect me to believe that?"

"Yeah," Freya said. "Nothing happened. We're friends."

"Right," Flynn said again. She took a drink, then set her glass down and turned to Freya. "You know, this isn't fair. When Tucker and I went through all that crap last year, I told you everything. And now I have to pull this all out of you."

"There's nothing to pull out," Freya said, her entire body feeling tense. "We're just friends. Really. Now drop it, okay?"

"Fine," Flynn said. She raised her hand and waved at Jake, who walked over, smiling.

"You're gonna have to leave the bottle right here," Flynn said.

"Thought I cut you off," he said, his entire existence focused happily on Flynn.

"It's for her," Flynn said. "Freya's brokenhearted and won't admit it."

"I am…not," Freya said. Both Jake and Flynn stared at her, sympathetic but not buying it.

"Fine. I'm miserable. Are you happy now?" She sighed and leaned her head on Flynn's shoulder.

"Oh, baby." Flynn reached her hand up around Freya's head and smoothed her hair.

"I'll get over it," Freya said. "I just need to go home and get back to work. Get my feet on the ground again."

"Yes," Flynn said, her voice flat. "Work. The miracle cure."

Jake took Freya's hand in his and smiled at her.

"Whoever this guy is, if he let you go, he's an idiot," he said.

Freya squeezed his hand and tried to smile. Jake was a good man, but she had a feeling he might be wrong about who the idiot was in this scenario.

Nate sat on the porch swing, staring out at the peaceful June morning. Brody's Camp and RV had been closed for two full weeks, and his money from the restaurant buy-out was burning a hole in his bank account. The folder Freya had left with her business plans still sat in his office, untouched, and he didn't plan on opening it. Somehow, that would feel like an admission that she was gone, never coming back, that he'd never have the chance to get her advice in person. He knew it was the truth, but still. No need to put salt on the wound.

His father's dusty Ford pickup came around the corner, rumbling over the gravel until Ruby parked it in the driveway and stepped out. She walked up the porch steps and sat next to Nate.

"Well," she said, "I dropped Piper off at the rec center. Brandy's mom said she'd bring her home when the girls were done giggling. Should be a couple of days."

Nate nodded. "Thanks."

"I also dropped by the PO box." She dumped some mail on his lap. "Nothing interesting."

He met her eye. Code for *nothing from Boston*. He nodded.

"And," Ruby said, "I stopped by the bank."

Nate kept quiet, just sipped his coffee.

"I told you I don't want that money," Ruby said.

"And I told you you don't have to move to Oregon with

your sisters," he said. "But you lived here with my dad for eight years. You deserve to be compensated."

"Been compensated," Ruby grumbled.

"I'm not having this discussion again."

"Fine," Ruby said. "Then I've got a proposal for you."

Nate cut his eyes at her. "I already can't wait to hear this."

"I want to invest in this place," she said. "I want it to be mine, too. And I think we should develop it. You know." She paused. "Freya left some good ideas in that folder."

Nate looked at her. "You opened it?"

Ruby shrugged, not contrite in the least. "You weren't doing anything with it. And Freya had a good idea about opening up a restaurant. I also think we should maybe hire a consultant to help us figure all that stuff out."

Nate shook his head. "No."

"Well, what are you gonna do? Sit here and run an old campground?"

Nate sipped his coffee. "It's what my dad did."

"You are not your dad," Ruby said. "And if we got the right help, just the right person—"

Nate turned on her. "Don't call her."

"What?" Ruby said, very bad at acting innocent. "Who?"

"Freya."

"Did I say Freya? I don't remember saying Freya."

"Ruby, stop. Okay? Just . . . stop." He didn't mean to be short with her, but he had a hard enough time not thinking about Freya without Ruby making it worse.

"Well, someone has to call her. You're too stupid and stubborn—"

Nate shot her a look.

"Yes, that's what I said, and I'll say it again. Stupid. Stubborn. I don't know what happened between you two that day, but you've been moping around here ever since—"

"I'm not moping."

"—and it's not good for Piper."

Nate let out a bitter laugh. "I thought you were the one who wanted Freya to go for Piper's sake."

Ruby pulled on her shirt, smoothing it. "Well, it's possible I was wrong. It's been known to happen, time to time. And Piper's fine. She's all excited, planning a trip to Boston. It's you that's moping—"

"I'm not moping," Nate said again.

"—and making everyone around you miserable. You haven't cooked in weeks. Some days you don't get out of bed until past ten. It's not who you are, Nate, and it's not good for your daughter, so just call Freya and, whatever happened, work it out."

"I tried," Nate said. "She doesn't want me, okay? She said no, and she's gone, and she's not coming back, so just…" He sighed. "Just stop, okay? This isn't helping."

Ruby stared at him for a while, then patted him on the hand.

"Let me freshen up that coffee for you," she said, reaching for his mug.

"It's fine," he said. ·

She took it anyway, started for the house, then turned back to look at him.

"I'm going grocery shopping this afternoon," she said, "and tonight, you're cooking."

Nate smiled. "Look, I'll do it tomorrow, okay? Today, I just—"

"You're cooking tonight, and that's final," she said. "No more pining. No more moping. I won't have it. I'm gonna be a partner in this business, and I'm telling you right now, tonight you're lighting bananas on fire if I have to stick a torch up your ass to make it happen."

Nate looked at her, and her serious expression as she threatened him made him laugh. "All right."

Ruby went into the house and Nate stared out at the trees, trying to get excited about cooking, but he couldn't.

Pining and moping, he thought. *Great.*

Then he pushed up off the swing and went inside.

CHAPTER TWENTY-THREE

FREYA STOOD at her father's desk and waited while he read her letter. He finished and raised his eyes to hers.

"If you need some time off," he began, but she shook her head.

"It's not that," she said.

"It's only been a month since all that...happened," he said. "It would be perfectly acceptable for you to take some time off."

"That's not what I need, Dad."

He sat back and nodded. "Well, then, I guess I accept your resignation."

"Good." She forced on a stiff smile. "You should start the search to replace me with Suzanne. She's very sharp, and I think she can slide right in so you won't even miss me."

"Okay, then," he said, in his regular business tone. "Thank you for everything. You've been an exemplary employee."

"Right," Freya said, wondering how many girls dreamed of hearing that from their dads. Not that it mattered. Richard Daly was who he was, and it was time to accept that.

"I'm selling my apartment, too," she said.

He looked at her. "Why would you do that?"

"It's a clean-slate thing," she said. "Starting over. I'm going to stay with Flynn in New York while I figure it out."

"That's not New York," he said. "That's upstate."

"You talk like the country is this terrible place," Freya said. "I think you need to get out more, Dad."

He nodded. "You might be right."

Freya turned toward the door, then stopped herself. Things were never going to change for her until she changed them; she'd learned at least that much. So she turned back to face him.

"I'm really proud of you, you know."

Her father raised his head to look at her but his expression was, as always, unreadable.

"The way you confessed to everything," she went on, "and are working so hard to retrieve all the stuff for the museum. You're handling the bad press with dignity, too. I think you're a good man, Dad. I really do."

He didn't meet her eyes. "Thank you."

"You're welcome." She hesitated. "So, I'll see you next month in Boise, when we testify for Malcolm's trial, right?"

He nodded and stood up, walking her to the door. "Yes. We'll go out for dinner?"

"Sounds like a plan."

He opened the door for her, and she was about to leave, then turned and kissed him on the cheek.

"Thanks, Dad," she said.

He nodded. "You'll always have a place here if you change your mind."

"Thanks." *I won't.* Then she turned and left the offices of Daly Developers, Inc., for the last time.

Nate leaned against the marble wall of Freya's apartment building, paper bags in his arms. Once again, the doorman eyed him suspiciously, so Nate walked over.

"Okay, when you called up, she really wasn't there, right?" he said. "It wasn't that she told you she wasn't there because she didn't want to see me? Because all you have to do is tell me, and I'm gone."

The doorman shook his head. "She was not there."

"Okay." Nate took a deep breath and went back to his spot, juggling the bags to check his watch. Five-thirty. When he'd called her father's office earlier, Richard said she'd left the office early that day. So...where the hell was she?

"Ruby and her stupid ideas," Nate muttered. He should have just called. It was so much easier to get shot down long-distance.

Christ, he thought, then set the bags down at his feet. *This was a bad idea.*

"Hi, Marcus."

"Good afternoon, Ms. Daly."

Nate looked up. There she was, looking...damn, so far out of his league. No wonder the doorman had eyed him like that. She was in a sharp dark green suit, tailored perfectly to her body. He was wearing a T-shirt and jeans, which was what happened when you hopped on a plane on the spur of the moment, but still.

Bad, bad idea.

Freya waited for Marcus to open the door and for a moment, Nate held his breath, hoping that the doorman would forget about him, just let her in and let Nate sneak away unnoticed. He could donate the food at a shelter and get the hell out of there with his dignity intact.

But then Marcus pointed, and Freya looked over at him. Nate watched her, his breath catching in his chest at the sight of her. Then she smiled and the air around him started to move again.

"Hi," she said, walking over to him.

"Yeah, um, hi," Nate said. *Smooth.*

"What are you doing here?" she asked, but didn't seem mad at all, which Nate thought might be a good sign.

"Well," he said, his heart beating way too fast to be justifiable. "I, um, I realized after you left that, uh…" He glanced down at the grocery bags at his feet. "I made you a promise that I didn't keep."

Her eyebrows knit. "What promise was that?"

"I said I'd teach you how to make an omelet," he said. "And I realized this morning that I never did." He met her eyes. "And you know how I am about keeping my word."

Her face broke out in the most beautiful smile he'd ever seen.

"So," he said, smiling back, "are we gonna cook or what?"

She nodded. "I'd like that, Cap'n."

Freya turned the key in her apartment door, her heart flip-flopping as Nate stood behind her. She hadn't stopped smiling like a fool since she'd seen him outside her apartment building, and the only thing that kept her from throwing herself at him in the elevator was the grocery bags in his arms.

"I have to warn you," she said, pushing the door open. "I don't have a lot of kitchen things. I'm not much of a cook."

"We don't need much," he said, stepping in past her

and beelining to the kitchen, "and what we do need, I bought." He set the bags down on the counter and grinned at her. "It's the Boy Scout in me. Always be prepared."

"Yeah?"

He whipped a crisp, white apron out of the bag. "Yeah."

He hooked it over her head and then reached around her waist to grab the strings, tying them over her stomach. She watched his face as he did, so happy she almost wanted to leap in the air.

He cinched the apron and looked up at her. "Too tight?"

She shook her head. "No."

"Good." He turned and went back to the bags, and she almost felt grief at his being that far away again. *No fair,* she thought, and trailed after him. He tied his own apron around his waist and clapped his hands.

"So," he said. "Omelets with goat cheese and spinach, right?"

He pulled a heavy frying pan out of one bag and set it on the counter. "Before we get started, I have a confession to make."

Freya stood next to him at the counter and reached into another bag, pulling out some eggs. "Oh, yeah? What's that?"

"Well, I'm kinda here on business," he said.

"Business?"

He stopped unloading groceries and turned to face her. "Yeah. Turns out, I have this big piece of land, and I have no idea what to do with it." He angled his head to the side a bit, looking like a little boy trying to get something past the teacher. "And I was thinking you could help me with that."

She crossed her arms over her stomach. "You want my...professional help?"

"Yeah," he said. "I'd like to hire you. And then..." He paused and cleared his throat. "Then I'd like you to come back with me."

"What?" she whispered, her breath gone.

"Yeah," he said, and the smile disappeared from his face as he looked down at the counter. "I know I've already asked you to stay, and you've already said no, but I am nothing if not a glutton for punishment. I figure, even if you shoot me down again, it can't be worse than being back there without you, so..."

She opened her mouth, but nothing came out, and Nate laughed nervously.

"You know what?" he said. "I was gonna cook this whole meal before dropping that on you, so let's just do that first, okay? I want to enjoy some time with you before anything goes bad." He pulled the spinach out and put it on the counter. "I was much smoother when I practiced that in my head, by the way."

He reached back into the bag, and she grabbed his hand.

"Nate, stop," she said, and he hung his head and sighed.

"Okay." He held her hand in his, and put it to his lips. "I can take a hint."

"No," she said, her eyes filling with tears as she looked at him, easily the most beautiful man that had ever walked the earth. "I don't think you can."

She put her hands on his face and leaned in to kiss him gently. He kissed her back, tentative, unsure, and when they pulled back, he put his hands on her waist and leaned his forehead against hers.

"Don't toy with me," he said. "It's not nice."

She kissed his lips and then his cheek and pulled him into a hug, unable to believe how good it felt to have him close to her again.

"I didn't think it was possible to miss someone so much," she said. "Every day, I woke up thinking it would get better, but it never did."

"You, too?" He tightened his hold on her and kissed her on the shoulder. "Thank god."

He pulled back and looked at her, then rubbed at his eyes.

"Sorry," he said. "It's just that I have this eye condition..."

"It's okay." She laughed and reached up, wiping the moisture from under his eyes with her thumbs. "It's temporary."

"Good to know," he said. "So...you'll come back with me?"

"Absolutely yes," she said, and kissed him. He wrapped his arms around her waist and kissed her back and then laughed when they came up for air.

"What?" Freya asked.

"That coin of Piper's," he said, shaking his head. "It really works, huh?"

Freya smiled. "You used it?"

His face flushed a bit. "Well, you know what they say about desperate times."

She put her arms around his neck. "So, what did you wish for?"

"It's kind of hard to explain," he said, then grinned at her. "I think maybe I should show you."

Much, much later, they finished cooking that omelet.

It came out perfect.

Dear Reader,

Hi, there! Thanks so much for reading *Wish You Were Here*. I hope you liked it. I had a great time writing it, which, sometimes with books...is not the case. It's funny, because the exact place a book lands on the *Hey, that was fun!* to *Someone-stick-a-fork-in-my-eye* scale often has little effect on the final product. You would think a book an author had to struggle with somehow would suffer for the struggling, but based on my experience, pain in the writing is not a predictor of the quality of the book. As a matter of fact, I have a friend who, when I tell her which of her books is my absolute favorite, always gives me a deadpan look and says, "Really? *That* one?" because it gave her fits to write.

So, now I've gone and blown the lid off a big secret about writing—it's hard. Okay, okay, *okay*...it's not coal-mine hard, or cardiac-surgeon hard, or even answering-the-phone-for-a-boss-who-speaks-to-your-boobs hard. But it presents its own challenges in its own ways, just like every other job. Bonus—you get to work in your pajamas. Drawback—it's not a rare Thursday when you realize you're still wearing your pajamas from Tuesday. Ew.

Oh, hell. I'm tarnishing the sheen on writing, aren't I? Leave it to me. Big Mouth. So, you're probably wondering, "Well, Miss Writerpants, if it's so hard, why don't you just get a real job?" Only you're thinking it in much nicer terms because you're a much nicer person than me, which I can say with pure conviction because...well, let's just say everyone benefits from a low bar.

And here's the reason why I don't get a real job. You. Oh! You just rolled your eyes, and I don't blame you, but hand to God, it's the truth. I've said it before and I'll say it again—readers are miracle workers. See, here's the thing. I got this story in my head and I got all excited about it and stayed up nights and made sound tracks and got up (yes, really) at 4AM every morning to write it. I laughed and I cried and I had a fabulous time, but it didn't have meaning until you did what you just did.

You read it.

It's easy to be unaware of how incredible that is, but the fact is, readers give writing meaning, and the whole point of this letter is to make sure you know that. Hard as it is, you make it all worth it. Thank you, truly, sincerely, from the bottom of my heart, for partnering with me to finish this process.

I hope we get a chance to do it again sometime.

With deep appreciation,

Lani

THE DISH

Where authors give you the inside scoop!

From the desk of Elizabeth Hoyt

Gentle Reader,

The hero of my book TO SEDUCE A SINNER (on sale now) Jasper Renshaw, Viscount Vale, had quite a rocky road on his way to the altar. In fact, TO SEDUCE A SINNER opens with Vale being rejected by his fiancée—the *second* fiancée he's had in six months. Thus, it should be no surprise that once married Vale endeavored to pass on some of his marital wisdom to other gentlemen. I'll reprint his advice below.

A GENTLEMAN'S GUIDE TO MARRIAGE AND MANAGING THE LADY WIFE

1. Chose carefully when selecting a bride. A lady with a sweet disposition, engaging smile, and full bosom is a boon to any man.

2. However, should a gentleman find that he has been left at the altar yet again, he may find himself accepting the proposal of a lady of less than a full bosom and rather too much intelligence.

3. Surprisingly, he may also find himself attracted to said lady.

4. The marriage bed should be approached with delicacy and tenderness. Remember, your lady wife is a virgin of good family, and thus may be shocked or even repulsed by the activities of the marriage bed. Best to keep them short.

5. However, try not to be too shocked if your lady wife turns out *not* to be shocked by the marriage bed.

6. Or, even if she is wildly enthusiastic about her marital duties.

7. If such is your case, you are a fortunate man indeed.

8. The lady wife can be a mysterious creature, passionate, yet oddly secretive about her feelings toward you, her lord and husband.

9. The gentleman may find his thoughts returning again and again to the subject of his lady wife's feeling for him. "Does she love me?" you may wonder as you consume your morning toast. Try not to let these thoughts become too obsessive.

10. Whatever you do, do *not* fall in love with your lady wife, no matter how alluring her

lips or seductive her replies to your banter are. That way lies folly.

Yours Very Sincerely,

Elizabeth Hoyt

www.elizabethhoyt.com

♥ ♥ ♥ ♥ ♥ ♥ ♥ ♥ ♥ ♥ ♥ ♥ ♥ ♥

From the desk of Marliss Melton

Dear Reader,

Sean Harlan, the hero of my latest book TOO FAR GONE (on sale now) is a killer. Surprised? I thought you might be. How could such a charming, sexy, fun-loving man with a sunny disposition and a special way with children be a sniper for his SEAL team? How could he be so ruthless and merciless, taking lives without remorse?

Oddly enough, this all began with one of my kids. I wanted to create a hero with the same re-laxed and irrepressible charm as my son. So Sean was born. But I did a little research into that "re-laxed" personality type and learned something that blew me away: it's the one and only personality type that makes up a natural born killer! Did you know that in battles, only 15 to 25 percent of infantrymen ever fire their weapons? And most fire over the heads of the enemy! Those who actually shoot to kill comprise less than 4 percent of those in battle yet they do half the killing!

When I discovered this, I knew exactly who Sean was, dark side and all. He was a man that was indispensable to the military. After all, without men like Sean, armies would crumble and decisive battles would be lost. But I wanted Sean to be indispensable to a woman who needed him, too; so, I created Ellie Stuart as the perfect foil. As hesitant as she is about Sean's killer instinct, she soon realizes that without Sean, she stands little chance of reclaiming her kidnapped sons. She also comes to see that her mother's instinct makes killing a viable option and that she and Sean are not so different after all.

It is my hope that you'll love Sean as much as I do. Oh, and by the way, my son is a perfectly nice young man . . . so far.

To learn more about Sean and Ellie's personalities, visit the FUN STUFF page at www.marliss melton.com.

Thanks for reading,

Marliss Melton

From the desk of Lani Diane Rich

Dear Reader,

Most often, when you write a book, people ask you why you chose that particular setting. All I can say about northern Idaho, the setting for my latest book, WISH YOU WERE HERE (on sale now), is that I drove through it once while moving with my family from Anchorage, Alaska to Syracuse, New York, and I was absolutely entranced. Given the hard-nosed business woman Freya was, I figured there would be no greater fish-out-of-water situation for her than being stuck in the middle of all those trees.

One of the challenges of Freya's story was where I'd left her at the end of CRAZY IN LOVE—on a road toward something of a mental breakdown. Like her sister Flynn, I felt it was high past time for Freya's life to buck her off like a mechanical dive bar bronco; and so, it was with great relish that I saddled her with a rare "condition" and placed her in an impossible situation. While writing CRAZY IN LOVE, Freya was one of those magical secondary characters who just begged for her own book, and it was so much fun to spend this time with her and watch her grow into her own person.

As for Nate, he was a lot of fun to write as well.

Where Freya was hardened and tough, Nate was open, sensitive, and honorable. His relationship with Piper was especially fun for me to write, especially against the backdrop of Freya's relationship with her own father. Nate's a classic cleft-chin hero, but there was a lot of depth under those still waters, which made him a pleasure to write.

I hope you enjoy reading the story as much as I did writing it. Thanks so much!

Lani Diane Rich

www.lanidianerich.com